DARK KISS

"You are the daughter of my enemy. You should hate me. You *see* the beast in me, yet you are not afraid. Why, Jane? Why are you not afraid? You know what I am."

"I see no beast. You are a man." Jane closed the distance between them and laid her palm against his cheek, desperate to understand, to heal the great gaping hole that threatened to suck away his humanity. "Do you think that I fear you?"

"You should." He touched her, a brush of his knuckles against her cheek; and she nearly moaned at the hot, sweet current that invaded her blood. "Be wise, Jane. Find that fear and hold fast to it."

Leaning close, he touched his face to her neck, breathed deeply. Wild emotion careened through her, leaving her trembling. With a cry, she stepped away, her back colliding with a large, rough boulder. He advanced, pressing the palms of his hands to the rock on either side of her, trapping her between a wall of cold stone and hot, muscled man. She breathed the scent of him, citrus and spice, and she wanted to press her nose to his skin and breathe in until she was filled with him.

A smoldering spark flared and roared through her, burning away common sense, leaving a trail of molten need in its wake. Should she let him, he would consume her. His name escaped her lips on a sigh. "Aidan."

Arching her body, she raised her face to him, beguiled, mesmerized, wanting him so badly that her limbs trembled, and the world spun dizzily. With a low groan, he leaned in, pressing his open mouth to hers. The tip of his tongue traced her lips then thrust inside, licking her, tasting her . . .

Books by Eve Silver

DARK DESIRES

HIS DARK KISS

DARK PRINCE

Published by Zebra Books

Dark Prince

EVE SILVER

ZEBRA BOOKS
Kensington Publishing Corp.
www.kensingtonbooks.com

ZEBRA BOOKS are published by

Kensington Publishing Corp.
850 Third Avenue
New York, NY 10022

All Kensington titles, imprints, and distributed lines are avail-
able at special quantity discounts for bulk purchases for sales
promotion, premiums, fund-raising, educational, or institu-
tional use.

Special book excerpts or customized printings can also be cre-
ated to fit specific needs. For details, write or phone the office
of the Kensington Special Sales Manager: Attn.: Special Sales
Department, Kensington Publishing Corp., 850 Third Avenue,
New York, NY 10022. Phone: 1-800-221-2647.

Zebra and the Z logo Reg. U.S. Pat. & TM Off.

ISBN-13: 978-0-8217-8128-9
ISBN-10: 0-8217-8128-6

First Printing: August 2007
10 9 8 7 6 5 4 3 2 1

Printed in the United States of America

Acknowledgments

To my phenomenal editor, John Scognamiglio,
and my marvelous agent, Sha-Shana Crichton.
I am so grateful for your guidance and support.

To Nancy Frost and Brenda Hammond
for critiques, camaraderie, and friendship,
and to the "debs" for being
there to pass me the bucket.

To my parents, brothers and sisters-in-law,
nieces and nephews,
and my wonderful friends
for celebrating my writing and
supporting my dream.

To Sheridan, my joy, and Dylan, my light.

To Henning,
my hero, my love.

Chapter 1

Desperation made for a poor walking companion.

Jane Heatherington studied the horizon, dread gnawing at her with small, sharp bites. The sky was a leaden mass of churning gray clouds that hung low on the water, and the ocean pummeled the shore with a strength that heralded the furor of the coming storm. Breathing in the tangy salt scent of the sea, Jane clenched her fists. The edges of the delicate pink shell in her hand dug into the skin of her palm, grounding her as she struggled to hold her misery at bay.

Life was burdened by tragedy. Naïve girl, to have believed that fate had dealt out all her cruel jests years ago. Jane shook her head. No, not fate. She could blame no one but the true perpetrator of this terrible thing that had come to pass. Her own father had consigned them both to uncertainty and despair.

How much money?

Five hundred pounds.

Yet fate *was* there too, lurking, laughing, playing

her horrible game. Was not Jane's presence here this morning some act of chance?

Ill chance, to be sure.

Less than an hour past, as the cold, gray dawn had crawled into the heavens, Jane had left her father's hostelry, needing a few moments to understand, to accept the terrible choices he had made, the dreadful consequence he had brought down upon them. She had walked along the beach, mindless of any destination, seeking only to calm her concerns and fears.

She shuddered now, studying the two men who stood in the churning surf. They waited as the waves carried forth a grim offering, a single dark speck that dipped and swayed with each turbulent surge, growing ever larger, taking on defined shape and macabre form.

Indeed, desperation made a poor walking companion, but death even more so.

Wrapping her arms about herself, Jane watched the dark outline float closer, closer, discernable now as human, facedown in the water with arms outstretched, long tendrils of tangled hair fanning like a copper halo.

A woman, bobbing and sodden.

And dead.

Heart pounding in her breast, Jane took a single step forward as the men sought to drag their gruesome catch from the ocean's chill embrace. She was held in thrall by the terrible tableau unfolding before her, and she swallowed back the greasy sickness that welled inside her. 'Twas not morbid curiosity, but heart-wrenching empathy that froze her in place.

Most days, she could look at the ocean as a thing of great beauty.

Most days.

But not today.

Today there were disquieting clouds and churning surf and the icy kiss of the mist that blew from the water's surface to touch land. Too, deep in her heart, there was the awful knowledge of her father's actions and the terrible feeling of foreboding, of change, unwelcome and unwanted.

It seemed all too similar to a day long past, a day best buried in a dusty corner of her mind. The sea. The storm. And there, just beyond a great outcropping of rock, the brooding shadow of Trevisham House, looming silent and frightful against the backdrop of gray water and grayer sky.

Separated from the sweeping curve of sandy beach by swirling waves, the massive house was a lonely, empty shell balanced atop a great granite crag that rose out of the sea like the horny back of a mythical beast, a fearsome pile of stone and mortar that offered no warmth. Trevisham was linked to the mainland by a narrow causeway that was passable at low tide or high. Unless there was a storm, and then it was not passable at all.

Chill fingers of unease crawled along Jane's spine, and she tore her gaze away, glancing to her right, to her left, feeling inexplicably wary. She was given to neither fanciful notions nor wild imaginings, yet today it appeared she was subject to both. Her heart tripped too fast, and her nerves felt raw as she scanned the beach, searching for the source of her unease. She could swear there was someone watching the beach. Watching *her*.

This was not the first time she had suspected

such. Twice yesterday she had spun quickly, peering into darkened corners and shadowed niches, finding nothing but her own unease. She sighed. Perhaps it had been a portent rather than a human threat, a chill warning of the news her father had been about to share.

"She's been in the water less than a week, I'm thinking," Jem Basset called grimly, drawing Jane's attention to where he stood thigh deep in the water, the corpse bobbing just beyond his reach.

"Where's she from?" Robert Dawe asked, wading a step farther into the waves. "A ship, do you think?"

"There's been only fine weather for more than three weeks. No ship's gone down here. If she's from a ship, then it was wrecked on the rocks to the north, I'm thinking."

The two men exchanged a telling look.

Jem grunted and reached as far as he could, but the waves carried the body just beyond his grasp. He glanced up, saw Jane, and shook his head. "Go on now, Janie. No need for you to see this."

He was right, of course. There was no need for her to watch them drag this poor, unfortunate woman from her watery grave, but Jane could not will her feet to move. The talk of wrecks and rocks haunted her.

There had been whispers of late that the coast to the north was safe for no ship, that in the dark of the night wreckers set their false lights where no light should be. They were vile murderers bent on luring the unsuspecting to their doom, tricking a ship into thinking it was guided by a lighthouse's warning beacon, only to see it torn asunder on jagged rocks.

Torn asunder like the fabric of her life.

But at least she had life, Jane thought fiercely as she watched the corpse bob down, then up; long, copper hair swaying in the current like snaking tendrils of dark blood.

Pulling her shawl tight about her shoulders, Jane blew out a slow breath, steadying her nerves, battling both her fears for her future and the ugly memories of her past. Dark thoughts. Terrible recollections of storm and sea and Trevisham House.

Jem lunged, and this time, he caught the dead woman's arm, and then Robert came alongside him, and together they wrestled her from the frothing waves.

"You think there'll be others?" Robert asked, breathing heavily as they slogged toward the shore, the sand sucking at their booted feet, the woman's body dragged between them, her head hanging down, legs trailing in the water.

Shaking his head, Jem cast a quick glance toward Jane. "Not likely. Bodies usually sink into the deep dark. Strange that this one didn't."

"They sink only until they fill with bloat, and then they float up again like a cork, don't they?" Not waiting for a reply, Robert waved his free hand and continued. "Her skirt. See the way it's tangled about her ankles? It must have caught the air when she went into the water and held her afloat. That is why she did not sink."

Drawn despite herself, Jane took a step along the beach, and another, gripped by the image of this poor woman, her limbs growing heavier and heavier as she was tossed about on a cruel sea. Struggling, gasping, praying.

And finally, dying.

Such an image.

Such a *memory*. She could *feel* the tightness in *her* chest. The great, gasping breath that brought only a cold burning rush of water to fill her nose and throat and lungs. With her heart pounding a harsh rhythm in her breast, Jane struggled against the strangling recollection, determined to hold it at bay.

Jem laid the drowned woman in the back of a rough wooden cart, mindful of her modesty, though such was long past any value to her. With a twist of pity, Jane saw that the woman was both bloated and shriveled at once, her face white-green, in frightful contrast to her copper hair, and her eyes . . .

With a cry, Jane stumbled back a step, pressing her palm to her lips. Horror seeped through her veins, a terrible dismay that chilled her to her core.

The woman's eyes were gone from her skull, leaving only empty black sockets.

Jane wrenched her gaze away, swallowing convulsively as she stared at the wet sand dusted with a smattering of white and pink shells.

Shells.

She had come to walk on the beach to soothe her soul, and to fetch a handful of shells to carry with her. Just a handful of shells for her mother. Those were her reasons for being on the beach. Now, instead of shells and ease of mind, she would carry the memory of the dead woman's bloated face and the empty holes that had held her eyes.

A new nightmare to haunt her rest, Jane thought. Imaginings of another woman's suffering, as though her own was not companion enough in the darkest hours of the night.

Suddenly, she froze, and her head snapped up. The hair at her nape prickled and rose. Jane rubbed her hands briskly along the outsides of her arms as apprehension chilled her from within, swelling in tandem with the rolling waves.

Someone *was* watching them.

Lips slightly parted, the tip of her tongue pressed between her top and bottom teeth, Jane turned to face the great wall of sea-carved cliffs that rose alongside the long, slow curve of sand. Tipping her head up and back, she studied the stark precipice with measured interest. The sound of the waves hitting the shore surrounded her, punctuated by the cry of a lonely gull high overhead. From the corner of her eye she caught a hint of motion, a shadow, far, far to her left, up on the cliff.

There was a blur of movement, a dark ripple of cloth that might have been a man's cloak.

She spun so quickly, her balance was almost lost. Reaching down, she pressed the flat of her palm to her left thigh, adding sheer will and the strength of her arm to the paltry force of the muscles that would straighten her knee and hold her upright. If she was lucky. If not, her leg would crumple as it was often wont to do, and she would sink to the sand in a graceless heap. After a moment, she righted herself, and turned her attention to the place she had glimpsed the shadowy stranger.

The cliff was barren. There was no one outlined against the ominous backdrop of gray sky. The man—if in truth she had seen one—was gone.

But the sinister unease that clutched at her remained.

Leaving the beach, Jane inched along the narrow dirt path that hugged the jagged cliffs, her thoughts awhirl with both her own personal turmoil and the horror of the drowned woman's tragic and pitiable fate. She climbed to the top and paused, her attention snagged by her father's cousin, Dolly Gwyn. The frail woman stood by the edge of the cliff, arms raised, her wild gray hair unbound, whipped by frantic eddies of air, her form swathed in layer upon layer of faded black cloth. Before her lay the roiling turmoil of the angry sea, above her the leaden sky that pressed its ominous weight down upon her as she perched there atop her precarious roost, summoning the storm.

Jane sighed. "Cousin Dolly!" she called, cupping her hands about her lips to amplify the sound. "Come away from the crag!" The wind and the crashing sea swallowed her cry, or perhaps Dolly chose to ignore her. 'Twould not be the first time.

As Jane reached her side, Dolly stretched out a thin arm, waving her hand to encompass the storm-washed beach and the sea cliffs that extended as far as the eye could see.

"I saw a light, oh, about a week past," Dolly said, diving into the topic without preamble. Her voice was strong, though her body was beginning to weaken as years and hardship took their toll. "Far to the north it was. An evil light. A false light." She cast a glance at Jane. "A wrecker's light."

"Never say it," Jane whispered, a sick feeling rising inside of her.

"I say it because I saw it," Dolly insisted. "We'll be hearing the tale of a ship gone down within a short time, my girl. You heed me now. We'll hear of a ship gone down and all aboard her dead. What can that be but wreckers, I ask you? What?"

A wrecker's light, so close to Pentreath. Earlier, as they dragged the woman from the ocean, Jem and Robert had guessed that she'd been in the water but a few days. They had hinted with brief words and subtle glances that they believed she had come from a wreck on the northern shore. And if Dolly spoke true . . .

Enough. Jane wanted no more heartache, no more sadness this day.

"I pray you are wrong," she said.

"As do I, Janie. As do I. But I tell you . . . the woman that was pulled from the waves this morning . . . she came from that ship. She died for men's greed." Dolly wrapped her thin arms around herself and swayed to and fro in the wind as they stood, shoulder to shoulder, facing the crashing surf, listening to the building furor of the ocean.

"And it's *him*, his coming, what's brought the evil down upon us," she continued, stretching out one gnarled finger toward the sea, and toward Trevisham House, guiding Jane's unwilling gaze. This of all days, with the horrible news her father had shared and the image of that poor drowned woman so fresh in her mind, Jane would have preferred not to think of Trevisham, not to remember. But wasn't that ever the way of things, with one tragedy recollecting others?

"He is in league with the devil. I feel it in my bones." Dolly pulled back her lips in distaste, revealing the uneven outline of her three remaining teeth.

"The new owner?" Jane asked, loath to tar and feather a man without cause. "We know nothing about him."

With a careless shrug, Dolly shuffled a short way along the path, clutching her tattered cloak about her hunched shoulders.

"What do we know? What do we know about him?" She slanted a sly glance at Jane. "We can guess that he has a very, very *large* fortune, for Trevisham surely cost him more than most could ever imagine. But how he came by his money . . ." Dolly's voice trailed away, leaving her allusions all the more sinister for being unspoken.

"I am sure that is none of my concern," Jane chided gently. She knew from experience exactly where this conversation would lead. Dolly loved nothing better than to sniff out her neighbors' secrets, and if she smelled naught of interest, she was not averse to providing details from her own vivid imagination.

"His money's ill-gotten, if you ask me. Smuggling. Wrecking. Mayhap murder." The old woman turned a jaundiced eye to the heavens.

Wrecking. Murder. Jane could not help but think of the terrible bloated face of the woman she had seen dragged from the sea, and that image tweaked the memory of the dark shadow she had sensed high atop the cliff earlier that morn. Dear heaven, was there to be only darkness today and in the days to come, only sadness and loss and fear?

"There's an ill wind blowing," Dolly said, as though in answer to Jane's unspoken question. "You mind me well . . . it blows from Trevisham"—she stabbed a finger in the general direction of the house—"and from the man who will be master there."

"The man who will be master there," Jane repeated. She could not recall a time when Trevisham had been inhabited. The previous owner had left more than two decades past, before Jane had come to Pentreath, and the house had stood empty all the time since. Curiosity surged in her breast, an interest in who he was, this man who had purchased a crumbling, forgotten pile of rock and mortar, a man of mystery and shadow.

He was a man of great fortune, if Dolly was to be believed. A pirate. A smuggler. A wrecker.

With a shudder, Jane turned and stepped forward, moving closer to Dolly's side. Fierce breakers pummeled the jagged rocks that surrounded Trevisham House, then crashed against the stretch of beach, churning the sand. She felt Dolly reach for her, age-twisted fingers curling about her wrist.

"Have you seen him, Dolly? The new owner?" Jane asked, though for certes she already knew the answer. If Dolly had seen him, the entire village of Pentreath would have known within the quarter hour.

Speculation about the newcomer was rampant. Even without the man having actually put in an appearance, people had talked of nothing else for more than a fortnight. Her father welcomed the gossip, for the villagers needed somewhere to meet and discuss their conjectures, and a pint of ale at her father's hostelry was usually the venue of choice.

"I've not seen him. Other than old William, no one has," Dolly replied, hooking her arm through Jane's. "He arrived under cover of night, never stopping at the pub for drink or conversation. I wonder what kind of man shuns the company of his neighbors."

"A man who prefers his privacy." Jane pulled out her black wool gloves from the small pocket she had sewn on the inside of her cloak near the slit for her arm. She slid them onto her hands, keeping her arm linked with Dolly's throughout.

"Aye. But *why* does he prefer his privacy? There's a good question." Narrowing her eyes, Dolly tapped the tip of her forefinger against the sagging skin of her wrinkled cheek. "And why did he choose *this* place?" she mused. "There are less isolated houses about, and in better repair."

Jane thought she understood such a choice. She had long ago learned to appreciate the magnificence of the stark and lonely countryside that had been her home for more than a decade. She knew the splendor of the moors, the harsh appeal of the wind-and-salt-spray-etched faces of the precipices that jutted into the sea, the tors with their caps of jagged granite. And she knew that Trevisham House called to those who would listen. "Perhaps he views isolation as privacy."

Dolly grunted. "Isolation is good for certain activities . . . those that are carried out on a barren rocky coast with none to bear witness."

A heaviness settled in Jane's chest, stalling her breath. She shook her head, and said firmly, "Perhaps he chose Cornwall because this is a place of beauty."

"Aye. That it is. Barren. Lonely. Beautiful." Dolly hooted at some secret jest. "But that is not why he came. Mark my words. This man is cloaked in death. I feel it in the depths of my old soul."

"Death is no stranger to Pentreath. No stranger to Trevisham," Jane replied, thinking of the pitiable, nameless woman whom she had watched Jem and Robert drag from the ocean.

She dared not let her memories wander farther back than that.

No, death was not a stranger.

At length, Dolly gave Jane's arm a gentle squeeze. "I'll leave you now. I have mending to do and I need what there is of the light on this dreary day to do it.

You'd best see to your visiting, Janie, and make your way home before the storm."

Yes. She would do well to make her way home before the storm. The lesson was one well learned. Cold fingers reached forward through the years to touch her skin, making her shudder. She would have done well to hurry home another day, far in the past, to hurry home before that long ago storm. Memories nipped at her like a beast poked with a stick.

Gathering her thoughts, Jane spoke her farewells, and Dolly hobbled off in the direction of her small cottage nestled at the edge of the village. Watching her go, Jane tried to stifle her unease, to tamp down the restless urgency that gnawed at her, the sense that great misfortune was soon to come to Pentreath.

She sucked in a breath. Grand calamity had already come, not to Pentreath but to *her*, carried on her father's foibles and poor choices. Yet, she sensed something bigger, stronger, something worse than even this wretched circumstance that had been thrust upon her. The thought was terrible indeed.

Dolly had seen a light to the north, where no light should be.

A dead woman had washed ashore, her very presence testament to some horrific event.

Wreckers.

Only once before had Jane felt such a strong forewarning building inside her until it seemed to take on a life of its own. On that day her world had tilted and all she knew as safe and good had shattered. Gone in an instant. She remembered the storm and her mother's voice calling out to her, then the sharp crack of sound, and the pain. She remembered the pain.

She remembered Mama dead, calling out no more, broken like a porcelain doll on the merciless rocks, her long dark hair hanging wet and limp like seaweed.

Her fault. Her fault. Her fault.

"No." With a whispered denial, Jane tore her thoughts away from the cheerless remembrance, away, too, from the terrible guilt, for if she allowed it to surface it would easily overwhelm her. She had learned over the years to control it, rather than letting wave after wave of crushing sorrow control her.

Her grief was old now and tinged with bittersweet recollection, misty memories of joy and warmth tempering the horror of her loss.

Turning, she shambled with her uneven gait toward the tall square bell tower that loomed in the distance, its crenellated cornice reaching to the menacing sky. The way was familiar to her. At least once each week she made this journey to the church, to the graveyard that lay in its shadow.

She paused beside the low stone wall that surrounded the building, and rested a wool-gloved hand against the chilly surface, silently acknowledging the ever-present dull ache in her left knee. The winter damp seeped right through the joint. She could barely remember a time when the muted pain had not been her constant companion.

A noise caught her attention. Frowning, she turned and looked over her shoulder. A chill chased along her spine. But, no. There was no one behind her on the well-traveled dirt path.

She stood for a long moment, staring at the

empty trail. For an instant, she had been certain that she was no longer alone.

Opening the ancient iron gate, Jane set her teeth as the rusted hinges emitted a strident squeak. The gate was in need of oiling. She would mention it to the vicar's wife, who in turn would mention it to the vicar. Such was the way of village life.

Fallen autumn leaves, brown and parched, tumbled end over end, whipping between the headstones with a dry, rustling sound as Jane walked through the graveyard.

Suddenly, the wind died, and all was still. Uneasy in the eerie silence, she glanced about, her gaze coming to rest on the dead and blackened elm that stood in the far corner of the cemetery, its lifeless limbs arcing over the etched stones. High upon a narrow branch perched a solitary raven, watching her.

She let her gaze wander away, across the rows of gravestones. Something felt strange this morning: the silence in the face of the brewing storm; the portent of the raven; Dolly's doomsaying; and the faint whisper in the darkest corner of her mind that had haunted her since she had jerked from fitful slumber at the first rays of dawn. There was a wind of change swirling over Pentreath, carried by the storm. A wind of change, bearing menace and danger.

Chilled to her marrow, Jane fastened the highest button on her cloak and pulled her shawl tighter about her shoulders as she slipped between the graves, making her way to the carved granite headstone that marked her mother's final rest. Pausing, she reached into the pocket of her cloak to pull out the small, perfectly coiled pink shell that she had taken from the beach. With a sigh, she trailed her

fingers along the stone to the engraved words that
were her mother's epitaph.

> *Sacred to the memory of Margaret Alice Heather-*
> *ington the wife of Gideon Heatherington of this*
> *Parish who departed this life 18th day of July in the*
> *year of our Lord 1802 aged 29 years. In this life a*
> *loving wife, a tender mother dear.*

Silently mouthing the phrases, Jane closed her
eyes against the insidious tide of sadness that flooded
her heart. There were still days that she awakened
expecting to hear her mother's voice.

"Good morning, Mama dear," she whispered as
she placed the shell on the top of the tombstone. A
hazy memory flitted through her mind of her
mother running barefoot along the beach, laughing as she paused to gather shells. That night she
had strung them on a length of yarn, making a
necklace for her daughter. As a child, Jane had
treasured the gift; as a woman grown, she treasured
it still more.

Her touch strayed to the small, painted miniature—
fronted in glass—that her father had ordered embed-
ded in the stone. An exorbitant expense, but one her
father had insisted upon. Jane ran her finger over the
glass, noting that the winter's harsh kiss had forced a
jagged crack. Her heart twisted and a tear escaped to
carve a path along her cheek.

The glass would remain as it was, broken, for
there were no funds for its repair. Her father's folly
had seen to that.

She traced the twining vines that the mason had
carved about the picture to frame her mother's
likeness. The artist had done a wonderful job. The

minute painting resembled Margaret Heatherington in all details, just as it resembled Jane, who took
after the woman who had borne her to an uncanny
degree.

Mother and daughter shared the same tall, slim
build, the chestnut hair, the ready smile. Jane well
remembered her mother's flashing dark eyes, tipping up just a bit at the corners. She could see
those eyes looking back at her in the mirror each
morning. And she could see the subtle differences,
too. Her nose was smaller, her lips fuller, her chin
slightly squared where her mother's had been soft
and round.

"Oh, Mama. I miss you so."

Her only answer was the mournful howl of the
wind, which had renewed itself and bit through
Jane's cloak and shawl with pitiless vigor.

With a single piercing cry and a great flapping of
feathers, the raven took flight from its lofty perch.
Startled, Jane spun about. Her gaze sought the
source of the sound and she watched as the bird
spread its wings and soared above the secluded
cemetery, flying free and unfettered.

Oh, to be that raven. To be free of the situation
her father had thrust upon her. Free of her twisted
limb. Free to roam the world and see all manner of
wonderful things.

She watched the bird until it was only a dark
speck in the distance, and then she shivered. Again,
she felt the sensation that she was not alone.

Slowly, she lowered her head. Her breath caught
in her throat as her blood rushed hot and rich in
her veins. Taking a stumbling step back, she felt the
unyielding solidity of the granite stone at her back,

and she leaned against it, touched by an equal measure of trepidation and fascination.

Her heart stuttered, and then raced.

Because, no, she was most definitely *not* alone.

Chapter 2

Jane's breath escaped her in a rush. There, at the
far edge of the churchyard, separated from her by
the low wall, stood a man.

He was broad and tall. The stone fence reached
nearly to the top of his thighs, while it rose all the
way to Jane's waist. The new owner of Trevisham
House. He could be no other. His proud bearing,
the cut of his coat, the confident tilt of his head, they
bespoke wealth. And power.

The wind caught the tiers of his long black greatcoat, making it billow about him. His hair was long,
past his collar, honey-brown shot with gold, the rich
color telling her he was no stranger to the sun.
Hard, unsmiling, his face was as harshly beautiful as
the Cornwall landscape.

He was a vision from a fairy tale, Jane thought, a
battle-hardened knight. A man of mist and dreams.
A young girl's hero. She swallowed, reminding herself that such fantasies were not for her. Her story
did not include a prince. Even the men of Pentreath who knew her so well, who laughed at her
tales, who valued her kind words, even they saw her

as the innkeeper's crippled daughter. Surely a man of means and station would spare no notice for her.

Nor did she want him to, she thought defiantly.

Well, perhaps a single thought . . . It was *her* girlish fantasy, after all.

She stood, frozen, watching him warily as he turned and made his way around the perimeter of the graveyard, following the course of the stone wall. He opened the gate and stepped inside, his stride confident, his boots crunching the dry, dead leaves. All masculine grace and power, the way he moved was unutterably appealing.

The pace of her heart accelerated with each step that brought him closer, and she waited, her feet rooted to the ground.

"Good afternoon," she said, offering a tentative smile of greeting as he approached. Years of work in her father's pub called up a friendly salutation as a matter of habit.

Stopping some three feet from her, he inclined his head politely but did not return her smile. "I did not mean to disturb you," he said.

There was a subtle shade to his vowels, some peculiarity to his pronunciation. Jane could hear that he was not a Cornishman, but she could not place his origin. His voice was low, a touch gravelly. The sound reached deep inside her, made her want to lean closer, to touch his smooth lips, to *feel* the words pour from him. With a frown, she pressed her palm against the icy granite at her back, girding herself against such odd and ridiculous notions.

"No. You did not disturb me." She gestured toward the headstone. "I came to be with my mother."

She had no idea why she told him that.

The silence stretched and grew thin. Jane cast about for some topic of conversation.

"Do you . . . that is, are you here to visit someone in particular?" she blurted, not at all certain why she felt so nervous in his presence.

"Yes." He watched her intently, elaborating no further, and making no move toward any of the graves.

Her eyes widened as she had the bizarre thought that he had come here to see *her*. How absurd.

Unnerved, Jane looked away, scanning the distant clouds, looking anywhere but directly at this glorious man whose mere presence somehow left her feeling both exhilarated and wretchedly confused.

"I fear we are in for a storm," she said hurriedly. "You'll want to make your way back to Trevisham House before the crossing becomes impassable." As the words left her lips, she realized that she had given away the fact that she had surmised his identity. Darting a quick glance at his face, she found him regarding her with an expression that hinted at amusement. The emotion seemed awkward for him. The carved planes of his face, so handsomely etched, had the look of a man who rarely smiled.

"I could seek shelter at your father's inn." There was a discernable undercurrent to his words. Sarcasm? But that made no sense.

Seek shelter at her father's inn. His suggestion reminded her of the dire uncertainty of her situation. Regret was bitter on her tongue.

Yes, for this night, and perhaps the next, the Crown Inn belonged to her father, but one day soon his rash debt would come due.

What would happen then?

Likely, the inn would no longer belong to

Gideon Heatherington. Likely, the inn would be
sold for whatever coin it could fetch. And then . . .
No, she would face *that* tragedy only when it arose
in truth, rather than in the haunted uncertainties
that plagued her.

"Do you know my father?" she asked.

"We have met." His tone was brusque.

"He never said." How odd that her father had not
mentioned having made the acquaintance of the
new owner of Trevisham House, for such personal
association would have brought in many curious pa-
trons for a pint or a meal, and a spot of conversation
and gossip.

"It was a lifetime ago." He smiled darkly. "Somehow, I doubt he will remember the occasion."

Jane raised her head, and her gaze locked with
his. Indigo ink. Polished granite. His eyes were a
stunning mixture of blue and gray, changeable,
dazzling, rimmed by thick lashes, set beneath
straight honey-brown brows. Beautiful eyes. But
shadowed. Eyes that had seen much; windows to a
soul that had suffered.

She shivered, inexplicably uneasy. And then she
wondered why she was not *more* uneasy in the presence of this man, this stranger. Had she learned
nothing from the lessons of her past?

"I am sorry. I do not believe that you introduced
yourself." She frowned, suddenly aware that he
knew who she was, who her father was, yet she had
never told him her name.

His expression became shuttered. "No, I did
not."

"I think I should go." Jane made to step past him,
and then paused, unable to restrain her curiosity,
however foolhardy. She turned her head to look at

him. "How did you know who I was? That my father owns the Crown Inn?"

He gestured at a spot behind her. Turning, she found herself facing her mother's gravestone, the name Heatherington clearly stamped in the granite.

"Oh. Of course." Had she thought him prescient? Perhaps imagined that he was the one who had been following her, watching her from the cliff that morn? Stalking her for some nefarious and unspecified reason? The idea was laughable. He had only to read the stone to know who she was. Despite the fact that he had yet to visit Pentreath, he would have heard of her father, who owned the only inn for many miles. There was not another to be found until one reached the New Inn, which sat smack-dab in the middle of Bodmin Moor.

"Have you ever been to Trevisham House, Miss Heatherington?"

At his politely spoken question, she shifted to face him once more. A tingle of awareness danced across her senses as she realized he was a step closer than he had been before.

"Do you mean inside the house?" she asked, startled by the thought.

His brows rose.

"No, I have not been to Trevisham." She had never been to the house itself. Had not been to the island since that one terrible day, the waves crashing her against the rocks, and the pain—

She shook her head. "I was quite small when my family moved to Cornwall. The previous owner left some years before that. He never returned. Trevisham has been vacant until, well, until you, Mr. . . ."

"Warrick," he supplied. "Aidan Warrick."

She thought the name fit quite well. He did not

look like a Charles or a William. Definitely not a Harry. *Aidan Warrick*. A dashing name that suited him as perfectly as his well-tailored coat.

"Well, Mr. Warrick, I must confess that I have seen Trevisham House only from the outside."

"That will change."

"I beg your pardon, sir?" She felt disoriented. Was he inviting her to visit his home? The thought was extraordinary. Much less than proper. And frighteningly appealing.

As her thoughts tumbled one over the next, she saw the nonsensicality of such notions. Most likely, he meant to offer her a position in the scullery or the kitchen.

He looked up at the sky, and she followed the direction of his gaze. Angry clouds gathered overhead, no longer a distant threat on the horizon.

"We should be away," Mr. Warrick said, cupping Jane's elbow with one leather-gloved hand.

She gasped at the contact. He was touching her. *Touching her.* And it was like no touch she had ever known. Despite the leather of his glove and the layers of her clothes, she felt the connection arrow deep, as though, somehow, she had waited her entire life for him to touch her, to warm her, to send fire licking through her veins.

He inhaled sharply.

Jane found her breath coming in rough little panting gasps as she stood pinned by the intensity of his regard. His eyes were suddenly dark and heavy lidded. For an instant, something almost frightening flickered there, wild and strangely seductive, and then he blinked and it was gone. Yet she was left with an unfamiliar awareness, a wish that he would look at her like that again.

"We should be away," he repeated, dropping his hand to his side, breaking the contact. "I will see you back to your father's inn."

"That is not necessary, sir. I have traveled this path more times than I can count. I assure you, my safety is not in question." Her protest was a bare whisper. She was mortified by the thought of this man going out of his way to accommodate her, the innkeeper's lame daughter.

Gesturing for her to precede him, he shook his head decisively. "I insist. One never knows the harm that can befall the innocent in a place such as this."

Jane took a step back, her left heel dragging on the ground with a soft shush.

"My footing is sure," she insisted, feeling hideously awkward as her statement was belied by her obvious infirmity.

"I do not refer to your footing. There are greater dangers here than a rutted path or a loose stone."

His words conjured an image of the poor drowned woman from the beach with her flesh bloated in death and her eyes pulled from their sockets, gnawed out by the fish, like as not. Jane shuddered and wrapped her arms about herself.

Again, he moved his hand to indicate that she should precede him toward the gate. "Please."

Deciding that this particular argument was hardly worth her energies, Jane did as he bid. She could not fathom the reason for his firm insistence, but she could not fault a man for behaving chivalrously. As she stepped past him, she caught the faint scent of citrus and spice, and something else . . . The scent escaped her. Bemused by the outlandish thought that she would like to lean close and sniff him, to press her nose to the solid column of his neck and inhale to her heart's content, she bowed her head and walked on.

They followed the path that Jane had taken with Dolly not an hour past. She cast surreptitious glances at her companion, curious as to his purpose in walking with her thus. He strolled at her side, measuring his tread to match her own uneven gait. His presence made her heart beat a little faster than normal.

She pressed her lips together, struggling to find a pleasant and acceptable topic for discussion, but only the weather leapt to mind and they had already exhausted that subject with their discourse of the imminent storm.

The path descended toward Pentreath, curving smoothly. Behind them lay gently rolling hills and fields, muddy from the winter rains, dotted with fluffy sheep. Old Magworth's run-down cottage came into view, and then Dolly Gwyn's tidier one with its clean whitewashed face and neat yard. Mr. Warrick glanced at each, making no comment, and then Jane saw his gaze stray to her feet. Mortification washed over her. He would comment now on her limp, she thought, feeling the tension creep across her shoulders.

"There are wild ponies on the moors," she blurted, anxious to draw his attention to something other than her imperfection.

He stopped and laid his hand on her arm, halting her progress as he regarded her curiously. Again, his touch sizzled through her, confusing her, making her feel oddly restless and a little breathless.

"Do you dream of running free on the moors, Miss Heatherington? Like the wild ponies?"

She met his gaze for an endless agonizing moment, wondering how, from her innocuous statement about the ponies, he had divined her most secret yearning. Wondering, too, if he meant his question to be as heartless as she found it.

Fettered by her mangled limb, burdened now as well by her father's terrible choices and financial ruin, her world was a narrow cage. Never again would she know the joy of running free. Never.

"Yes, you will," he said, his words a promise, low and rough.

She gasped as she realized she had voiced her thoughts aloud. Or had she? There was something about this man, this stranger, that made her feel as though she was stripped bare to her soul; as though her thoughts were as transparent to him as clear water on a sunny day.

"Please," Jane whispered desperately, gathering the tattered remnants of her poise as he watched her, his expression unreadable. She glanced at the sky. "We must hurry if we are to find shelter before the storm."

He waited a heartbeat, and then said, "Yes, of course. Let us proceed."

They resumed walking, side by side, and Jane was increasingly aware of *everything*. The breadth of Mr. Warrick's shoulders. The easy grace of his every step. The tantalizing scent of him, so subtle, so clean.

The shimmering impression of danger and power that clung to him.

Oh, this was madness, this inexplicable fascination with a man she had met only moments ago. Such thoughts were so far outside her normal character that she wondered if she had caught a chill, if the heat generated by Mr. Warrick's proximity was in fact a fever in her blood, an evil humor or the ague.

With a casual movement, he took her arm, helping her over a rock that disrupted the smooth flow of the path. The contact crackled through the cloth of her sleeve, and she stared at the back of his gloved hand, broad and strong. As he withdrew, her gaze dropped to the ground, and she resumed walking, numbly keeping pace with him as her blood pounded in her veins. She wanted to touch him again, to feel that connection, and that unfamiliar wanting baffled and alarmed her.

As the Crown Inn came into view, Jane felt an odd twinge at the sight of it. Ambivalence. Though she and Mr. Warrick had not shared any significant conversation save for that one fraught exchange, she was loath to see their brief journey end, even as she knew there was no reason for it to continue. Her pulse raced in a rhythm that far surpassed the mild exertion of their walk, and she could not stop herself from casting sidelong glances at his handsome face, the hard line of his jaw, cleanly shaven and smooth, the shadowed hollows of his cheeks.

She found their silent companionability exhilarating. She found him unimaginably fascinating. Never had she looked at a man thus, only to admire the perfection of him, to take pleasure in his form. But then, never had she seen a man such as Aidan Warrick.

Mr. Warrick paused, studying the inn with careful attention. Jane wondered if he saw the beauty of it, the simple practicality of the cobbled courtyard and slate roof. The building was shaped like the letter *L*, with a stable, a tack room, the pub and dining room, and sleeping chambers above. A row of casement windows lined up tidily along the upper floor, and a second row along the lower. Her father had purchased the place a decade and a half prior.

Jane knew nothing of his profession in the time before he became an innkeeper, only that he had disliked whatever it was that he had done previously and that it had paid well enough for him to become an innkeeper.

More than once she had asked him about their lives before Cornwall, for she vaguely recalled a small house in a crowded city, where neighbors rubbed shoulders and tempers. She remembered that her father had been gone from the house for long periods of time—weeks, if not months—and those absences had made her mother cry. His homecomings had made her cry all the harder.

Each time Jane pressed Gideon Heatherington for answers, he sidestepped her questions, saying coldly that he wished she would not badger him so.

She thought he must sorely regret the weeks and months he had been away, for surely he saw them as time stolen from a wife who had died too young. He raged against that loss still, the passage of time offering him no ease. The predictable bout of drunken melancholy that invariably followed her queries always made Jane feel both guilty and anxious.

Eventually, she had stopped questioning him about a past that was so obviously painful.

Yet even without her prodding and poking, her father was gruff more and more of late, drank too much and woke up surly. She well knew his excuses: he had suffered much, lost much. Jane would forever bear the guilt of that, and so she endured her father's weaker traits. Ever practical, she cleaned up after his messes as best she could.

Now she swallowed the worry that thickened in her throat as she thought of their newly revealed debt. Desperation shifted and swelled, a live thing deep in her belly. This time, she would not be able to set things to rights. This time her father had gambled away their very livelihood.

A shiver chased through her as, with a shrill squeak, the shingle hanging over the door of the Crown Inn shifted back and forth in the wind. Jane looked up to find a bird, black as coal, perched on the metal frame that held the sign. A raven. Had it followed her down the hill, an ill omen?

The feeling of foreboding that had plagued her earlier returned, wrapping icy tendrils round her heart. Such a strange and melancholy day, heavy with ill news and peculiar happenings, and memories best left buried.

Resolutely, she thrust aside her anxious thoughts, and laid her palms against the heavy wooden door of the inn, her actions accompanied by a distant rumble of thunder. The heavens opened and the rain began, landing in fat round drops on her hair, her face, her shoulders. She glanced at Mr. Warrick.

"Please, come inside," she said, pushing the door wide.

He followed her, close enough that she felt the brush of his greatcoat on her back. The pub was empty, though Jane knew the villagers would gather there come evening. Sooner, if those who had seen her cross the village square spread the tale of her companion.

Shrugging out of her shawl and hooded scarlet cloak, she shook the water from them and hung the garments on a hook by the door.

"Father," she called. "I am home."

After a moment, Gideon Heatherington strode from the back of the inn, his bulky frame filling the narrow hallway that led from the kitchen to the bar.

"Glad I am that you made it before the storm," he said. "You know I worry, Janie."

So he said often enough. But that day, that long ago day, he had not worried enough to come find her.

Jane opened her mouth to introduce their guest, but her father continued in a rush. "'Tis late. I'll need you to chop the carrots and potatoes for tonight's stew. I know your leg's been poorly, but you'll make do. Mary's sent her oldest to say she has a chill, so you'll be helping me in the tavern tonight as well as the kitchen."

He moved toward her along the corridor, and then paused as he caught sight of her companion. Gideon's eyes narrowed, and the tip of his tongue poked out from the corner of his mouth.

"Well," he said. "Well."

Jane saw the distinctive gleam of avarice as he took in the quality of their guest's attire. She saw, too, the reddened nose and puffy eyes. He had indulged in a dram or two, she realized, though noon was not yet upon them.

A brief flare of desperation nipped at her. She squelched it, knowing there was nothing she could do to sway her father from his course. When faced with adversity, he turned to his drink. It had ever been his way, and ever been the path to their downfall. The more he drank, the poorer his decisions became, and the more belligerent his temper. Best to stay out of his way, then.

"Father, this is Mr. Aidan Warrick," she said, injecting as much enthusiasm as she could into her revelation. "He is our new neighbor, from Trevisham House."

She had expected her announcement to win her father's favor and draw a smile, for Mr. Warrick's presence would surely attract a bustling crowd this evening, and a crowd meant good coin, which could only be seen as a boon. Instead of expressing his pleasure, Gideon stared at their guest, his brow growing stormy.

"Warrick. Mr. Aidan *Warrick*," he mused, as though the name held some special meaning. He turned to Jane. "Go to the kitchen," he ordered. "You've vegetables to chop."

Jane jerked in surprise, her gaze shifting back and forth between the two men. Her father did not spare her a glance. His attention was fixed on Mr. Warrick, and there was no welcome in his eyes. The corners of his mouth turned down as though he had tasted something foul, and high ruddy color flooded his neck and cheeks.

For his part, Mr. Warrick stood ramrod stiff, his expression stony, his jaw rigid.

"Go. Now," her father barked.

Jane dared not disobey. With a last furtive glance over her shoulder, she limped hurriedly to the kitchen at the back of the inn. Reaching its familiar confines, she rested her palms on the edge of the scarred wooden table and paused to steady her nerves. Her heart was like a drum, pounding a harsh rhythm, her agitation over her father's dreadful humor mounting as she struggled to determine a cause.

Taking up her apron from where it hung on a large nail hammered into the plaster wall, Jane tied it on with shaking hands. She glanced around the kitchen. There was nothing unusual, nothing out of place. Only her father's temperament had gone awry. She longed for an explanation. 'Twould take something terrible to make Gideon Heatherington offend a customer, particularly one who was clearly flush with coin, and especially now, when they needed money so urgently.

The murmur of her father's voice drifted along the narrow hallway. Jane edged toward the doorway of the kitchen, straining to hear his words. Taking pains not to be seen, she shifted forward, eavesdropping on their conversation. A part of her was ashamed that she would breach her father's privacy this way, disobeying his command. Yet, she was driven to discover the reason behind his unforgivably rude treatment of a complete stranger.

Unless that was the answer.

The fine hairs at her nape lifted. Perhaps Aidan Warrick was no stranger. Had he not made mention of an acquaintance with her father a lifetime ago?

But her father had exhibited no sign of recognition until she had spoken the man's name. The situation was peculiar in the extreme.

"You cannot have her. She's my *daughter*, and I need her here." Gideon Heatherington's ire hurtled through the silent inn. "You are a madman if you think I'll agree to this scheme!"

Jane slunk into the narrow hallway, listening with nervous apprehension to the exchange of words.

"Perhaps." Mr. Warrick's gravelly voice was calm, reasonable, devoid of heat. "But the fact remains that you owe me a significant amount of money, Mr. Heatherington. More than you can possibly raise."

Understanding dawned, a cold drenching. Jane pressed the flat of her fingers against her lips. The money. Not owed to someone in far-off London, someone Gideon could avoid with promises and excuses— a lost letter, a great distance—someone he could play for extra time to find a way to settle their debt. Instead, they owed the vast sum to their new neighbor, a man who knew exactly where to find them.

Despair oozed through her. Any foolish dreams of a reprieve she had harbored were dashed. So soon. He had come to collect so soon, on the very heels of the letter demanding payment.

"You'll be taken to debtor's hell. Do you have any idea what prison is like, Mr. Heatherington?" Mr. Warrick asked, his tone harsh. "Crowding, desperation, disease."

"A strange question you ask, Mr. Warrick, for I doubt you've any better idea than me." Jane could hear the bitter anger in her father's observation.

"My knowledge, or lack thereof, is of no relevance." The words were smoothly spoken, bereft of inflection. "The fact remains that if you deny my offer, Squire Craddick will see you taken to Halifax, or perhaps the Fleet, there to rot until your debts are paid. That eventuality may never come to pass, for how will you obtain the funds to remedy your situation? There will be no one to watch after your daughter. You will lose the Crown Inn." He paused, the truth of his words hanging heavy in the air, and then he continued softly, his tone laced with a terrifying enjoyment. "You will suffer. And you will lose everything you hold dear."

Leaning her shoulder against the wall at her side, Jane feared that but for its solid support she would sink to the ground. They could lose their home, their source of livelihood. Her father could be dragged away. *The Fleet.* In far-off London town, or other, worse places like Halifax Debtor's Gaol where men were herded four or five to a bed with little food and no heat. Gideon could lose his freedom, she acknowledged sickly, and with it his health, even his life. The thought was too dreadful to consider.

Whatever his faults and flaws, he was all she had.

Oh, dear, sweet heaven. *She* had brought Mr. Warrick here, invited him in to the Crown Inn.

She had thought her father would be pleased to host such a distinguished guest.

She had thought Mr. Warrick handsome, interesting. A prince from a fantasy tale.

Foolish girl to be beguiled by a masculine form and striking face. He was no prince, unless she named him Dark Prince, the very devil come to Pentreath in the guise of a man.

"You could take *me*," her father said, and Jane heard both the sullen frustration in his tone, and the lack of sincerity.

"You?" Mr. Warrick laughed, the rough sound devoid of humor. "Would you leave her to run the inn alone? How long would her chastity last?"

A horrified gasp escaped her. They were talking about *her*. Mr. Warrick was discussing her *virtue* as though it was a subject open for public review. She could imagine her father's face, beet red with anger, a vein throbbing in his temple. Nerves and worry pricking her, she eased another step closer.

"Come now, Gideon Heatherington. 'Tis a simple business transaction." Mr. Warrick's voice was infinitely patient. "A purchase of a product, so to speak."

Jane heard her father's answering bellow of rage, and without considering her actions, she hurtled forward, stumbling on her weak leg in her haste. Bracing one hand against the wall to stop herself falling, she watched, distraught, as her father lunged at the other man, one fist raised in clear intent.

Terror and bitter bile clawed their way to her throat. Mr. Warrick was younger, quicker, stronger. There was no doubt in her mind as to who would be the victor in a brawl between the two.

Stepping neatly aside, Mr. Warrick waited, making no move to either attack or escape. With an angry growl, Gideon lowered his head and charged once more. Again, Mr. Warrick avoided the charge, and Jane drew a shaky breath as her father lumbered awkwardly past, his morning's libations working through him and leaving him less than sharply coordinated.

As her father rounded for a third attack, Jane looked from one to the other, feeling as though she had stepped into the midst of a Penny Dreadful, for surely this tableau was stranger than any work of fiction. She must stop it. Now. Before Mr. Warrick lost his temper. Before greater damage was done.

"Father, please." She moved forward and pulled on his brawny arm.

He rounded on her, fist raised, eyes bleary.

Mr. Warrick gave a sharp hiss, and she felt his coiled tension close beside her, as though he would step in should her father try to strike her.

A ridiculous thought.

She tugged again on her father's arm and he resisted but a moment, then gave in. Narrowing his eyes, he tried to focus on her face. She was only grateful that he was not so far gone as to ignore her altogether.

She knew how her father was. He relished nothing more than stepping in to break up a drunken brawl before it got out of hand, or grabbing an unruly patron by the scruff and hauling him out the door. But this situation was different. There was an undulating tension that snaked through the air, and she sensed that Mr. Warrick *wanted* her father to come at him again, wanted him to lose control. She shuddered, confusion and dismay spinning her thoughts into a tangled knot.

"What on earth has come over you?" she whispered, though she already knew the answer. Desperation and drink. An ugly combination.

Suddenly coming to himself, Gideon scrubbed his free hand over his face, and then turned a mournful eye on his daughter. "Nothing on *earth's* come over me, Janie. Rather, something from the fires of hell, the devil's own spawn."

He jutted his chin toward Mr. Warrick.

A clap of thunder rumbled beyond the walls of the inn, and a sharp flare erupted as lightning touched the earth, flickering through the window. For an instant, Mr. Warrick did indeed look as though he had stepped through fire, a nimbus of bright light at his back.

"Nay, not spawned by the devil," Mr. Warrick said, and then he smiled, a dark, forbidding curving of his lips that spoke of harsh lessons and bitter recollection. "But, aye, tempered by hell's fires."

She looked at him, his features cast in shadow as the blaze of lightning died. Jane felt a fearsome certainty swell in her heart.

Here was threat and menace and danger. *Here* was the force that would rip the last vestiges of her safe world to shreds.

"I know much of hell," Mr. Warrick rasped, his eyes glittering. "And I would gladly share my knowledge with you, Gideon Heatherington, in all its cursed detail."

Chapter 3

Lightning flashed once more, illuminating Mr. Warrick's face for a brief instant, revealing both his splendor and his cruelty. Jane shivered. He was frightening to her now.

She turned to her father, convinced that whatever progress this day would make, it could herald no happy outcome for her. The solid weight of her dread bore down upon her. "Father, please, tell me what this is about."

The corners of Gideon's mouth drew taut in a grim line, and his words were laced with hopelessness. "'Tis to him I owe the money."

"Yes," she said slowly, her thoughts spinning back to the previous night when, sodden with ale and three full bottles of wine, her father had divulged his terrible folly, his words slurred, his posture slumped.

How much money?

Five hundred pounds.

In her naivete, she had held out a single shimmering ray of hope. "This can be fixed," she had whispered, clutching at her father's hands as she struggled with her shock and dismay. "We have a good sum of notes issued on the West Cornwall Bank." Their entire savings, money she had put aside so carefully over the span of nearly a decade, mindful of her mother's long-ago teachings. "Surely that will satisfy until we can get more?"

She would never forget the strangled sound of her father's denial.

"No, it would not." Her father had shaken his head, and pulled free of her hold, taking up the bottle before him to toss back yet another long swig. "The West Cornwall Bank has gone bust," he had said savagely. "The notes are worthless."

"No. That is not possible." Yet, even as she had uttered the denial, she had known that it *was* possible. The same thing had happened to the Dorseys only last winter, but they had made a quick run across the channel and exchanged their notes for smuggled brandy before that bank's situation became widely known, and in doing so they had reclaimed their lost monies with a bit of less-than-legal trade. Of course, they could never return to that particular merchant again, for he was more likely to skin them than welcome them. But at least they had not found themselves in the predicament that now faced Jane and her father.

They were saddled with worthless notes. They were left with no way to pay their debt. That terrible knowledge had left her tossing and turning the night through, and sent her out early that morn to walk and think and wish for answers.

Instead she had found only more horror: a dead woman pulled from the surf, and whispered snatches of conversation that hinted at vile happenings and wrecks and murder. And then she had invited their nemesis into their home.

Jane glared at Mr. Warrick, feeling hopeless fury surge through her. Such an uncharacteristic emotion. Anger at her father for knotting them up in the weave of this predicament, at herself for having so long failed to see it, and, yes, at Mr. Warrick for . . . for . . .

For what?

That question was one she dared not answer.

Unsettled by the churning mass of her emotions, Jane took an uneven step toward him. She tilted her head back and held his gaze, aware of her unusually bold behavior, yet driven to it nonetheless. Before she could speak, could even conjure her thoughts into some worthy rhetoric, her father waved her away.

"Jane, go back to the kitchen. This is men's business," he barked. "'Tis no concern of yours."

"Ah, but it *does* concern her," Mr. Warrick corrected, his attention fixed on her. Beautiful, mesmerizing eyes. They should be ugly, small and mean. Jane blew out a breath.

"She seems a sensible girl," he continued. "Perhaps we should offer *her* the choice."

"No—" Gideon interjected, even as Mr. Warrick said, "Yes."

"Yes," he said again, low and confident. She thought he had no doubts as to the outcome of this scene. He merely walked through his part in the tragedy.

His lips curled in a cynic's smile as, catching the edge of his greatcoat, he tugged it aside to reveal a large pistol in his belt. Jane drew a shuddering breath and rubbed her damp palms on the worn fabric of her apron. With a careless gesture of one blunt, strong hand, Mr. Warrick smoothed the butt of the firearm, his gaze locked on her father.

His meaning was clear. He felt no sorrow, no regret. He would do whatever he deemed necessary to collect the debt her father owed.

Jane swallowed and wrapped her arms about herself, her emotions roiling like a pot on full boil. *And it's him, his coming, what's brought the evil down upon us . . . He is in league with the devil.* Dolly's words skittered through her thoughts. Her earlier girlish fascination was cold, gray ash in her heart.

She glanced up to find Mr. Warrick watching her with those beautiful, changeable, astonishing eyes, cold now and flat. For fleeting moments at the graveyard and on the walk to the village, she had thought him extraordinary.

She had been horribly mistaken. How had she thought him anything other than a cruel monster, despite his handsome shell?

"By all means—" Prodded by desperation, she held up one hand to still her father's protest, calling upon vestiges of valor she had never dreamed she possessed. "I overheard enough to know that there is something in this discussion that involves me"—she slanted a derisive glance at her tormentor, amazed at her own temerity but quite unable to hide her bitter resentment—"and my chastity, was it not, Mr. Warrick?"

With a strangled growl that made Jane turn, Gideon strode to the bar and reached over for a bottle. He cast a baleful glance at Mr. Warrick, and then he took a great gulp and another. Wine dribbled down his chin, droplets falling to stain his shirt.

Narrowing his eyes, he slammed the bottle down on the bar, then pointed his index finger at Jane.

"Your fault, girl. The whole of it can be laid at your door. I sent all that blunt to London, for the opinion of that Dr. Barker on what to do with your damned leg. For nothing. All for nothing. I spent the money, and still was saddled with a crippled gel." He laughed, and ugly, twisted noise. "A crippled gel that killed her mother."

"No." Old wounds ripped open to bleed a rapid torrent.

Jane stumbled back a step, feeling the accusation as though it were a blow in truth. To her horror, she fell against the hard wall of Mr. Warrick's chest. He closed his hands around her arms, steadying her.

Mortified, she jerked away, the echo of her father's words flaying her, all the worse because she knew they were true. Her insides twisted like a wrung-out cloth. There was not a day that she did not revisit the guilt of her poor choice, and the tragic results. But here was something new. Her father had told her often enough that he had paid good coin for Dr. Barker's worthless opinion, but she had not known that he had sunk them into debt on her behalf.

She felt remorse heap upon remorse, for she had been the one to hear of Dr. Barker, the one to plead with her father that he make inquiries of the man.

"I took a mortgage on the inn that year," Gideon bit out, the muscles of his jaw tight. "A Mr. Aidan Warrick of London bought up my chit. I made my payments, regular as rain. Then I missed an installment when I . . . er . . ."

He spread his hands in a gesture of supplication, and his tone grew cajoling. "I ran afoul of an investment or two, Janie. Gave funds to my brother. It was a sure thing with a fine return. He promised me. Then he lost his money, and mine right along with it." He sighed. "When I heard nothing from Mr. Warrick here, I thought he'd forgotten about me. So I missed the next payment and the next. Warrick never said a word, so I never sent another payment."

Gideon slammed his fist on the bar. "Your own damned fault, Warrick," he snarled, his face twisting with rancor and bitterness. "If you wanted your money, you should have asked sooner. Not my problem that you let it get out of hand."

With the sound of the rain drumming hard, and the pounding of her heart keeping pace to it, Jane battled for calm. Her father had *known*, she realized now. For weeks and months he had known that ruin was upon them. He had said nothing, done nothing, and now he blamed everyone but himself.

Fear and hopelessness tugged at her, a great, sucking bog. What would happen to them now?

She fisted her hands at her sides, forcing a calm demeanor she was far from feeling. "Maybe there is some way—"

"There is a simple solution," Mr. Warrick interjected.

"No. I need her here. In the kitchen. In the pub. Who'll make up the rooms if she's gone? Tend the chickens and the garden?" Gideon slammed his fist on the bar once more, making Jane jump. He grunted, narrowing his eyes as he studied the younger man. "It is almost as though you knew exactly how much I was worth, and waited until I owed you everything. So, now, you'll get nothing, my handsome, because there's nothing to get."

My handsome. A common Cornish term applied

to any who visited the pub, but in this case it was
painfully apt. Mr. Warrick was without doubt fine-
looking of face and form. She shuddered as she
met his cold gaze, so very certain that beneath the
façade he was anything but handsome.

Pressing her lips together, Jane took a deep
breath. Her thoughts were in turmoil, her world
unraveling at its poorly darned seams, with Aidan
Warrick pulling carelessly at the threads.

Realization dawned, and with it came utter mortification. "You knew who I was at the cemetery."

"Yes."

"You went there to seek me out." The words
almost choked her, catching thick and rough in her
throat.

"I did." A curt nod accentuated his reply.

His agreement sent hot tendrils of humiliation
coiling through her. She had thought him a prince.
He had made her a fool.

"And this morning?" she whispered. "Was it you
upon the cliff this morning?" Had he watched her
then, on the beach? Watched Jem and Robert pull
the corpse from the waves?

Dolly's earlier assertions clawed to the forefront
of her thoughts, and Jane was struck by the coincidence of Mr. Warrick's arrival in Pentreath, in perfect conjunction with the rumors of wreckers, and
the body of the dead woman.

Wrapping her arms about herself, she took a step
back.

"I was at the beach this morn," he said, and again
the hint of a cynic's smile twisted his mouth. "I had
business that I needed to see to its conclusion."

At his admission, Jane's breath caught in dawning horror. She could not dismiss the whispering

certainty that there was some gruesome link between Mr. Warrick's presence and the woman's
death. She wondered if he had come to gloat over
the proof of his evil handiwork.

She had heard that Squire Craddick and his men
were determined to find the company of wreckers,
to see their leader hung by the neck. She stared at
Mr. Warrick, her blood thrumming wildly, her
breath coming fast as wretched uncertainty lashed
her with knotted cords.

Was the business he referred to that of wrecks
and murder?

Gideon made a sound low in his throat, drawing
Jane's gaze. Feeling as though she had been pummeled by brutal fists, she studied him in the dim
light. He suddenly appeared so old and worn, his
face marked by lines she had not noted until this
moment, his eyes pouchy and his skin sallow. Sadness sluiced through her. Her father was no bulwark of strength and stability, no safe harbor. How
ever had she convinced herself that he was?

Her expectations and assumptions were built on
a rickety foundation indeed. She had learned a par-
tial truth the day her mother had died, learned that
the world was not kind, not fair, not safe, and she
had spent the years since pretending that her
father was her protection. She had nurtured a
lovely fantasy, she acknowledged now, one that did
not stand well under the harsh light of reality. 'Twas
as if Mr. Warrick had ripped the blinders from her
eyes, robbed her of the rosy brush she had used to
paint her world.

Her father was no paragon, and he could not
keep her safe. She had *never* been safe. It was all an
illusion. Somewhere deep inside, she had known it,

but, oh, she had not wanted to see it, had preferred to hide behind a wall of delusion.

Evil, wretched man, Aidan Warrick, to have stolen this from her.

She found the barren truth an awful thing to face.

"Why?" she asked, turning her head toward him, her heart shrinking from the fact that earlier she had imagined a special connection to this inscrutable man whose brooding elegance seemed painfully out of place in the familiar and homey surroundings of the pub. "Why did you seek me out?"

"To offer your father a solution."

"I do not understand—" Jane began.

"No," Gideon grunted. "I've no coin to pay a girl to see to her responsibilities. She has no part in this."

"But she does," came the gruff reply.

"What is my part in this?" Her gaze remained fixed on Mr. Warrick. Her heart pounded hard against her ribs.

"Your father has not the means to pay his debt, which leaves him few choices." Mr. Warrick lowered his voice. "I can demand that he sell the Crown Inn."

"Can't take a man's home to pay his debt," Gideon snarled.

Jane nodded slowly. "That would leave us without a home, without a livelihood." *And without a penny to our name*, she added silently.

"It would." Mr. Warrick's tone was cold as a frozen pond, laced with neither sympathy nor glee.

She closed her eyes, battling to keep her rising desperation under control. When she opened them, it was to find Mr. Warrick's assessing gaze fixed upon her. There was no mercy there, only harsh resolve.

The room seemed to shrink and narrow until there was only the two of them, the only sound the frantic beating of her heart. "Go on," she whispered.

"I could have your father thrown in debtor's prison."

"Nooo," she moaned. The thought of her father lying in a cold dank cell was too horrible to consider. Away from the Crown Inn, from his friends, from his ale and his tales and the roar of the ocean, he would wither and die. Her fault. All her fault. Her poor choices those many years ago had paved the path for *his* poor choices. A circle with a sharp and jagged edge, to be sure.

Dropping her chin to her chest, Jane hesitated, staring unseeing at the floor as all manner of terrible imaginings flitted through her mind. "You have another option?" she whispered.

"He's come with an option I've no liking for," Gideon said, his voice crackling with emotion.

"I have offered your father the option of indentured servitude." The words fell, harsh and stark, like the clang of metal on metal. Jane raised her head, startled.

"I don't understand. You wish my father to sell himself into bondage, to work in the colonies?" The thought was absurd. She could not imagine that such an arrangement would garner adequate monies to satisfy the debt.

A bark of laughter rent the air, if indeed the discordant sound that tumbled from Mr. Warrick's lips could be named as such.

"No. I have not asked that of your father," he said. "Instead, I have suggested another option, a slightly modified agreement, one that would allow him to remain exactly where he is. A debt indenture."

At his words, Jane's heart lightened and hope sparked. There. He was offering a kindness. The situation was salvageable. She glanced at her father, the spark growing to a glowing ember, but Gideon's expression was dark and there was an ominous throbbing at his temple. He shook his head like a great shaggy dog trying to clear a buzzing from its ears.

"What does this option entail?" Jane asked, her hope abruptly snuffed.

"*You* will become my bondservant. You will commit to a debt indenture for a period of seven years." The unemotional pronouncement fell from Mr. Warrick's perfectly formed lips, the elocution flawless, so that there could be no misunderstanding.

Jane felt as though the callously uttered declaration tumbled down a very long tunnel before reaching her ears. She wove unsteadily as her legs wobbled beneath her. Foolish girl, to have thought he meant to offer a kindness.

His words chased head after tail through her thoughts. *You will become my bondservant.* Her hands felt cold, the fingers numb, and she could almost feel the chains heavy about her.

Sinking her teeth into her lower lip, she stared at Mr. Warrick, recalling their brief conversation about the wild ponies of the moors. He had known all along that he meant to chain her in bondage. She would never run free, fettered as she was by her weak leg. And now, this stranger, this coldly unfeeling man, hewn of granite, hard to his core, would shackle her so that her life would no longer be her own.

She felt unsteady, cast adrift, and she sent a desperate glance at her father. He stared at her in brooding silence, his brow furrowed, his jaw set, and in his expression she had confirmation of the

suspicion that had sprung to evil life in her mind.
There really were no choices to be made. Despite
his blustering pretense of denial, he intended to
sell her.

"If we lose the inn, we'll have no means of survival," Gideon muttered, his gaze sliding away.
"Were it only the two of us, Janie, we might find a
way. But think of the little ones, think of the money
I send to my wastrel brother's wife. That's her and
the six children I feed. And Dolly Gwyn. What'll
become of her without the food I put on her
table?"

Jane swallowed against choking desperation. She
wanted to break free of it, to shout that she didn't
care. That her father and the children and Dolly,
and the barmaid, Mary, whose husband drank away
most of what she earned here, and Will, the boy
who tended the stable . . . that none of them mattered to her. But it was a lie. They *all* mattered, and
she could not see a way to save all of them, and herself, too. Her gaze shot to Mr. Warrick.

Someone must pay the devil his due.

She could not speak, could not breathe. Her
father's every word had resounded like a hammer
blow to the nails of her coffin. He was burying her
with heartbreak, consigning her to a life of servitude to Aidan Warrick. She was to be little more
than a slave to him. He was terrifying, cold, and he
had come to Pentreath with death crawling in his
shadow.

Her father was selling her to a man who might
well be a murderer.

She shuddered.

No, she could not let her thoughts travel such a
path. It was merely unsettled emotion and ruthless

desperation that carried her frantic imaginings in such a wayward direction. He was a businessman come to claim a debt. She would be wise not to stray too far into macabre misapprehension, for such could only deepen her suffering.

What choice was there? What choice? The truth was that in the end, her fate would be tragic either way. If her father was sent to debtor's gaol, the Crown Inn would fail, and she would be left as prey for all manner of scavengers.

"Why do you hate us?" she whispered, her gaze locked on Mr. Warrick. She saw then the dark satisfaction, the grim pleasure he gained from his victory. "We have done you no harm. We have never met you before this day."

He turned his intent gaze to her father's tense-shouldered form. "Have we not met before, Gideon Heatherington?" He smiled, a cheerless twist of his perfectly formed lips. "Are you secure in the knowledge that you have done no harm?"

"You're the one what's doing harm." Gideon's voice vibrated with emotion: anger, resentment, futility. "Ripping my daughter from my arms when I'm in need of her service and care. What manner of demon are you?" He shook his head slowly from side to side. "You meant to strike me in my heart."

"In your heart? I think perchance you mean your pocketbook." Mr. Warrick paused. "What manner of demon are *you*, that you give her into my keeping?"

Jane sucked in a breath, struck by his argument, by the naked and ugly truth of it.

"Choose your path," Mr. Warrick ordered. "My patience is at an end."

"Janie," Gideon pleaded, though what exactly he asked of her, she was not certain.

The buzzing in her ears grew louder, a hundred, nay, a thousand angry bees. No choice to be made, really. There was no choice at all.

"I will go with you," she said in a rush, fearful that if she did not say them quickly enough, the words would lodge in her throat like fish bones and never break free, only sit there to dig at her with their pointed barbs.

Mr. Warrick gave a curt nod, and cast a glance at Gideon. "We are in agreement then. You lack the means to cover the debt, and so I will take an alternate payment. A simple business transaction—"

"A purchase of a product, so to speak," Jane finished, finally understanding the sentence she had overheard him speak earlier. "I am the product."

Mr. Warrick's jaw hardened. Withdrawing a prepared document from his coat, he bid her father fetch quill and ink.

Vibrating with anger, Gideon stalked off, leaving Jane alone with the man who had torn her world asunder. He did not speak to her, did not look at her, and she was almost grateful. What else was there to say?

Only when the vile transaction was done, Gideon's name—and, at Mr. Warrick's insistence, Jane's— drying on the page, did Mr. Warrick turn to face her, his expression remote. "You have precisely ten minutes to pack what you need. Do not make me wait," he said brusquely, and then he turned and strode from the inn.

The sound of his booted heels hitting the floor echoed through the empty pub.

For a frozen moment, Jane stood staring after him, her heart twisted in the tightest of knots. She turned to find her father watching her with be-

numbed confusion, as though he did not know
what to make of this, what to do, how to proceed.

And the allotted time was flowing swiftly like ale
on a busy night.

Goaded by the sharp edge of her desperation,
Jane tore her gaze from her father and lurched up
the stairs to her chamber. Pulse racing, she
crammed her belongings into a battered leather
portmanteau that had been her father's a lifetime
ago, one he still used for his occasional travel. Her
fingers were clumsy, her movements awkward. How
many minutes left? How many?

With both palms pressed flat against the pile of
clothing, she pushed down with all her weight,
cramming everything into the bag. She fumbled
with the closure, taking three tries before she got it
fastened.

Straightening, she did a quick perusal of her
chamber, taking in every corner, every tiny crack,
breathing in the familiarity of the room. An ache
began in the center of her chest and radiated out-
ward, a slow steady burn of wretched desolation.
Faced with the terrifying prospect of leaving her
home, she found that she could only wish for the
safety of the familiar. She was so very afraid.

A low moan escaped her, grief and fear mingling
bitterly inside her. *No.* She must *not* drown in the
thick miasma of her despair. She would survive. She
would flourish. She would overcome.

Blinking back tears, she dragged the portmanteau into the hallway and found her father hover-
ing halfway up the stairs, hands folded, his face a
mask of confusion.

"I'm thinking maybe you can find a way to pay
him, Janie, maybe you can work there days and

here nights, maybe . . ." His voice trailed away and he shrugged. A gesture of futility, she thought.

"Pay him with what?" she whispered. "Blood?"

She shook her head, her throat blocked by swallowed tears and, grasping the handle of her bag, she dragged it along behind her, making her way awkwardly, favoring her lame leg. The dull thud of the portmanteau as it hit each subsequent stair was like clods of earth tossed in a fresh grave.

Her father made no move to help her, just stared at her, and she wondered if he'd come a little unhinged.

Pausing on the bottom step, she breathed in the rich aroma of ale that permeated the air, wove through the fibers of the wooden beams that spanned the ceiling, clung to the walls and tables and chairs. Ale and smoke and men. She had grown up with that smell.

She would remember it. And return to it.

Seven years was not forever, she reminded herself. When her years of service were done, she would return here, to her father's inn.

But for now, her time here was done.

As she exited the inn, Jane noted that the storm had faded to a mizzling rain. Deceptive, she thought. The tempest would return.

She hesitated, sensing her father at her back. Her gaze lit on Aidan Warrick. Legs braced apart, he stood, his expression remote, impassive, his face marked by a hint of cruelty. The wind caught his hair and the long wings of his coat, making him appear even larger, more threatening.

And still she thought him beautiful.

Horrified by such thoughts, she sank her teeth into her lower lip. What beauty could she imagine in such a heartless, pitiless man?

She could feel the tension emanating from her father in shimmering waves as she took two halting steps forward. Her weak leg wavered unsteadily, and to her astonishment she saw the slightest movement of Mr. Warrick's hand, as though he meant to reach out and steady her. She jerked her head up to find him watching her with . . . admiration? She must be mistaken.

She frowned in confusion. Mr. Warrick's gaze shifted away from her, masking whatever emotion she had seen or imagined.

"You are most prompt." Words spoken in the same rumbling, gravelly voice that she had found so attractive earlier that day. Was she going mad that the sound of it pleased her still, despite her dire circumstance?

Steeling her nerves, she glanced at her father, and found him standing rigidly behind her, his face flushed a dull red.

"I have tarried long enough. Come." Mr. Warrick swung her case from the ground at her feet, carrying it with ease as he strode toward a gleaming black coach that stood now in the courtyard.

Jane flung herself against her father's broad chest, and he stood rigid, his rasping breaths ruffling her hair.

"Look out to Trevisham. Tonight," she choked out. "I will hang a sheet from the window. Watch for my signal. You will know all is well."

Though he did not hug her in return, she gave him one last, desperate squeeze. Calling on all her reserves, she pulled away.

With leaden tread she followed several paces behind Mr. Warrick, her legs trembling so badly that each step required a Herculean effort. She dared not cast a last glance at her father, for she feared that it would be her undoing. With a heavy heart, she walked toward the black coach and four well-matched horses. Conveyance and animals glistened, wet from the recent downpour.

Where had they come from? Jane glanced at Mr. Warrick, wondering if he had assigned his driver a specific time to arrive here.

A specific time to slice her from all that was known and familiar.

The horses pawed and stamped the ground, the driver holding them still with a steady hand. The man made to approach, but Mr. Warrick waved him away and stored Jane's bag himself, then pulled open the door of the carriage. Balancing his movement by resting his open palm against the side of the doorframe, he swung inside with easy grace.

Jane hesitated, stumbling to a halt as she eyed the restless hooves of the dark beasts harnessed to the front of the coach. She was uncertain as to her new employer's intent.

No, not *employer*. He was her *master*, and she was a bondservant. The thought made an ugly knot of terror curdle in her stomach. She was bound to him, well and truly constrained. Fettered by her word and by legal sanction.

She stood, shivering uncontrollably, unable to decide if she was to follow the man into the carriage or if he meant her to walk the distance to Trevisham House.

"Hell and damnation." His softly spoken curse reached her ears just before he leaned forward and reappeared in the carriage doorway.

"Get in," he gritted, his expression unreadable.

Limping to the coach, Jane grasped the sides of

the doorway and hauled herself inside. With an awkward twist, she fell into the seat opposite Mr. Warrick. She felt the weight of his gaze upon her and straightened her spine, unwilling to display any greater weakness than she absolutely must.

He leaned out and pulled the door shut, then settled back to stare out the side window.

Jane twined her fingers together to still their shaking and followed the direction of Mr. Warrick's gaze. Her heart twisted with regret as she saw her father standing by the door of the inn, shoulders slumped in defeat. She longed to fling herself from the coach, to limp to her father's side and cling to him in desperate entreaty as she had when she was a child afraid of a storm or a dream.

I had a nightmare, Father. A monstrous creature came in the night . . .

Only it had not come in the night.

The creature had come beneath the overcast sky of a stormy day, wearing the guise of a fallen angel, so perfect of face and form as to be mistaken for the finest of men.

It had come for her.

And her father had let the nightmare take her.

Chapter 4

How long she stared at the floor of the carriage, Jane could not say, but slowly, through the fog of her despondency, she became aware that the drive was inordinately long, too long for the short distance to Trevisham House. Raising her eyes, she looked out the window. Gray earth and jagged stones stretched before her, broken by clumps of scraggly shrub. In the distance was a single twisted tree, bowed and shaped by storm and time, a survivor in the face of such unforgiving climes.

They were on the road that wended through the moor, she realized, though their final destination remained a mystery. A frightening one, to be sure.

Hazarding a glance at Mr. Warrick, she found him staring moodily out the side window of the carriage, and she wondered what it was that he found so very fascinating in the barren stretch of land.

The vehicle lurched and rocked as it rounded a bend in the road, the damp cold from outside leeching through unseen cracks, chilling the air. Jane braced herself into the far corner of the soft velvet upholstery. Digging out her black wool gloves, she dragged them on.

"Excuse me, sir," she whispered, wrapping her arms about herself, quelling the rising tide of panic that threatened her composure as the howl of the wind and the creak of the coach measured their travels.

Mr. Warrick turned his attention to her, focused, complete, formidable in its intensity, his blue-gray eyes glittering in the dim light. Jane stiffened, refusing to yield to the near overwhelming urge to shrink back into the shadows. She had chosen to draw his notice and, having done so, she would be wiser to ask the questions that hounded her than to hold her silence and suffer all manner of dire imaginings.

"Where do we go?" She swallowed, tormented by a multitude of terrible possibilities. Too quickly had she agreed to this scheme, taking solace in the assumption that she would spend her servitude a stone's throw from her home, at Trevisham House.

Laundry maid. Scullery maid. She had no fear of hard work. But as the wheels dipped and creaked on the rutted road, and her village was left far behind, a horrifying realization clawed at her. Aidan Warrick could do what he would with her, for there was none to gainsay him. The road was isolated, running through the center of twenty miles of moor, and she was his property by right of legal bond.

Nearly dizzy with escalating fear, she asked, "Do you take me to a ship bound for the colonies?"

The skin around his eyes tightened and he raised his head just a little. Her pulse raced as she waited for his reply.

"You have no reason to—" He broke off abruptly,

inhaling on a slow steady breath, and she wondered what he had been about to say.

"Are you hungry?" His voice was a low rumble. "Cold?"

Jane blinked. Whatever she had expected of this enigmatic man, it had not been a solicitous inquiry as to her comfort. Following her first instinct, she shook her head, and then she stilled.

He had not answered her questions, had given no indication of their destination. The omission was sinister somehow, and that very threat gave her the strength to give voice to the truth. If he meant her harm, why should she pretend comfort when her belly twisted with hunger and her limbs shook with cold?

"Yes," she said, lifting her chin. "I *am* hungry and cold." She waited a heartbeat before adding softly, "And afraid."

For an instant, he looked surprised at her honest admission, his eyes widening a fraction, and then he nodded. "You have had an unsettling day."

"An unsettling day," she echoed. The absurdly understated observation dragged forth a short, high laugh that did not bode well for her continued composure. In the space of a day, she had learned of her penury and watched a dead woman dragged from sea. She had been sold into bondage, taken from her home, from her father, from whatever illusion of safety she had clutched at. Unsettling, indeed.

She dropped her gaze, twined her gloved fingers together, wondered if she was brave enough to ask why he hated Gideon Heatherington so, why he perpetrated this evil upon her family. Pressing her palms against her thighs, she held her tongue. To

risk his anger was sheer folly. He had not been
unkind to her thus far . . .

Suddenly, the preposterous nature of her thoughts
slammed through her with staggering force. Not
been unkind? He had ripped her from her home,
torn her from everything known and familiar. What
was that if not unkind?

All her best intentions evaporated like fine mist,
and she gave voice to the heartache that gnawed
at the edges of every thought, every breath.

"You are cold-hearted. A monster," she whispered. "Cruel. We could have paid you over time,
but you chose this spiteful course instead." With
each word she grew more reckless, and though
some remnant of her common sense cautioned of
her error, she could not seem to still her tongue.
"When I first saw you, I thought you a prince—"

"No prince." He cut her off flatly.

She sucked in a breath, caught in the chill flame
of his icy regard. Oh, what excessive foolishness
had grabbed hold of her, that she had spoken so?
Yet, set upon her course, she forged on.

"Why?" she asked, her voice shaking with the passion of her despair. "Why have you done this?"

Leaning forward, he studied her. She gasped as
he reached out and caught a stray tendril of her
hair, twining the dark strand loosely around his
finger. Heart pounding, she jerked back, pushing
his hand away as she pulled her hair from his grasp.
The contact sent a wild shiver of awareness careen-
ing through her veins, and with it, a hot swell of
mortification.

"Why have I done this?" His mouth tightened as
he pulled away. "Vengeance," he said, and then

continued in a softer tone. "Your suffering is a regrettable consequence."

She jolted as if struck. "Vengeance against whom? For what imagined wrong?" she cried.

"Any wrong I might *imagine* can provide no contest for the injury done me in truth." The dark menace of his tone left Jane with a deep sense of dread.

An image of the drowned woman from the beach, copper hair floating about her like rivulets of blood, sprang forth. With a shiver, Jane blurted her question, half convinced that her companion was capable of any manner of dreadful recourse. "Did you bring me to the moor so you could drop me in a bog and leave me to sink below the mire, let the sucking mud wipe away all trace of my existence? Is that to be your vengeance?"

"I brought you to Bodmin Moor because I have business at the New Inn." Mr. Warrick slanted an amused glance in her direction, and for that instant, she was reminded of her first sight of him and how she had thought him unbearably handsome.

The devil wore many guises.

With a shake of his head, he leaned forward. He took hold of a large basket that sat nearly hidden in a shadowy corner of the coach. Jane had not noticed it before and she watched in apprehension as he dragged it across the floor with a soft shush of sound. Her anxiety turned to surprise as Mr. Warrick lifted a thick blanket that was draped across the top, carefully unfolded the cloth and arranged it over her legs. She stared at him, beset by confusion.

"You are no wilting flower," he said.

Their gazes met and held. His eyes darkened, and she froze, heart pounding as he reached out and touched her cheek. Fear, she told herself. Her pulse raced with fear. But she was hardly convinced, for a part of her wanted to rub her cheek along his hand, to lay her fingers on his skin and touch him as he touched her.

Madness. She was beset by madness.

"You say you are cold and hungry and afraid." He drew away with a look of bemusement. "The blanket should help with the first." He rummaged through the basket, then brought forth a Cornish pasty and held it out toward her. "This should help with the second." His gaze locked on hers, bright and intent. "And as to the third . . ." He shrugged.

She wanted to tell him what he could do with both his blanket and his pasty, but common sense prevailed. She *was* hungry, and the scent of the spiced meat made her stomach rumble. Best to accept whatever kindness he offered in the moment, for there was no certainty of when she might eat again. Taking the small pie, she bit into it, closing her eyes as the flavors of the meat and potatoes touched her tongue. Delicious.

Head lowered, she finished the pasty with slow, steady bites, studying her companion with sidelong glances.

He had turned his face to the window once more, and she noted that he had taken nothing for himself.

Swallowing the last of her meal, Jane brushed away the crumbs and gathered her courage. In information lay strength.

"Why did you not take me to Trevisham House and set me to my tasks before you came away on your . . . business?" she asked.

For a long moment, she thought he would not

answer, and when he finally spoke his tone was gruff. "You meant to send some signal to ease your father's concern"—he made a dismissive gesture—"if indeed he is even capable of such."

She gasped. "How did you know that? I gave that reassurance for his ears alone." Shocked, she digested his words, opened her mouth to defend her father, and then thought better of it. Instead, she said, "So you have brought me here, to Bodmin Moor, to stop me from sending him a sign of my well-being. You wish him to suffer, to have no knowledge of my welfare, no reassurance of my safety."

"Yes."

"And will his suffering make you happy?" she whispered. "Will it give you peace?"

Oh, she had gone too far. She read it in the tightening of his shoulders and the hard cast of his jaw. Swallowing, Jane shrank back against the seat, wondering at her own reckless audacity.

She was normally a most prudent girl, one who guarded her every word and action with a careful eye toward possible consequences. Life and heartbreak and years of serving ale to bleary-eyed men, some with heavy fists and quick tempers, had trained her to be that way. Yet here she sat, poking at a most dangerous beast.

"Peace? Yes." Mr. Warrick's cold smile bore acquaintance with neither mirth nor joy. "Gideon Heatherington's suffering *must* bring me peace. It is my only hope for peace."

"What—" Jane struggled to find her equilibrium. He spoke of peace, yet he was a heartless, unfeeling man.

A man she should hate for what he had done to her.

A man who had draped a thick blanket over her cold legs and fed her a rich pasty to stave off her hunger.

"What manner of man are you?" she whispered, pressing the back of one hand to her cheek where he had touched her, half convinced that he was no mortal, but a demon sent to torment her and tempt her and leave her fit for Bedlam.

He ran the pad of his thumb across his lower lip, his gaze fixed on her face, and something flickered in the depths of his mercurial eyes. She thought it might have been regret.

"I am your employer," he replied.

"My master," she corrected softly, unable to keep the rancor from her tone, unwilling to let the lie stand. "An employee may choose to leave. A slave may not."

He made a soft sound of impatience, but offered no denial. Instead, he reached out and settled a corner of the blanket more securely across her lap before turning his gaze to the desolate landscape once more.

Bleak emotion bulged against the confines of Jane's restraint. She both feared and loathed Aidan Warrick. He blurred the boundaries, and in that instant she hated him as much for his kindness as for his cruelty.

"Jane, wake up. We have arrived."

Jane opened her eyes, feeling groggy and out of sorts. Slowly, she became aware of her surroundings, the feel of the velvet squabs beneath her fingers, the darkness, the sound of rain drumming on the roof. Recollection of her situation rushed at her headlong, cold and ugly. It stole her breath.

Turning her head, she saw that Mr. Warrick stood just outside the open door of the carriage, a shadowy form, rain running in heavy rivulets down the rich material of his greatcoat. She had the strangest urge to pull him inside where it was dry.

"Where are we?" she whispered, pushing aside a stray lock of hair with the back of her hand.

"Wait for me," he said, ignoring her question. "Do not leave this carriage until I return. Hawker is here. Should you need him, just call out."

"Hawker?"

"My driver."

Her mind still muzzy, Jane opened her mouth to question him further, but he closed the door firmly behind him, leaving her in inky blackness.

They had traveled until nightfall, she realized. She must have fallen asleep. Leaning forward, she pulled up the shade that covered the window. Against the rain-drenched night sky she saw the darker silhouette of a large building, interrupted by lit windows along the upper and lower floors. The shape was vaguely familiar to her, and she thought she recognized the New Inn on Bodmin Moor. She had been here once before with her father.

Just the thought of him brought a pang of homesickness. What twists and turns her life had taken in the span of a single short day. With a sigh, she wrapped her cloak about her shoulders and sank back against the seat.

Her thoughts were awhirl with supposition and concern, but it was not long before the reality of nature made her shift uncomfortably. She had traveled many hours in this coach, and she thought now that she would be hard-pressed to sit patiently much longer without attending to her personal needs. Sinking her teeth into her lower lip, Jane listened to the sound of the rain drumming on the roof of the carriage, which only served to make her discomfort and her pressing need all the more significant. She twisted her fingers in the material of her cloak and then untwisted them. She counted to five hundred, forward, and back. Finally, she pushed open the carriage door.

"Mr. Warrick," she called uneasily. When there came no response, she clutched the handle by the side of the door and carefully levered herself from the carriage. Her ruined leg screamed in protest, stiff from the hours of disuse. "Mr. Warrick? Mr. Hawker?"

Limping forward, Jane looked to and fro for some sign of Hawker, but he was nowhere to be seen. Slowly, she turned full circle, blinking against the beads of water that gathered on her lashes. Behind her stood the carriage and the horses, their heads bowed against the rain. Before her was a large wagon, its massive bulk sitting squarely between herself and the door of the inn. She paused, uncertain, the sight of the wagon making her vaguely uneasy. She glanced about nervously, but found herself alone.

"Mr. Hawker?" she called again, forcing as much volume as she could. Still, her voice was swallowed by the wind. She stepped toward the door of the inn, her soles slipping on the wet cobblestones. The rain pelted her hair, her face, soaking her to the skin.

She walked forward until she reached the wagon. Curling her fingers over the side, she paused to rest her leg. A tarred canvas pall covered the contents

of the wagon, but she could clearly see the outline
of several large kegs. The nervous conviction that
she was not safe here skittered through her.

With a sharp intake of breath, Jane shifted sideways. Her weak limb jolted in protest, and she
slipped on the wet stones, reaching out blindly to
steady herself. Her fingers clutched at the side of
the wagon, sliding along the stiff cloth, inadver-
tently pulling it aside to reveal keg after wooden
keg stacked beneath.

Uneasy, she tried to drag the slick material back
to its original place, to leave the wagon as she had
found it. She swallowed as a knot of fear tightened
her throat, and all manner of troubling possibilities
danced lead-footed through her thoughts. Huge
kegs hidden beneath a tarred cloth . . . The likely
nature of the wagon's contents was no challenge to
her imagination.

Smuggler's goods.

And Mr. Warrick had chosen *this* night for his
business at the New Inn. What conclusions might
she draw from that?

Suddenly, hard fingers curled about her wrist,
making her cry out in panic. She was yanked against
a solid mass even as she struggled to free herself
from the painful grasp that imprisoned her. Hot
breath fanned her cheek. "We got us a spy, Gaby."

"Seems we do, Davey," came the reply.

"No!" Jane gasped, writhing as she tried to
wrench free. Memories assailed her of another time,
another man who had grabbed her roughly with violent intent. Jagged slashes of terror flayed her.

She tried again to pull away, twisting to look at her
captor, to search for any means of escape. He was of
medium height, with a great barrel chest and a wild

shock of white hair. He bared his teeth as he yanked viciously on her wrist, pulling her about until her back pressed against his front. He wrapped one beefy arm around her neck, pulling tight enough to make Jane choke and gasp.

"Know what happens to spies, girlie?"

"Please," she croaked. "I am no spy."

Frantic, she tugged on her trapped hand, her gaze darting about as she searched for some sign of Hawker. The second man, Gaby, took a step forward. Grabbing a handful of Jane's hair, he tugged sharply. Tears pricked her eyes. She struggled harder, felt her elbow connect with a soft belly. The first man grunted in pain.

"Dead Man's Pool's good enough for the likes of her," he said. "But first a bit of fun, eh?"

Again. It was happening to her again. Horrible memories of her past oozed into her present until there was only fear and horror and the feel of rough hands pulling at her. Frantic, she wrenched and jerked against the brutal grasp that held her. Not again. Never again.

Harder still, she slammed her elbow into the soft mass of his belly, and the pressure about her throat released. Almost did she wrench free, but at the last instant he caught her once more.

"Aidan!" Jane cried, mounting terror stealing all reason as she struggled against the smuggler's hold, kicking and scratching, and again almost tearing loose before he renewed his grip with bruising force. She screamed, louder, her voice a panicked crescendo. "Aidan! Aidan Warrick!"

At her cry, Davey stiffened.

"Shut yer maw. Don't you go calling him," he snarled. "Shut yer maw."

Hooking one arm about her waist, he dragged her toward the back of the wagon. A deep and chilling dread lashed her. She set her heels against the wet cobblestones, but found no purchase, and he pulled her along as easily as a wet puppy.

"Move the tarp," he grunted at his companion.

"The only thing you'll be moving is your hand, Davey. Or I'll move it for you." The command was spoken in smoke and brandy tones, and Jane thought she would weep at the joy of hearing that low, gravelly voice. Aidan Warrick had come back for her. Relief was sharp and sweet.

Davey loosed his hold around her neck, but still kept a harsh grip on her waist. Gasping for breath, she pushed against him, desperate to be free. Over the pounding of her heart, she heard the distinctive sound of a pistol being cocked, and raised her eyes to find Mr. Warrick standing before her, his face hard as hewn stone, his gaze locked on her captor.

"Davey," he cautioned, "is she worth your life?"

The arm about her waist disappeared, leaving her to slump against the side of the wagon. Relief was a swimming tide as she hung there, panting.

He had called the man by name. Davey. Pressing her palm against her throat, Jane swallowed, left with few illusions as to what that familiarity might mean.

With two long strides, Mr. Warrick reached her and dragged her up against him. He was hard and warm and solid. She turned her face into the wet folds of his coat.

"What is mine, I keep," he said. "This girl is mine and mine alone. Spread the word, boys. The man that touches her is the man I'll gut. A nice, slow death, that."

Jane knew his words, both his claim of ownership and his threat, should bring shame, horror, repulsion. Instead, they brought solace, and she was left stunned by that realization. She heard the sound of the two men's scuffling retreat, but she could not seem to turn her face from the comfort of Mr. Warrick's shoulder, nor uncurl her fingers from the material of his coat.

One black-gloved finger came to rest beneath her chin, and he tipped her head back gently until she met his gaze. His eyes glittered in the darkness, and his mouth was drawn taut and ruthless.

He would have killed them. To protect her. Oh, dear God.

"You did not wait in the carriage," he observed with no more expression than he might use to comment on the weather.

She could not help it. She laughed, a high-pitched sound that ended in a hiccoughing sob. "I had to— to—to—oh, the coach ride was so long . . ." Her voice trailed away in an agony of embarrassment.

His brows drew down in confusion, and then rose abruptly as understanding dawned. Mortified, she looked away.

"My apologies," he said softly.

He scooped her up, lifting her in his arms as though she weighed no more than a mite, and then his long-legged stride ate up the distance to the door of the inn, the wind and the rain drowning out her cry of surprise.

Moments later, Jane stood in the middle of a room on the upper floor, staring unseeing at the closed door.

Aidan Warrick had apologized to her. Upon realizing her desperate need to use the privy, he had carried her through the common room of the inn, up the stairs to this chamber. Setting her on her feet, he had closed the door firmly behind him as he withdrew, leaving her alone with her waning terror, and her confusion.

He was an enigma.

What manner of man forced a woman to make terrible choices, to leave her home, to sign away seven years of her life, and then begged her pardon for failing to see to her needs? She was less than a servant, a bondswoman, little more than a slave. Yet, he had apologized to her.

His actions left her bemused, fluctuating between extremes of emotion: fear, acute embarrassment, heartfelt gratitude.

Shaking her head at the quagmire of her thoughts, Jane looked around the chamber. It was clean, simple, with a decent-size bed in the center, two straight-backed chairs and a table next to the window and, on it, a lamp with a glass chimney. The flame cast flickering fingers of light and shadow to creep along the wall, and the peat fire in the brick hearth cut through the chilling damp.

In the far corner was a washstand adjacent to a screen, behind which Jane was relieved to find— and make grateful use of—the chamber pot. She then washed her hands and her face, concentrating on her task rather than the recollections of the terrible encounter she had endured.

Her breath came fast and harsh. What would have happened had Mr. Warrick not heard her cry?

She froze, one hand snaking to her throat, coming to rest against her wildly thrumming pulse. Dead. She would be dead, her throat slit, or perhaps strangled but not before they—

A soft knock interrupted her, and she jerked back, sending water sluicing over the edges of the basin. Rubbing her damp hands along her equally damp skirt, she quickly assessed the contents of the room for anything she might use as a weapon to defend herself.

"Who is it?" Her voice quavered.

"Hawker, miss."

Relief quenched her agitation. Jane opened the door and found the tall, lean form of the carriage driver, Mr. Hawker. He stood awkwardly in the hallway, her bag clutched to his chest. One unruly lock of sandy hair fell in his eyes. He met her gaze, a sheepish expression clouding his features.

"Sorry I left you alone, miss. Thought to answer nature's call myself, and forgot you likely needed to do the same." He ducked his head and then met her gaze once more. "Himself is in a temper about it. Not that I blame him."

"Oh, well, no harm done, Mr. Hawker," she replied, squelching the memory of what had almost come to pass. She pressed her lips together, feeling somewhat abashed. Obviously Mr. Warrick had taken him to task for his oversight.

"Harm was almost done, though." His eyes were wide and somber. "I shoulda been smarter. His Lordship nearly took a strip off my hide."

Though the words held ruthless meaning, Mr. Hawker's tone carried admiration but no true fear.

"I hope you were not treated harshly," Jane blurted.

Hawker tipped his head to the side, studying her. She suddenly realized that despite his height, he was impossibly young, little more than a boy. "His Lordship treats me fair," he said defensively.

"I am certain he does," she replied, astonished to realize that she meant those words. She *was* certain that Aidan Warrick treated this boy fairly. The concept was unsettling, for she did not want to think of him as good, fair, kind. She did not want to think of him at all, but the more she tried to expunge him from her thoughts, the more clearly his image formed in her mind.

"Why do you call Mr. Warrick His Lordship?" she asked after a moment.

"He has our respect, and other reasons," Hawker said, thrusting her bag at her. She took it without thinking, tensing her muscles against the sudden pull of its weight. "But more than that I cannot say. You'll have to ask himself."

With a shuffle and a nod, he turned and strode away. Halfway along the dim corridor, he stopped and looked back. "You lock up now. No sense inviting trouble."

Baffled, Jane retreated into the room and after placing her bag on the floor by the bed, she slowly walked back to the door and turned the key in the lock. Wariness tramped icy steps along her spine as she swiftly changed into her nightclothes, and she glanced around the edge of the screen more than once just to be certain she was still alone. Coming round from behind the screen, she carefully laid her damp dress over the back of a chair.

The sound of a horse's whinny carried upward on the night air. Curious, Jane moved to the window and pulled the drapery aside, just a hand span, no more, caution whispering that she have a care.

At first she saw only the ghostly reflection of her face in the glass, but after a moment, she found she could see beyond that to the courtyard, awash in the glow of the brightly lit windows of the inn. The rain had let up, she noticed. She let the curtain fall back and moved to snuff her lamp, leaving the chamber lit only by the paltry glow of the fire.

Returning to her place, she peered out once more. Her view was clearer now, and she watched as three large carts, each drawn by a pair of horses, pulled into the yard below to join the wagon she had clung to earlier. A shudder shook her frame as she thought of that wagon . . . of the men who had terrorized her . . .

And of the solid warmth of Aidan Warrick, the rough threat in his voice as he warned them off.

Crushing the cloth of the curtain in her clenched fingers, she dragged her thoughts back to the tableau before her. Men spilled from the inn. They gathered round the wagons, spoke in hushed voices that did not carry. She could hear little more than a soft murmur of sound, their words lost to her.

One man swept his arm before him, a gesture of haste, and the others complied, hurriedly unloading one cart and carrying the contents inside. With equal speed, the men transferred the contents of another cart to the one that now stood empty. There was a cry and the creak of a wooden axle and the newly laden wagon moved off.

Shivering, Jane stood, transfixed. They were like ants, so very industrious and focused on their task. Her heart kicked at her ribs, thumping a frantic rhythm, certainty settling in a leaden lump. What she witnessed was not a few local men finding a bit of extra coin in occasional smuggling. *This* was con-

traband on a grand scale, a planned operation of
routes and passages, with the New Inn at its core.
Here was no harmless bit of quiet trade, but something far greater. And far more sinister.

She wrapped her arms about herself, rubbing
her hands up and down to ward off the chill that
seemed to come from deep within.

The silent men made short work of the third
wagon, unloading it with sober and swift precision,
and soon all the carts had been divested of their
burdens. Less than a half hour after their arrival,
the wagons moved on, creaking out of the yard to
the narrow ribbon of road that was quickly swallowed by the darkness of the night.

Yet, one cart remained, the one that had been
there since Jane's arrival. It stood alone, untouched, menacing in its mere presence.

Beset by unease, tormented and exhausted by
the events of the day, Jane stared out at the darkness, wondering what she should do now. Cold
night air seeped through the window to touch her
skin and make her shiver. Practicality and exhaustion bid her seek warmth and rest in the large bed
that dominated the room. Yet, sleep seemed an unlikely eventuality, so twisted and churned were her
thoughts, the scene she had just witnessed adding
another layer to her disquietude.

She was about to turn from her clandestine perusal of the yard when a movement in the shadows
caught her eye. Dropping the curtain until she
peeped through an opening of less than an inch,
she paused.

Apprehension oozing through her, she held her
breath and watched as a large shadow separated
itself from the overall gloom, tails of a greatcoat

fluttering in the wind, broad shoulders and tall form identifying the man even before she saw his profile.

Aidan Warrick.

Dark prince.

And, it would seem, king of thieves.

Chapter 5

The sound of the hall clock striking the midnight hour yanked Jane from a deep slumber. She bolted upright, every sense strummed to heightened sensitivity. The misty swirls of her dream—she thought it had been more a nightmare—receded as sleep gave up its hold. An unfamiliar sound nagged at the edges of her awareness. There, it came again, a soft scraping noise from outside her door. Her breath caught in her throat, and she sat, tense and alert.

Reaching over the side of the bed, she groped for the fireplace poker that she had placed on the floor when she retired. With shaking hands, she gripped the cool metal.

She had relit the lamp earlier, her inner turmoil too great to withstand the darkness in this unfamiliar and frightening place. The sound came again, a definite scratching. Now, the light of the lamp glinted off the door key as it fell from the lock, pushed aside by something thrust through the keyhole from the opposite side.

For an endless second the key tumbled end over

end before it landed with a metallic clink on the wooden floor. The door handle turned slowly and, with a lazy squeak, the portal swung inward.

A thick and choking terror assaulted her. Jane tightened her hold on the poker, her breath held suspended as Mr. Warrick stepped into the room.

"What are you doing here?" The words croaked past her too-dry lips. She was uncertain if she felt dismayed or relieved.

Balancing a heaping plate on one hand and a bottle of wine in the crook of his arm, Mr. Warrick hunkered down to retrieve the fallen key. After locking the door once more, he tossed two keys on the small table, placed the plate of food and bottle of wine beside them, then doffed his heavy coat and hung it on a wooden peg next to her own scarlet cloak.

"Why are you here, Mr. Warrick?" Bolstering her courage, Jane repeated her query, and she raised the poker to make clear her intent to defend herself should the need arise.

He glanced at her. The flickering light accentuated the planes and hollows of his cheeks, the sensual curve of his lips, the chiseled perfection of his features. With a kind of bitter detachment, Jane noted these things.

"The inn is full." The rough texture of his voice sent a shiver down her spine. "I am here to share the bed."

Surely he spoke in jest. She tightened her hold on the poker, and watched him warily as he removed his waistcoat and hung it over the bedpost. She noticed that there was one shiny brass button missing, and she focused on that lack, barely daring to breathe as from the corner of her eye she saw that he undid the lacings of his linen shirt and pulled it from the waistband of his breeches. Her pulse jumped as the open shirt bared the solid expanse of his naked chest. He lifted the hem and pulled his pistol from his belt.

She felt hot and strange at the sight of his skin and the thin line of light brown hair that ran down his midsection. Her blood felt too thick, and her lips too dry.

Reflexively, her fingers curled tighter still around the poker. "Here to share this bed? I think not, sir."

Their eyes locked and held.

"Planning to cosh me on the head?" He gestured at the poker.

Her reply caught in her throat, and then she forced it free. "If I must."

He grunted. "Move over."

At the softly voiced command, Jane's heart stuttered to a stop, then restarted, bounding at an accelerated pace that left her light-headed and a little woozy. She could scarce fathom that he had saved her from those men outside only to then perpetrate the same vile act they had intended upon her person. Was her virtue to be a part of the price he was set on exacting from her father?

She wriggled back against the solid wood of the headboard and brandished her makeshift weapon in what she prayed was a daunting manner, though her arms quaked with nerves.

"What manner of monster are you?" The words were out before she could think to stop them. Oh, cursed, cursed impetuosity.

"A tired one." He laid the pistol carefully on the floor beside the bed, and then turned to look at her. "Now be a good girl and scoot over."

Jane stared at him in amazement. He expected her to welcome him as easily as that. Scoot over, he said, and she was to allow him into her bed. Resentment, cold and pure, poured through her, and self disgust that a part of her *wanted* to touch him, to press her palm to his hot flesh, and her mouth to—

Fury at herself, and at him, lent her courage that she had not dreamed she possessed.

"I will fight you," she breathed. "I *will* cosh you on the head."

Mr. Warrick studied her for a protracted moment, running the first joint of his thumb across his lower lip. "I wish you wouldn't—"

Girding herself for defense, Jane reared up. "I will not easily yield to your unnatural—"

Her words died as he leaned forward and took the poker from her as deftly as a breeze snatching a leaf. He tossed the thing to the floor where it landed with a sharp clatter, and then braced one hand on the edge of the mattress. With the other, he caught the long, damp braid that hung down her back.

Leaning close, he stared down at her, eyes glittering in the meager lamplight. She could smell his hair, his clothes, his skin, rain-washed, a whisper of citrus, and underlying that the tantalizing hint of a scent that was his alone. Her chest felt tight, constricted by some unseen band. She could hear her blood rushing.

Despite her innocence she recognized the sharp twist of yearning in the pit of her belly for what it was—her own accursed longing for this man. This terrible, beautiful man.

He recognized it as well. His awareness was there, in the darkening of his eyes, the deepening of his breathing. She caught her lower lip between her teeth, her own breath coming in short, sharp gasps.

Pulse beating a wild rhythm, mind screaming that she must retreat, must flee from his dishonorable intent, she sat where she was, mesmerized by the heat she read in the mercurial depths of his eyes. Oh, dear heaven! What was wrong with her that a tiny secret corner of her soul reveled in his obvious desire, even as fear made her galloping heart nearly burst from her breast?

She opened her mouth to demand that he unhand her, that he remove himself immediately, that he—

He kissed her. His mouth slanted across hers, his tongue tasting the edge of her lips, her teeth, and beyond. She smelled spiced wine, tasted it.

Only in her secret dreams had she ever thought to be kissed, and never had she imagined such a lush and shameless claiming.

The taste of him, cloves and wine and man. The room spun away until there was nothing but Aidan, kissing her until she forgot to hate him, forgot all but the thrust of his tongue, the feel of his mouth, the wicked heat that poured through her like molten honey. She reached for him, hands fisting in the loose fabric of his shirt, her only anchor in this swirling storm.

"Jane." He wrenched away, the soft linen of his shirt sliding through her fingers. Taking a step back, he ran one hand through the thick, long strands of his hair in a gesture of frustration.

The wide expanse of his chest broadened as he drew in a deep breath, and his hands dropped to his sides, clenched into fists. Jane thought he struggled to master some great emotion. After a moment he looked at her, appearing bemused, then his lips tightened in displeasure.

With her?

When he spoke his voice was gruff. "Forgive my trespass."

With himself then.

She looked down at the tangle of sheets and nightclothes that bared her feet, her calves. She had not fought him as she had vowed she would, but rather had yielded with humiliating ease. Tears pricked her eyes. With frantic, jerky movements she tried to thrust the bedsheets back into place, desperate to cover her naked limbs, to hide the evidence of her wanton abandon. Her imprudence. Her wretched acquiescence.

With renewed zeal she jerked the sheets.

He stepped toward her. "Here, let me. You're making a tangle of it."

She slapped his hand away when he grasped the edge of the sheet, then snatched her own hand back in horror as she realized what she had done. "Mr. Warrick—"

"Aidan."

Aidan . . . Aidan . . . Her gaze flew to his. "You are Mr. Warrick to me."

He said nothing, only tugged the sheets from her hand and quickly rearranged them in perfect order, leaving her modestly covered.

Damn him. Why did he have to be kind? It would be easier if he treated her badly. Easier to hate him. Easier to protect herself . . . *from* herself. Was she so weak-minded that a kiss could so befuddle her?

Straightening, he picked up the plate of food he had brought with him and stood gazing down at her. "As I was saying . . . I wish you wouldn't fight me. I want to eat, and sleep, and in the morning I want to wake with the dawn and see to business. There is no room in my plans for argument."

Nor was she in a position to argue, she added silently. She was his bondswoman, his servant, surely less than nothing in his eyes.

As though reading her thoughts, he spoke casually. "If you insist on a fight, I can always tie you to the bedpost."

His words left her feeling cold. This from the man who had just kissed her with such passion?

Yes, of course. For there was not a necessary link between passion and affection, or respect. She would do well to remember that.

With a sigh he put the plate back on the table, bent forward at the waist, and planted both palms flat against Jane's right side. She imagined she felt the heat of his touch through all the layers of cloth that separated her skin from his. Stiffening, she watched him warily, uncertain of his intent. He cocked one brow, and then with a single shove he pushed her to the far side of the bed. Before she could respond, he lay down atop the sheets beside her. With one hand he plumped a pillow at his back, then shifted until he half reclined.

There was a span of several inches between them, as well as the layers of sheets and the blanket that covered her but not him. Still, she felt the overwhelming threat of his presence.

"What is it that you plan for me?"

"I know what I did not plan." His gaze moved to her lips, then slowly back up to her eyes. The way he looked at her then made her skin heat and confusion buffet her.

She looked away, at the wall directly across from

her. There was a thin crack high in the left corner, and she stared at it until her breathing came back under her control.

"Why did we come here?" She wondered that she dared question him, that she courted his ire without bridling her tongue. Perhaps it was because she was used to her father, who had left so much in her care while he drank and joked and often slept away half the day. Always when she questioned him, he had told her what she needed to know.

Except he had not told her of their debt. Their impending ruin.

And so here she was, lying in bed beside a man who was not her husband, but, in fact, her captor.

"We came because I have business here."

His words provoked a distinct wariness. She had watched his *business* from the window, though she had no intention of telling him so.

Rocking his torso forward, he pulled up one trouser leg to reveal a leather sheath, the handle of a knife protruding from the top. She watched in silence as he undid the straps that held it in place, and then laid the weapon carefully on the small table beside the bottle of wine. He lifted the plate of food with his right hand, and twisted to settle it on her lap. Helping himself to a chicken leg, he glanced at her. "And soon my business will be done. Now eat up."

Jane blinked. There was a pistol on the floor and a knife on the table. Mr. Warrick was not the gentleman that the villagers of Pentreath had conjectured he might be. Nay, she was rapidly becoming convinced that he was the smuggler, the pirate, that Dolly had foretold.

Taking a deep breath, she stared at the mountain

of food before her and was astounded to find herself tantalized. She was hungry. Biting her lip uncertainly, she glanced at Mr. Warrick from beneath lowered lashes. He lifted the bottle of wine from the table and settled it between his legs, the long glass neck protruding several inches above his thighs. Swallowing, she looked away.

This man, this stranger, had stolen her from her father. He had bullied her, terrorized her, brought her into danger.

He had seen to her comfort, staved off her hunger, kept her warm. He had chased off her attackers, saving her virtue, likely even her life.

Jane turned her head and watched him. He seemed to have forgotten her. His head was tipped slightly back, resting against the wooden headboard, his eyes closed as he chewed. She had the strangest urge to run her fingers along the rigidly carved line of his jaw. Her gaze drifted to his lips.

She thought of his kiss. Dark and lush, a kiss to lure her from rationality.

Her world was no longer sane. Perhaps she was no longer sane, for she could not summon the bone-numbing terror that had withered her heart when those two men had grabbed her outside. Here, lying next to Aidan Warrick, a man of questionable morals and admittedly wicked intent, she felt no fear.

Forgive my trespass. The knowledge that she *did* forgive him was bitter poison. Yes, she forgave him, though she could find no logic in such largesse. He was her enemy, a cold, cruel man who represented all she should despise. Yet after a mere handful of hours spent in his presence, she was half smitten with him.

The realization left her feeling pitiful, wretched.

She despaired to think that she longed so desperately for the things she would never have that she wove fantasies about a monster who had torn her world apart.

For that, she could not forgive herself.

"Jane, you need to eat." Mr. Warrick lifted a chicken leg from the plate and offered it to her.

She took it and gnawed daintily. The skin was crisp, the meat moist, and before she knew it she had devoured the whole thing, along with a chunk of soft bread.

His own meal complete, Mr. Warrick took the plate from her, setting it aside before lifting the bottle of wine from between his legs and tipping it in her direction. Wetting her lips, she shook her head. With a shrug, he brought the bottle to his mouth and tilted his head back to take a long, slow pull. He dragged the back of his hand across his mouth, his eyes locked on hers, and he offered the bottle once more.

She stared at the rim, knowing his lips had touched that spot, his tongue had licked away the last drops of wine.

Her pulse banged a hard rhythm as she slowly extended her hand and took the wine from him. She took a tentative sip. The rich, red brew slid smoothly down her throat, and she took a deeper drink, swirling her tongue around the neck.

Raising her gaze, she found him watching her, his eyes dark pools, heavy lidded, assessing.

"Have you had enough?" His voice was deeper, more gravelly than before.

She nodded and held the bottle out toward him. He took it, and after setting it aside, he snuffed the lamp. In the darkness, she shrank from him, shifting as far as she could to the edge of the bed. Wariness seeped into her thoughts, tensing her body, chilling her heart.

What would he do now?

"Good night, Jane. Sleep well." With those softly spoken words Mr. Warrick turned on his side away from her, and within seconds the slow, even cadence of his breathing told her he was asleep.

The morning sun woke her. Jane stretched and marveled at the strange dream that had inhabited the darkest hours of the night. A most beautiful man, a most wondrous kiss . . .

She opened her eyes and let out a sharp squeak. No dream then, for he stood at the foot of the bed watching her, bare chest peeking from between the open edges of his shirt, his jaw darkened by dark gold stubble. The sight of him in such dishabille unsettled her, for he was all the more perfect in his rough and ungroomed state.

"Wake up, Jane. I must leave for the span of a day. Stay in this room. Keep the door locked. Meals will be brought to you."

A spark of elation flared as she registered his meaning. He would leave her here. Alone. But as quickly as the thought of escape flickered and roared to life, it was doused by harsh reality.

There was nowhere for her to go.

Resentment nipped at her. "Do you not fear that I will flee?"

She held her breath. Why did she goad him? Such foolhardiness was against her character.

"Flee?" He made no attempt to hide his incredulity.

"There is nowhere you can go that I will not find you, sweet Jane. You are mine. Bought and paid for."

A sharp pang of despair slapped her at this harshly stated truth.

"Please do not call me that," she whispered. "Sweet Jane."

"Why not?" He looked at her mouth, and she raised her hand to cover her lips. "You *are* sweet."

She shook her head, at a loss for any rejoinder.

Lifting one booted foot, he rested it against the seat of the chair and tugged upon his trouser leg. With swift ease he fastened the leather dagger sheath in place, then pushed the chair aside and strode across the room. The door closed firmly behind him, the sound of the lock turning barely audible against the noises of the wakening inn.

Jane scuttled from the bed and dragged on her dress. She crossed to the washstand and was surprised to find a tin of Partridge's Peppermint Tooth Powder sitting next to the pitcher of fresh water. Bending, she retrieved her own tooth powder from her portmanteau and quickly performed her ablutions, her eyes constantly straying back to the tin on the washstand.

She supposed that even a monster had cause to use tooth powder. For a moment, it made him seem remarkably human.

After washing her face, she stepped to the window, pulling the edge of the curtain aside. His coach was at the ready in the courtyard, but there was no sign of Mr. Warrick. She refused to acknowledge the tiny niggle of disappointment that she would not catch a glimpse of him before he left. Suddenly, the door swung open and she whirled about, dropping her hold on the curtain.

Mr. Warrick strode back into the room, a full plate of food in one hand, a thick tome in the other. She watched him warily as he tossed the book on the bed and offered the plate to her. Reaching out, she accepted the breakfast.

"I've brought you a book . . ." He paused, frowned. "You do read?"

She looked at the book and then back to his face. "Yes, my mother taught me."

"And how did she come to know?"

"She was not always an innkeeper's wife. Once, she was the twelfth daughter of a country squire," Jane said softly, and then she lifted her chin a notch in challenge. "How did you learn to read?"

A stillness came over him. "I was not always what I am today. Once, I was the son of a mother who taught me my letters." His tone turned brusque. "I will likely return by dusk. For your own safety, do not leave this chamber unescorted." He studied her carefully. "I mean what I say, Jane. The moor has hidden dangers. It would give me no pleasure to pull your corpse from the marsh."

As Jem and Robert had pulled the corpse from the sea . . .

With that warning, he left, and Jane stood numbly staring at the locked door long after he was gone. Finally, her gaze strayed to the book on the bed, and she frowned in confusion. What manner of servant was she, that her master brought her entertainment to ease the passage of the hours?

Upon finishing her morning meal and tidying the room, Jane lifted the book that Mr. Warrick had left and settled in the chair by the window. *The Mysteries of Udolpho*. The title beckoned, and she began to read. Falling under the spell of Count Montoni and the castle of Udolpho, she did not notice the time as she sank deeper into the story and the rather frightening world the tale divulged.

After a time, she paused and rose to stretch her legs, wondering at Mr. Warrick's purpose in leaving her this chilling story to occupy her hours. There was a certain dark irony to the deed.

Hawker appeared mid-afternoon to take her on a lengthy stroll outdoors. The sky was clear, the air brisk, but the environs were far from welcoming. Despite having been to the New Inn once before with her father, Jane had never noticed until now how harsh and bleak and vast was the landscape about the place. On all sides the inn was encircled by stark and barren terrain that rolled endlessly to the east and west, and in the distance, great hills rose to meet the heavens.

Behind the New Inn, she noticed a chicken run and a small vegetable garden that invited a wave of melancholy as she thought of her own garden at home. Turning away, she let her gaze roam the gray stone wall that surrounded the yard, the stable set at the far end, and the drinking trough that sat in the center. There was nothing welcoming here.

'Twas a place drawn from a dark yarn. A frightening place. Jane sighed. Perhaps her impressions were clouded by the story she had been reading and by her own private turmoil. Surely there were good folk about, farmers and hard-working souls.

After they had walked a reasonable distance, Hawker pointed at a granite crag that rose above the marsh. "That there is Kilmar Tor." He glanced at her, his gaze dropping to her feet. "You all right then?"

Her limp was pronounced this afternoon, her

muscles aching from the lengthy carriage ride the previous day.

"I am quite well, thank you. The more I walk, the less stiff I feel." She took several steps to support her assertion.

"Not that way, miss." Hawker caught her arm and gently turned her direction. "Marsh lies that way. Marsh, and death."

Something in his tone made her shudder. "Whose death?"

Hawker sent her a wry smile. "Mine, nearly. A boy can easily lose his way, especially after dark. I thought my direction was good, inherited 'cause I'm a country lad, but I was wrong. There I was, walking along, whistling a happy tune, and next thing I knew, I was up to my arse—er, beg your pardon, miss—up to my . . . hips in slime and wet."

Staring out at the grass stems of the marsh where they waved softly in the breeze, masking the danger beneath the surface, Jane could see it in her mind's eye, see Hawker struggling against the sucking mud, trapped in what threatened to be his murky grave.

"How did you manage to pull yourself free?"

"I didn't. It was His Lor—I mean, Mister Warrick what pulled me free. And him a stranger to me. He waded right in, bold as you please, and let me tell you, I was down to my shoulders by then"—he shuddered—"and he grabs my shirt and hauls me out. I've been with him ever since. He was captain; I was his cabin boy, then worked my way up to mate."

Captain. The appellation caught her attention as much as Hawker's story. So now she had two more pieces of the puzzle that was Aidan Warrick. He was the captain of a ship. And he was a man who would risk his own life to save a boy he did not know.

Strange how pieces of the solution only made the riddle more confusing.

Chapter 6

Two more days passed much as the first. Jane was allowed only the limited freedom of Hawker's wardenship. They walked on the moor, talked of insignificant things, and Jane was left to wonder . . . Why were the tasks of a bondservant not assigned to her? What was it that kept Mr. Warrick so very busy during the daylight hours?

At night, he came to share a meal and to sleep by her side. Once, lying next to him with the layers of sheets between them, she bluntly, and foolishly, asked what his business was here at the New Inn. Mr. Warrick stared at her for a length of time, his mouth tense, his eyes narrowed, and she felt a flicker of unease as the silence stretched and grew.

There was something in his eyes . . . something . . . tormented.

When he finally doused the light and bid her roll over and sleep, she shifted to her side, moving to the very far edge of the bed. Tense, wary, she lay there, the scent of him, citrus and spice, teasing her. She felt restless, wound tight, and she thought back to the first night at the New Inn, the first night she had shared a bed with him.

The night he had kissed her.

What terrible lunacy overtook her that she longed to roll over and touch him, to lift her face to his, to feel the hard press of his mouth against hers once more? This *wanting* of him was a dark and frightening thing, for he was in a position of great power, and she was in a position of none.

Yet, he had chosen to kiss her only once and then pressed her no further, and as she called to mind every nuance of that kiss, the warmth of his mouth and the luscious taste of him, she had the horrid thought that she had far more to fear from herself than from him.

Sleep was a long time coming.

The next day was a repeat of the others, and Jane felt a growing disquiet, fed by her unfulfilled hours. She longed for some task to busy her hands and mind. Hawker took her out for a lengthy walk, but her pointed inquiries were met with evasion of a most obvious nature.

Upon her return, she took up the novel Mr. Warrick had left her and read the remainder of the afternoon away.

Night fell, a blunt and heavy press of darkness. Alone in the chamber, Jane closed her book, resting her palm flat against the leather tome, her concentration broken by the clatter of wheels on stone. Nervous unease pricked her, and some instinct whispered that 'twas no farmer's wagon come to the inn.

She pinched the flame of her candle and crossed

to the window in time to see a covered cart roll to a
halt, reminiscent of the wagon she had seen that
first night. The driver climbed down, peered round
into the shadows that laced the yard, and finally
strode into the inn. Such caution seemed vastly out
of place for a simple driver of a simple wagon.

With a sharp tug, Jane began to close the draperies,
only to still her movements as two figures separated
from the gloom to make their way furtively to the
heavily laden cart. A shock of white hair stood out like
a beacon against the black sky.

Davey.

The man who had attacked her that first night.

Jane shuddered, a miserable distress oozing through
her. With her heart tripping a frantic rhythm, she studied his sly, stealthy progress. She thought the companion slinking at his heels might be Gaby, though
there was no distinguishing thing that marked his
identity.

Fear and anger mixed in a glutinous brew, stirred
by a slew of terrifying memories. She could almost
feel their hands on her again, sense their ghastly
intent. Bile rose in her throat as she thought of
what might have happened if Mr. Warrick had not
come when he did.

Her savior.

Her tormentor.

As if conjured by her thoughts, a third form
glided from the shadows. Tall and broad, with his
black coat billowing about him, he was unmistakable. Jane sucked in a sharp breath and pressed
deeper into the cover of the velvet curtain, her
clenched fingers crushing the soft cloth. Mr. Warrick strode toward the two shadowy forms that
slunk about the wagon, his steps sure, his posture

that of a man in control. She could not hear the exchange, but Davey and Gaby appeared belligerent, argumentative, their tone carrying through the glass, if not their words.

Mr. Warrick advanced as they retreated. Davey lunged, and Jane gasped as she caught the glint of what she thought might be a blade. Bodies collided. There was a scuffle, dark forms blending and shifting in the night shadows, limbs flailing.

A single strangled cry drifted upward to raise the fine hairs at her nape.

Clinging to the curtain as though it was a solid bulwark in a storm-tossed sea, Jane pressed her face to the glass, lured by the terrifying scene, unable to tear her gaze away.

One figure lurched away from the others in a crooked dance. Drunk. Or hurt.

Jane pressed her palm against her lips. Oh, dear heaven. What tragic act did she witness?

The shadows parted, and two men moved off, the one supporting the other, the wagon left untouched. She had no doubt as to the identity of the man who remained behind.

Seconds crawled past as Jane pressed her shoulder to the cold wall, her thoughts in disarray. Mr. Warrick turned his face toward the inn and stepped into a halo of light cast from a window on the lower floor. It was then that Jane saw the unmistakable shape in his hand: his knife, held with the confidence of a man who knew what he was about.

She stared in dreadful fascination, horrified by the possibilities that knife promised. He took a light-colored cloth from his pocket—a handkerchief, she thought—and slowly, so slowly, he wiped the blade, a solid stroke on one side and then the other, the movements both graceful and awful. With a ragged exhalation she dragged the curtain shut as she stumbled back.

What had she witnessed? What? A drunk subdued, or something far more sinister?

Despite the façade of civility he presented, Aidan Warrick was a mystery, and a threat. She would do well to remember that she had no idea what he was capable of. No idea at all. So she reminded herself again and again, whispering the litany aloud as she paced to and fro and rubbed her palms along her upper arms, unable to chase away the chill.

Only when Mr. Warrick pushed open the door and entered the room a few moments later did she still her frenzied march.

"Good evening, Jane." He looked at her quizzically.

Jane stared at him, tormented by suspicion and wariness, appalled by the inexplicable burst of joy that blossomed at the sight of him. For a moment, she questioned her own sanity. She must see this man for exactly what he was, a criminal, a smuggler, mayhap a wrecker and murderer.

A man to fear.

A man who brought her dinner.

Madness. Madness. 'Twas the only explanation for the inapt and unseemly thoughts that dogged her.

He held out a tray toward her, and she wondered how he had collected a meal so quickly. Perhaps he had requested it before he went out into the night with his frightening demeanor and his knife.

She wasted little thought on why he brought their meal himself rather than summoning a serving maid. The likelihood was that he wished to offer her no opportunity to find a kind-hearted ally.

With a sigh, she took the tray from him and set it down on the table, aware of the rich scent of well-seasoned mutton stew and fresh bread.

"Good evening," she replied at last, watching him doff his coat and hang it on the peg.

Her heart hammered as he again followed the ritual of the previous nights, removing his pistol and his knife. Her gaze followed his movements as he placed the sheathed blade on the table near the bed.

If she drew nigh and examined the piece, would she find it stained red with blood?

A shudder crawled along her spine. She raised her gaze to find him studying her with narrowed eyes.

Flustered, she set her hands to laying out the plates from the tray, and soon they were sitting on the two rough chairs, facing each other across the table by the window.

"Are you enjoying the book?" Mr. Warrick asked some moments later.

"Yes, thank you." Such civil conversation.

Jane poked at a potato, and then a carrot. What would he say if she asked him about the strange and frightening scene she had just witnessed? Would he tell her the truth?

He leaned forward and filled her glass with wine. "What do you think of Emily?"

Jane stared at him. She had spent the past moments in an agony of uncertainty, wondering if she had just witnessed him gutting a man, while he had spent that time pondering literature.

"She values life's simple beauties, and that I can understand," she said at length, thinking about

Emily, the heroine of *The Mysteries of Udolpho,* thinking, too, of Emily's trials and tribulations, perhaps a metaphor for her own. An indelicate snort escaped her. "She does tend to faint a great deal."

Mr. Warrick let out a laugh, the sound brief and clear, as though startled from him. Jane closed her eyes, pleased by the cadence of it, perplexed by her pleasure. When she opened her eyes, she found him watching her, his mouth curved in a small smile.

That mouth had kissed hers. Warm, firm lips. The delicious thrust of his tongue. She dropped her gaze to her plate, dismayed both by her inability to expunge the episode from her thoughts and by the secret truth that she had enjoyed his kiss, that she desperately wanted him to kiss her again, despite all her rationalizations and silent admonitions why he must not.

"Yes, I suppose that is true," he agreed.

Jane's head jerked up and for endless seconds she wondered if he had divined her most private thoughts. But no, she recalled the direction of their conversation . . . Emily, the fainting heroine.

"I found her honorable," he said.

"Do you admire that? Her deep sense of honor? You do not seem a man to value morality or honor—" Jane stumbled to a halt and drew a breath as she realized what she had implied. That he was not a man to value honor, that he was not a man of principle. "Oh! I—"

His gaze settled on her, and she thought he delved deep inside her soul, seeing more of her than she ever intended him to.

"Morality," he mused. "No, I have no time for the social morality imposed by a tainted civilization. But I am not a man who equates false morality with honor. Let us just say I have my own personal code." His tone was rife with some emotion she could not place.

Jane opened her mouth, but could summon no reply. Did he mean that he chose to live outside the bounds of civilization? Was this a confession to his illegal deeds? Yet, he implied that he *was* honorable, measured by some secret standard he did not choose to define. The possibilities tormented her.

They finished their meal in silence, their companionability now strained and palpably uncomfortable. At length, Mr. Warrick rose and crossed the room. Jane stared at his broad back as he took up his pistol and his knife, thinking that she had somehow offended him deeply. She almost laughed aloud at the absurdity of it; she questioned the honor of a man she suspected was a smuggler and thief, and he would take her to task for it. Worse, she took herself to task, feeling that somehow she had behaved the churl.

Returning to the table, he lifted the now-empty plates and set them on the tray. He did not look at her. "I will allow you a moment of privacy, Jane." With that, he lifted the dirty crockery, strode to the door, and exited the chamber. She heard the turn of the key in the lock.

Her mind awhirl with the odd tenor of her situation, Jane swiftly divested herself of her dress and donned her nightclothes. Scurrying beneath the sheets, she lifted them to her chin as she had the previous nights. She knew what to expect now, knew that Mr. Warrick would return and take up his place beside her. The thought both thrilled and distressed her. She turned to one side then the other, nervously awaiting his return, wondering if he tarried because she had insulted him. A strange possibility, and one that left her restless and troubled.

She found her thoughts skittering hither and yon. The frightening scene she had witnessed through the window haunted her, and then, somehow, the novel she had read took on sinister significance. She wondered if he meant her to read it and draw some deep comparison, or if the book was meant as an innocent entertainment. And all the while, she tossed on the bed, preoccupied by images of ghosts, souls ripped from life by violent and terrible deeds, of menacing strangers who skulked in the shadows, and of frightening castles and catacombs that snaked their way deep into the ground.

Sounds floated upward from the common room below. A shout, a raucous laugh. Her eyelids drifted shut, heavy with the lateness of the hour. At some point she fell into a light slumber, oblivious to the noises of the inn, unaware of Mr. Warrick's return.

She was in a dark passage, deep under the ground, and then she was calf-deep in a gray and angry sea. A woman rose up from the waves, her red hair writhing like living snakes, her eyes gaping black holes in her skull, her raw flesh hanging in ribbons. Hands reached out, clawed fingers draped with rotted entrails, and there on the cliff a cloaked figure watched and laughed.

As she struggled against the nightmare, half-aware that she had but to rouse herself in order to escape, an image shimmered and coalesced, a stranger not borne of imagination, but of terrible and unkind memory.

The cloaked figure on the cliff disappeared, replaced by a man garbed as any common tar. He was on the cliff and then he was halfway along the familiar stretch of beach, in the shadow of Trevisham House.

"Oy, girl. Which way, then, to the inn?"

Young, nondescript, he appeared to pose no threat, but the breakers churned and roared behind him in a terrifying fury.

Be home before dusk. Her mother's rules drummed through her thoughts and she felt the weight of the sky, tinged with the coming of night. She glanced back at the man, uncertain. What harm in telling a stranger the way? What harm?

Terror was a thick miasma, wrapping her in its choking hold.

Too late. Too late to see the harm, to heed the warning that snaked icy tentacles through her veins. His hands were on her, hurting her. She struggled. Screamed.

His hands were on her. His hands . . .

With a cry, Jane jerked upright, her chest heaving as she sucked great gulps of air. A memory. A dream. She had not suffered its coming for so long that she had dared to hope it would never return.

There *were* hands on her shoulders, not rough, but gentle, soothing, reassuring. Aidan's hands. He had wakened her. She shuddered. The New Inn . . . She was in a room in the New Inn.

Grasping at that thought, she tried to chase away the frightening recollections that snapped at her, crossing the boundary from dream to wakefulness. Rigid and distraught, she stared at nothing, haunted by images that yet felt real, memories that refused to rest. The fire had died and the room was couched in blackness, chilled as the frost-kissed winter ground.

"Jane, lie against me, sweet. I will let none harm you, not even the demons of your dreams." The low and gravelly whisper of Aidan's voice calmed her flayed nerves. His big, warm hands guided her as he drew her against his muscled chest and wrapped her in the safe harbor of his arms. She did not resist, drawn by his strength and the kindness of his touch.

"Sleep now," he commanded, his breath caressing her cheek as he tucked her close, warming her with the heat of his body.

She could feel the steady rhythm of his heart, the even cadence of the rise and fall of his chest. He was solid against her back, his hand gentle as he stroked her hair.

The horror of past memories faded, and she drifted toward sleep, strangely comforted by the embrace of the monster who was her present.

I am unhinged, like mad Letty, who sang to her babies though they had never been born, and spoke to a husband who had drowned decades past, Jane thought as she drifted toward sleep. Surely she was unbalanced, that she felt soothed by Aidan's embrace.

No, not mad. Safe, for this moment, at least.

Because the nightmare had come for her, and he had not let it take her.

Morning found Mr. Warrick up and dressed, prowling the confines of the small chamber like a caged beast. Jane felt certain that he had been awake for some time. She thought he might have gone out and returned while she slept.

"My business is concluded and I would be away from the New Inn," he said. "I am for home."

Home. Jane stared at him uncertainly. She did not go to *her* home, but to *his*. The thought of the unknown terrified her. He had been nothing but kind to her, but she was not lulled into security. *He was not a kind man.* Was he merely playing some game of torment, waiting until they reached Trevisham House to mete out whatever harsh future he planned for her?

Why? Why would he do that? For some twisted satisfaction?

Or was she spinning dark meaning where none existed?

Surely her features hinted at her inner torment, for his expression grew cold and distant.

"You have seen too much." His voice was soft, musing, his words alarming.

Her chest tightened and she struggled for breath. "What—what do you mean?"

"You have witnessed much on this little excursion. In truth, you have seen far more than I would have liked. And so you study me with veiled glances and a wary gaze. Do you think me ready to pounce, sweet Jane?"

His words left her more confused than ever. Did he mean that she spun fantasy from what she had witnessed? Or, more likely, did he mean that she had borne witness to nefarious deeds and unspeakable crimes?

She could not imagine how she might ask.

"I will wait for you directly outside this door. Make haste, if you please." He strode across the room.

Jane crushed the blankets in her tightening grasp. Directly outside this door . . . A promise or a warning?

Good as his word, Mr. Warrick was in the hall waiting for her, along with Hawker who hurried inside to gather their belongings.

As they made their way through the common room, Jane saw Mr. Warrick glance at a darkened corridor that led toward the back of the inn. She paused, squinting into the gloom, and wondered if smuggled barrels and goods were stored in some dusty chamber at the far end, or if they were already on their way to the city, destined to sell for a goodly amount.

After a moment, she realized that Mr. Warrick had moved on. With a shake of her head, she hurried after him, following him outside to the courtyard.

"Oy, Mr. Warrick!" the owner of the New Inn, Joss Gossin, called out as he stepped through the door. He shot a look at Jane, and she saw his eyes widen in recognition, for this was the first time since her arrival that they had met face to face. She was acquainted with this man. He had been to the Crown Inn twice that she recollected, and she had once visited this inn with her father.

Her cheeks burned with embarrassment as she realized that he knew she had spent the past nights in the same bed as Mr. Warrick, that he likely believed she was nothing more than a lightskirt.

And then a new thought struck, one with far more sinister implications. Mr. Gossin was the keeper of this fine establishment. It was highly unlikely that Mr. Warrick plied his nefarious trade at the New Inn without the knowledge of the innkeeper. The thought was disturbing in the extreme. Not for the issue of smuggling in the simplest sense. Most Cornishmen believed that what the sea gave up was theirs by right, and believed, too, that a small bit of smuggling harmed none.

But all she had seen made her certain that this was not that sort of trade. No harmless petty crime that the revenue men might ignore.

The New Inn must be part of an elaborate smuggling ring, one that snaked through the countryside, a sinister poison. Too, there was the horrific

possibility that the company of thieves turned to
luring ships to the rocks and to bloody murder, for
it seemed strange that both a group of wreckers
and a second group of smugglers would ply the
coast at the same time. 'Twas far more likely that
they were one and the same.

A shudder took her. Whatever their nefarious
deeds, she had little doubt as to the identity of the
serpent's head. Her gaze strayed to Mr. Warrick's
broad back, and she hastily looked away as he
glanced at her over his shoulder.

As the men entered into hushed conversation,
Jane walked beside the crumbling stone wall that
surrounded the courtyard, wishing that she could
be anywhere but here. Behind her was the inn itself,
and the stables and tack room. Ahead of her, at the
very far end of the wall, was a great pile of rubble
and rock, as though the wall was unfinished and
meant to be built upon some time in the future.

She walked, head high, face turned to the meager
sun that poked periodically through the clouds. She
passed the drinking trough, and the patch of grass,
and then she went up the low rise toward the pile of
rock.

Once, she paused and turned to look behind
her. Mr. Warrick stood in a small group of men, listening as they spoke. He dipped his head. Spoke
briefly in reply to someone's words. But his eyes
never left her.

She felt the heat of his gaze upon her as she
walked on.

When she reached the pile of rock, she toed it with
her boot, watching small pebbles roll down the slope.
Her gaze wandered to the small knot of men—
Mr. Warrick and Hawker and Joss Gossin among

them—and then idly over the ground. Something glittered, catching the sunlight, and she rounded the far end of the heap of rock and bent forward to examine her find. It appeared to be Mr. Warrick's button. The missing one from his waistcoat that she had noticed that first night.

Leaning forward a bit more, Jane picked it up, and then gasped as she made a second discovery. Two booted feet protruded from the very far side of the pile. Someone sleeping off a drunk, she imagined. Frowning, she stepped closer, and immediately wished she had not.

A wall of acrid stink slammed into her. Her breath left her in a whoosh and her gaze locked on the dark stain that had all but soaked into the ground, nearly invisible against the brown soil. Staggering back, she pressed her hand against her lips, her fingers closing reflexively around Mr. Warrick's waistcoat button as her eyes traveled from booted feet to coarse coat to the shock of white hair that stood out in contrast to the earth.

Recognition dawned, and she bit back the churning ball of nausea that roiled in her belly. *Davey*. She had no doubt that he was dead. Stumbling back another step, she began to shake as she conjured the recollection of the exchange she had witnessed last night, the one that left Mr. Warrick wiping his blade and Davey lurching off into the night.

Dragging in a painful breath, she tried to call out, but her throat clogged against the formation of sound, and she stood, frozen by her horror of the corpse that stretched before her. Dead. He was dead. And the rocks had rolled down the mound, covering a part of him and leaving the rest exposed.

Blood. Blood. So much blood. A stain soaked deep into the soil.

She whirled, took three uneven steps, her gaze seeking Mr. Warrick's tall form.

As if sensing her desperate need, he turned, his eyes finding hers.

"Jane!" He reached her in a few long strides. "What is it?"

"There," she rasped, feeling as though a thick, sticky ball of bread and honey clogged her throat. "A man. Behind the rocks."

Mr. Warrick's expression hardened. "Did he frighten you?"

A sob caught in her throat, and she refused to let it free. Swallowing her distress, she shook her head. "No. I think he is quite dead."

His eyes roamed her face, assessing. Then he smiled. "Quite dead? You mean he is not partially dead?"

She stared at him, appalled. He was making a joke of it? Stiffening, she jerked her chin up a notch.

"That's my girl. Strong as forged steel," he said softly. "You won't swoon on me."

She blinked, strengthened by his praise and appalled that she cared at all.

Looking around, she realized that Hawker was there, and Joss Gossin, and several others she did not recognize. She stepped back as they pulled Davey's corpse free of the debris. His arms were above his head, and she stared at the gashes dug by his fingers in the loose, damp earth. He was face down. She was grateful for that, for she thought she might retch if she looked upon his lifeless eyes.

She could well recall Mr. Warrick's voice, low and menacing as he demanded her release that first night. *Davey, is she worth your life? . . . The man that touches her is the man I'll gut. A nice, slow death, that.*

Though she knew with certainty that Davey would have killed her, she could not find satisfaction in his demise. Drawing a shaky breath, she forced herself to look at the dead man once more, and was sickened by the sight of the back of his shirt, dark and stiff with the stain of his blood.

He had been stabbed in the *back*. Or perhaps shot. But it appeared that he had not faced his killer as he died. Stepping away, she turned her face from the sight.

Shock and dread gnawed at her. Had Mr. Warrick killed him as he had threatened? Shot him? Stabbed him in the back? Had she witnessed the man's murder from her window last night?

She glanced about the circle of men that had formed, wondering what any one of them would do if she spoke of that now.

Nothing. They would do nothing, for she had not seen anything that definitively proved blame. And even if she had, she suspected that none would speak against Aidan Warrick.

Surreptitiously, she pushed the button she had found deep in the pocket of her cloak. Certainly it proved nothing, for Davey had been hale and hearty for days after Mr. Warrick's waistcoat had given up the button.

"Stabbed from behind," one of the men said, confirming her suspicion.

Stabbed. Oh, dear heaven. A frantic buzzing sawed at her, and she felt as though a dark tunnel closed in. She could *see* him, Mr. Warrick, as he had been last night, slowly, methodically wiping the long, wicked blade that he kept always close at hand.

Someone's hand came to rest on her shoulder. With a gasp, Jane jerked around to find Joss Gossin watching her with a strange expression, his gray brows drawn together in a frown. "Are you going to be sick, girl?"

"No." She shook her head. "I am well. Truly."

She thought of all that had passed since she had first laid eyes on Mr. Warrick standing at the edge of the graveyard, his coming heralded by the stark cry of the raven, and she thought that she was not well at all.

Sinking her teeth into her lower lip, she glanced nervously at her employer. His back was toward her as he spoke quietly to Hawker. In that instant, she realized that this was her chance. She had been unable to fulfill her promise to hang a sheet from Trevisham House and notify her father of her well-being that first night. *This* was her opportunity to remedy that lack, to take control over at least one small thing in the turmoil that had become her life.

"Please, Mr. Gossin," she whispered. "I beg you send word to my father. Tell him I am well. Tell him—"

"Nothing." Mr. Warrick's rough voice cut her off coldly. "You will tell him nothing."

Her heart sank as Joss pulled his hand from her shoulder and looked uncertainly between the two.

"Miss Heatherington is—" Mr. Warrick paused. "Under my protection."

She cringed at his choice of words. He made her sound like his mistress. Kicking up her chin a notch, she turned to Joss.

"I am his *bondswoman*, Mr. Gossin."

The innkeeper's bushy eyebrows waggled in surprise. "Are you, now? Well . . . er . . . well . . ." He looked to Mr. Warrick for confirmation.

Her employer was in no mood for civility. He ignored Joss and turned to Hawker. "You know what to do with him," he said, nodding in the direction of the body.

"I do, sir."

"Should we not call the magistrate?" Jane protested, a small bubble of hysteria floating close to the surface. "Find the perpetrator? Return the man's remains to his kin?"

"Davey's got no kin we know of. One of the boys"—Hawker jutted his chin in the direction of the small group of men who stood nearby—"will take him to the church at Tintagel. Get him buried. We . . . um . . . that is . . . the vicar there is known to us."

Jane followed Hawker's gaze to the growing knot of men who stood some feet away. Like scavengers, their numbers increased the longer the corpse sat.

With a shudder, she strained to see those in the back, feeling a malevolent gaze locked upon her. Gaby, Davey's cohort. She thought she saw him lurking at the far edge of the group, though she had no clear view of his face. Wrapping her arms about herself, she took a steadying breath. She could remember the ugly sound of their voices, the rough grasp of their clawing fingers, and now one of them was dead. She shivered and looked away.

"As to the magistrate . . ." Hawker shrugged, his gaze flicking first to Joss Gossin, and then to Mr. Warrick.

With a dark curving of his lips that barely qualified as a smile, Mr. Warrick shook his head and said, "*My* law will suffice."

Chapter 7

They rode in silence for quite some time, Mr. Warrick frowning formidably as he stared out the carriage window at the surrounding countryside. Jane silently reviewed the terrible events of the morning. Her imagination added detail after macabre detail until she wondered at the veracity of her recollections.

Yet death was the indisputable truth.

Jane shuddered. The horrific sight of the grooves gouged in the earth by Davey's clawed fingers was branded in her mind's eye. Davey, dead. The woman pulled from the ocean, dead. A deep, gnawing certainty plagued her, one that whispered of connections and links, the voice ghostly and inescapable.

Suspicions.

"Did you—" Jane began. Her stomach plummeted. What folly took her that she dared question him? Taking a deep breath, she forged on. "Mr. Warrick—" Again, she faltered.

He turned and fixed her with a steady stare, and she could not look away. Such eyes. Blue and gray, a swirling storm, the color made all the more rich by the sun-kissed tone of his skin.

"Aidan," he said softly.

She blinked.

"We have shared a bed, sweet Jane." He gave a small, close-lipped smile. "My given name is Aidan. Use it."

Shared a bed. The words made a wave of heat spread through her. "We shared naught but a place to sleep," she corrected. "And I shall call you—"

"Aidan. You shall call me Aidan simply because I wish it. Consider it my command. Are you not answerable to me, Jane? Did you not agree to the bargain?"

Opening her mouth to respond, Jane found herself at a loss, unsettled by his questions and by the odd tone to his voice, low and rough and a little urgent, as though there was some import attached to her use of his name.

She *was* answerable to him, for she *had* agreed to the bargain. She was his bondswoman, though thus far he had treated her more like an honored guest than a servant bought and paid for. The why of it escaped her.

Strange man.

The moment stretched, tense and unnerving, until her curiosity overcame her anxiety and she pressed on.

"Mr. War—" His displeased expression made her swallow the remaining syllable. Turning her head to look out the carriage window, she silently tested his name. *Aidan.* Why did he wish to hear the word on her lips? She glanced at him, and found that he watched her still, his expression inscrutable. Something in his gaze tugged at her, drew her, made her heart race and her skin tingle.

"Aidan," she whispered, his name filling the small space that separated them.

He leaned closer, bracing one hand on the seat beside her. Her breath hitched and she froze, both attracted and repelled, her common sense bidding her shrink from his regard, her traitorous body aching to lean closer.

Closer. Her blood pounded a wild rhythm in her veins. She wanted to breathe the smell of him— soap with a hint of citrus and spice—to rest her hands on the muscled planes she had seen beneath his fine shirt. Her gaze shifted to the firm line of his mouth. A hard mouth. Just a little cruel.

Oh, God. What was wrong with her that even faced with the likelihood that he was a smuggler, a wrecker, a *murderer,* her heart, her body, yearned for him? Was there some flaw in her makeup? Was this heart-pounding need perhaps a failing that was passed through generations, the same instinctual urge that had made her mother love a man who was rough and harsh and far below her station?

It mattered not. Whoever, whatever, Aidan Warrick was, she wanted to *taste* him. To press her lips to his, to open her mouth as he had taught her. The memory was a molten river wending through her body until it puddled in the pit of her belly.

His gaze intent, he reached toward her, running the pad of his thumb across her lower lip, tilting his head ever so slightly. She drew a shaky breath, lured by the unimaginable urge to lick his thumb, to take it in her mouth and suck on it.

The carriage rocked. Jane was thrown back against the cushioned seat, and the small physical distance was enough to remind her exactly what dangers he

posed. She could not trust him, and—dear heaven—
it seemed she could not trust herself.

He was arrogant, unkind, molded of metal and
ice, and she could not seem to remember all that
when he turned his stare upon her, his thoughts,
his need, naked there for her to see.

Focusing on their earlier discussion in a desperate attempt to bring some sanity to her muddled
thoughts, Jane finally blurted the questions that
had haunted her throughout their long, silent journey. "That man . . . Davey . . . Did you—" No, she
would be wiser to rephrase. "Who do you suppose
killed him? And why?"

Aidan's face betrayed not a flicker of emotion as
he sank back into the corner of the seat and folded
his arms across his chest. He studied her. She refused to flinch from his frank regard.

"Ask again," he ordered. "But ask the question
you want answered, not a watered-down version."
His mouth tightened, and he looked away, letting
the silence spin a silken web between them before
he continued softly, "I would not have you fear me,
Jane."

His assertion verged on the absurd. Why should
it matter whether his bondswoman feared him?
Moreover, after all that had transpired, how could
he imagine she did not?

"Ask," he commanded.

"I do not know what you mean." She did know,
but did she dare ask? She pushed her hand into the
pocket on the inside of her cloak, her fingertips
testing the rim of the button she had found, her
memories spinning a dark web of the threat she
had heard him make and the blade she had seen
him wield.

Her pulse raced. Withdrawing her hand, she pressed damp palms to her skirt. All right, then. All right. "That man, Davey, did you kill him?"

He turned his face to her. A shiver chased along her spine as he smiled in a way that had nothing to do with mirth. "You are brave. There are few men who would dare question me."

"You bid me ask. I did as you said." She paused. "Besides, I am not a man."

"But I am." His gaze dropped to her mouth and he leaned forward so his knees brushed hers and his forearms draped casually across his thighs. "And damned if my senses are not full of you, sweet Jane."

Again the pounding tide of awareness flooded her veins, thicker and hotter than only moments before. He was so close, so big. So male. Her desperate attempt to avoid the tug of attraction had only brought her back to the same place she had started.

She held out one hand, palm forward. Such a paltry shield should he choose to press his advantage. He held his place, neither withdrawing nor shifting to crowd her further.

"You bid me ask, and yet you refuse to answer," she challenged, her chest tight, as though bound by chains.

With a casual twist of his wrist, he caught a loose tendril of her hair, winding the dark strand through his fingers before letting it slide slowly from his grasp.

"Answer," she whispered, the word sounding thick even to her own ears. What was it she wanted to know? For a moment she forgot, her attention fixed on Aidan Warrick, on the dark passion glittering in the depths of his eyes, etched in the chiseled lines of his jaw.

He wanted her. Of that knowledge she could not pretend ignorance, for she felt the answering call in every fiber of her being. There was neither reason nor wisdom in the yearning that spilled warm and viscous through her limbs, only mindless, foolish wanting. She licked her lips, wishing he would lick them for her.

He leaned closer, and she could feel the light touch of his breath across her cheek. A sharp, hard twist coiled deep in her belly. Her fingers clenched against the urge to touch his sun-burnished, silky hair, to trail over his skin and feel the texture of it . . .

"I did not kill him, Jane." Aidan's gaze locked with hers.

She wanted to believe those words. A lie would not serve him. So, if he spoke the truth, then he had not killed Davey. "But you could have."

He laughed in genuine amusement. "I would not choose the coward's road and stab a man in the back."

Now there was an untruth.

"You lie," she whispered rashly. "In all but the literal sense, you stabbed my father in the back. Oh, you did not use a blade, but rather the sharp edge of utter desperation, stealing his coin, his livelihood, and finally stealing me away, like some snake in the grass, rather than facing him, facing the man you call your enemy." The words were torn from her in an agonized rush, a barricade against her own convoluted emotions.

"I am a poor liar, Jane, so I never bother with it. The truth invariably suffices." His brows rose and he rocked back. "I faced your father." He waited a heartbeat. "And I stole nothing. Rather, he was too drunk and foolish to pay heed to the value of what he gave away so carelessly. I did not steal you, Jane. You came of your own free will."

He caught her chin and tilted her head so she could not avoid his piercing stare. "Remember that. Remember that you had a choice."

Sinking her teeth into her lower lip, Jane struggled with his assertion and her own confusion. Had she made a choice? At the time she had thought there was only one possible solution, believed that this cold, unfeeling man had offered no alternatives. And now? She had no idea what she believed now.

Beset by uncertainty, Jane deliberately shifted away from his touch and steered her attention to the landscape beyond the carriage window. The way was unfamiliar to her.

"We do not got to Trevisham House?" she whispered, acutely aware of the conflicting thoughts and feelings that Aidan roused in her.

"We do," he rumbled, his gaze flicking to her and then away. "By a circuitous route."

His reply only served to stoke the fire under the boiling pot of her emotions, and she laced her fingers tight lest she give away the trembling that beset her. A futile effort. She was very certain that he read her every thought and feeling.

A short time later, the coach slowed and rocked to a stop. Jane had been vaguely aware that they had left the main road, and now, as she gazed out the window, she saw a freshly whitewashed farmhouse with a neat black roof and well-tended front garden. Beyond the house, steep hedges of banked earth rose then fell toward the sea, creating a low hillock that obscured the view. The trick was an old one. Smugglers brought soil to build a wall between land and ocean, hiding them and their nocturnal activities from the prying eyes of the excise officers who patrolled the coast.

She glanced at Aidan. Gone was the intensity of only moments past. His features betrayed nothing of the desire that had bubbled between them, his expression now one of cool detachment. For a moment, she thought she had imagined the whole of it, the rampant need, their inexplicable connection.

And then his eyes met hers, and in their depths she saw the reflection of her own yearning, mingled with his. So he wanted her still. The realization was as frightening as it was thrilling, and even more terrifying was the knowledge that he intended her to see it, to recognize his desire.

He turned away to push open the door of the carriage. Jane swatted a wayward strand of hair, glad to be free of the intensity of his regard. Stepping down, Aidan turned and offered his hand.

"The other day . . . when you took me from my fath—" She hesitated, then continued. "From my home. You purposely left me to fend for myself, to climb into the carriage unaided. Why?"

He narrowed his eyes. "Why pose the query when you already know the answer?"

Jane pressed her lips together, certain now that his behavior that day, when he had callously entered the carriage without a glance in her direction, had been an act designed to grieve her parent. She digested the thought as she placed her hand in his, allowing him to help her down, just as he had done on every other occasion save one.

Aidan steadied her as she alighted, holding her hand far longer than necessary. His touch warmed her, nay, *heated* her, until she felt her skin flush.

From a single touch. She was left restless and tense, wanting to pull away, wanting to never let go. In truth, her instinct whispered that she step even closer, press herself against his hewn thighs and taut belly. She gasped, appalled by her thoughts, and her gaze flashed to his as she tugged her hand free.

He watched her with eyes hot and hungry. He *wanted,* but he did not *take.*

Why? Why did he show such restraint, such consideration of her? Bewildered, she turned away. Searching for calm, she inhaled deeply. The familiar tang of salt air washed in from the ocean.

Suddenly, the door of the farmhouse flew open and an older woman with an aura of barely leashed energy stepped out into the late-morning sun.

"Well, there you are." The woman bustled toward Aidan, her weathered face wreathed in smiles, her hands outstretched in greeting. "I expected you sooner. But no matter, no matter. You're here now, aren't you? The boys'll be along any time with the wagon. Will Hawker see to the horses?"

"He and I, both."

"Very good, sir. And then come along inside. I have a meat pie all ready."

Suddenly, she stopped, her smile fading as she caught sight of Jane. "Oh, dear." She rounded on Aidan. "Who do you have here?"

"She is mine, Wenna," he said gruffly.

Jane tensed.

"Yours?" Wenna nodded sagely, her shrewd gaze running from the top of Jane's head to the tip of her toes as she drew her own conclusions. "Well, a fine thing you've done, dragging your wife around the country like so much baggage. Couldn't leave her to home where she'd be comfortable. Men!"

To Jane's astonishment, Wenna rounded and glared at Aidan. He scowled, but said nothing.

The older woman stepped forward, linking one arm through Jane's and pulling her determinedly toward the open door of the house. "Name's Wenna Tubb. You just call me Wenna, Mrs. Warrick."

"I am not his—" Jane began, wondering how this woman had mistaken the situation so terribly. "That is, I am his—"

Wenna stopped abruptly and whirled to face Jane, her sharp eyes taking in her bedraggled appearance. "Which is it, dear? You're not his? You are his?" She threw her hands up in the air. "Doesn't matter. Come along. You look like you could use a nice rest and some good hot food."

Glancing behind her, Jane caught sight of Aidan leaning against the side of the coach, shoulders shaking, face turned into his collar. Why, he was *laughing,* Jane realized with wonder. Hard, cold Aidan Warrick had a sense of humor, if not a heart.

She turned to Wenna and spoke loud enough for her voice to carry. "Thank you, Wenna. You are quite right about needing a meal. My *husband* neglected to feed me this morning, and I find that I am both fatigued and famished."

"Oh! Didn't even bring along a little something for you? Just like a man!" Wenna sent a jaundiced look in Aidan's direction.

Over her shoulder, Jane watched as he lurched away from the coach, no longer laughing.

Wenna took Jane's cloak as they entered the house. The older woman moved to the left, into a large and airy kitchen. She paused to stand by the window that overlooked the front garden. Jane followed her gaze, watching Aidan and Hawker see to the horses.

"He's good with the animals," Wenna said, pride in her tone. "Wouldn't expect that from a man so long at sea."

Jane felt a spark of curiosity. "How long was he at sea?"

Though she tried to convince herself that she only wanted to know her enemy, the truth glared at her. She wanted to know Aidan for himself. He intrigued her. Kindled unfamiliar emotions in her heart. Made her someone other than the woman she had been before, the woman defined by her damaged leg and her role as the innkeeper's daughter. With Aidan she was not pitiable, crippled Jane. That was how *others* saw her.

Aidan saw her as a woman.

The thought was frightening, for despite her limp, there had always been a certain comfort, a safety in her ordinariness. So the question she was left with was: how did she see herself?

"You'd best ask himself about his years at sea. He would not like for me to tell you his story, I'm thinking." Wenna looked away, busying her hands collecting dinnerware. "You'd think he would have told me sooner about finding himself a bride," she grumbled, and sniffed as she handed Jane a pile of plates.

Jane took them and held the stack carefully. Fine china, she noticed, with lovely flowered detail. How odd. She limped through the open doorway to the adjacent dining room, aware of the other woman's questioning gaze on her as she walked.

"I am not his wife, Wenna," she said as she carefully laid a plate on the table. "I am his servant. His bondswoman. Bought and paid for."

She winced. The words sounded so much worse when spoken aloud. With a sigh, Jane set the second plate down, then the third, paying excessive attention to her task.

"Are you now?"

Raising her eyes, Jane found Wenna standing in the doorway staring at her with a quizzical expression on her round face.

"That boy's been to Hades, do not doubt it for a second. Life has taught him to never do anything without good reason. If you are his servant, well, he'll treat you as well as any other master. Better, most likely."

Jane smiled sadly, knowing the words were meant as a reassurance.

"My older boy, Cadan, served on his ship for a time, so I can tell you for certain there's no fairer master," Wenna continued, and then her voice dropped low. "But make no mistake, our Mr. Warrick does not shirk from a dark deed if the need be called."

Whatever small comfort had been offered by Wenna's words shriveled as she made her final assertion. Cold dread crawled along Jane's spine. The appalling truth was that she could not imagine Aidan dodging even the darkest deed if he felt it justified.

Jane realized her horror must have shown on her face, because Wenna shook her head and said, "It'll turn out in the end, child. Mark my words."

Blinking against the sting of tears, touched by Wenna's gruff but kind words, Jane set the last plate on the table.

She glanced out the window, watching as Aidan stroked a brush along the horse's side. Strong movements, but gentle, each stroke a perfect rhythm. The sight made a knot form in her throat.

Wenna thought all would turn out in the end, but Jane felt a cruel coil of desperation twist her belly. What Wenna said was likely true. Aidan *would* treat her as well as any master, if his behavior so far was an example. She would need no protection from him, for he guarded his actions with care.

Alas, it was only her foolish heart that needed protection for she was drawn to him in a way that she could not explain, to the strength of him and the kindness he had shown her. Strangely, to the sense of safe harbor he offered. And, heaven help her, to his dark and brooding depths. The need to fix him, to heal him, was growing inside her, and she could not fathom it. How was she to fix one so damaged when she could not even heal herself? When the raw wounds of her own tormented memories yet haunted her nights?

"I'm only saying that it's clear he means you no harm," Wenna said.

He meant her no harm? Did she know that in truth? Jane shook her head, swayed by the other woman's conviction, but wary nonetheless. She knew almost nothing about the enigmatic man who owned the next seven years of her life.

At Jane's continued silence, Wenna made a clucking sound. "Why, you heard him laugh. That's rare . . . not something he does often. I'd wager he cares for you."

Perhaps. As he cared for any possession. She could not imagine greater depth of feeling than that from him. Jane opened her mouth to say so. "He cannot. I—"

"Those boys'll be looking for their meal, dear." Wenna cut her off, gesturing toward a breakfront on the far wall. "Finish setting the table. There's good cutlery in that drawer there."

Following instruction, Jane opened the drawer, but seeing what lay inside made her draw back with a sharp inhalation. Fine plates and now the finest silver she had ever seen or imagined, here, in such a humble cottage. What deeds had brought such wealth to these people? Surely not honest work, for a single fork likely valued the same as a year's worth of food.

What manner of woman was Wenna Tubb, in truth?

The sound of wheels on the road drifted through the window, followed by a man's shout. Jane looked out to see a large wagon pulled by two sturdy horses coming toward the cottage. She frowned in confusion. It looked like the wagon from the New Inn, the one carrying the kegs of smuggled brandy. The one that had enticed Davey just before he was murdered.

The driver called out in greeting as a second man jumped down and inclined his head in greeting to Aidan. He tugged on his forelock, an archaic gesture of respect, but something about the man's posture gave Jane pause. There was a swagger to his walk, and an arrogance that laced his every action. . . .

"That'll be my boys." Wenna's voice warmed with pride. "Cadan. He's the one on the wagon. And Digory's the baby. A bit wild, that one is."

Wenna's baby was a good two inches taller than Aidan, and likely two stone heavier, Jane thought.

"Dig takes after his Da, God rest his soul. Big and

brawny he was." She sighed. "Well, I best get this meal on the table. Men hate to wait for their food. Makes 'em cranky."

"Not as much as they hate to wait for their drink," Jane replied.

Wenna sent her a questioning look. "And how do you know that?"

"I've helped my father in the pub since I was a young girl."

"The pub . . ." The older woman's eyes widened, then narrowed, and her expression turned cold. "I should have realized. You're her. The landlord's girl."

"And the fault of that is none of her making."

The sound of Aidan's voice made Jane gasp, and she turned to find him filling the doorway. Against her will, her treacherous heart gave a small jump at the sight of him. A lock of honey-gold hair fell forward across his brow and he raked it back impatiently as he pinned Wenna with a dark look, a clear warning.

Wenna stepped back and lowered her lashes as she clasped her hands before her, offering Jane the stark reminder that despite his apparent kindness, his play at joviality and sociability with these people, Aidan Warrick was first and always a man to fear.

The silence thickened. Jane caught the inside of her cheek between her teeth, gnawing nervously. Then she noticed the keg balanced on his shoulder, and she realized the men were unloading the wagon.

Digory came up against Aidan's back. He, too, balanced a keg on one massive shoulder. "Come on. Ma's got food ready. I can smell it. Let's get this lot stored before I die of hunger—" He paused, and then added, "Sir."

Aidan shifted to the side and turned, balancing the keg with one hand as he stared Digory down. "Manners, boy," he said with soft menace. "You would do well to learn some."

Melting back a step, Jane moved to a shadowed corner.

"Well, who've we got here?" Digory asked, peering past Aidan and raking a leering gaze over her. Jane shivered. The way he looked at her made her skin crawl. "Don't say you've gone and got leg-shackled, man!"

"In a manner of speaking."

The words gave Jane a start. Sensing Aidan's eyes on her, she raised her chin, and squared her shoulders. She had met worse than Digory Tubb in her day, and she knew that the most foolish thing she could do was shrink in a corner and show her fear.

"Ah, well, you can tell me over Ma's meat pie." Digory shrugged and then he crossed the small entry hallway to disappear through a door on the far side. Aidan watched her a moment longer, his perusal only adding to her confusion, and then he, too, strode through the door. The two men were soon joined by Cadan and Hawker as they made several trips through the house and back outside.

Through the window Jane watched until the wagon was empty and the men strode away. They rounded the side of the house, disappearing from view. After checking that Wenna was busy at her pots, she sidled to the open doorway on the far side of the front entryway and peeked through to a sitting room with two large wingback chairs and an overstuffed horsehair sofa. On one wall was an enormous stone fireplace. There was no sign of the many kegs that the men had carried through, and there was no other exit that she could discern. Confused, she glanced around the room but saw no evidence of the contraband brandy, and no possible hiding place.

"Curiosity killed the cat," Aidan whispered directly beside her right ear, his voice rich and deep. With a squeak, Jane jumped and whirled to face him, her hand instinctively rising to press against her breastbone. "And here you are, sweet Jane, curious as any puss."

Her stomach plummeted, true fear freezing her blood. "I was just—"

"Curious," Aidan finished for her, his voice velvet and smoke.

For a moment she said nothing, her heart pounding so hard she thought it might burst the confines of her ribs. Finally, she nodded. "Yes, I suppose I was."

He smiled at her, a dark, devilish curving of his lips that made him look more ruthless than amused. "What are you curious about?"

She took a step back, then another and another, into the empty sitting room. He strode forward with measured tread, stalking her as she retreated. Putting the bulk of one wingback chair between them, Jane shook her head.

"Come now. Ask your question, sweet."

The recollection of the way he had looked in the carriage when she had asked him who had murdered Davey filled her thoughts. So he would not have her fear him? He would have her ask at will, would he?

Squaring her shoulders, she met his gaze. "Are you a smuggler?"

His smile widened, a predatory flash of straight white teeth in his tanned face. "Of course. What Cornishman has not dabbled, at least a little?"

"You are not a Cornishman," she said.

"But I have done my share of smuggling."

Well, she should not have asked the question if she did not wish to hear the answer. She had expected a denial, and faced with such clear confirmation she was at a loss as to what to say next. She glanced around the room, feeling more than a little desperate, her thoughts in turmoil.

And then she wondered why he did not take the trouble to lie to her, instead baring his crimes with casual disregard. Had he no fear that she would run to the authorities, tell her tales and rejoice to see him hang? Or was he so very certain that she would never get away? Did he mean to kill . . . No, she could not think of that.

"I have no liking for smugglers," she whispered. For a moment she was twelve years old again, hurrying home with the dusk. A man had asked her directions and she, foolish girl, had stopped to give them, trusting a stranger—a smuggler, as it turned out—to do her no harm. That girl had been smashed on the rocks, her trust and naivete shattered like porcelain. It was no consolation that the sea had claimed the life of that smuggler, and it was the most terrible heartbreak that the churning waves had taken Mama as well. She had come in search of Jane, and found her daughter struggling against the smuggler's hold, her dress torn, her skin exposed. As the tragedy unfolded, Mama flying at the man with fists and nails and teeth, all three had been thrown into the sea. Only Jane had survived. The guilt of that was Jane's burden to bear.

She wrapped her arms tight about herself, feeling as cold as the iciest depths of the ocean.

So he was a smuggler, but was he something worse still? She could not bring herself to ask Aidan if he was a wrecker, if he lured ships to the rocks, if he bludgeoned the survivors to a bloody death, murdering them as they cried for mercy.

"Smuggler. Runner. Pirate. Though I prefer the term privateer." The admission hinted at neither shame nor remorse.

Dismay assaulted her.

"*Businessman* is better still. And a damned good one at that." There was mockery in his tone, but she was not certain it was directed at her. "Anything else?"

Are you a wrecker? No, she could not ask, for he seemed inclined to answer, and her terror lay in that. Repulsion crawled through her. To ponder the possibility was an awful sort of torture, but should he *admit* to the deed, to know such a thing for certain was more than she wished.

Instead, pushing the words past the tightness in her throat, she asked, "Where are the kegs?"

"Hidden away until I have need of them."

"Why do you tell me this?" she whispered. "I could turn you in to the excise men."

"The excise men." His tone was bland.

Reaching out he laid his palm against her cheek, and then he dragged his thumb forward, along the curve of her jaw, and lower until it rested on her pulse.

Oh, the way he looked at her, ravenous, such dark hunger.

Her breath was little more than ragged gasps, and her blood thrummed. Unbidden, the heated memory of his kiss surged through her, a raging and unwelcome storm. Her heart pounded madly in her breast, a wild thing trapped, desperate to be free. Just as she was trapped by the intensity of his gaze and the force of his will.

"Would you turn me in, sweet Jane?" He stepped closer still, his voice so deep and rough. "Watch me twist at the end of a rope? Hear the sickening snap of my neck as I fell? Would it give you pleasure to see my face turn a hideous shade of puce, my tongue bulge like the bloated carcass of a week-old carp?"

Her belly rolled at the horrific images his words conjured. Oh, God. She could see it, see the horror he described, hear the jeering crowd eager for a hanging, smell the stink of unwashed bodies and fear. She wrenched away from his touch, her fingers curling into the back of the chair to steady herself. Curse her vivid imagination, and curse her tender heart that she could not bear to envision the gruesome scene he described, could not bring herself to welcome the picture of his death.

And she could not imagine why the thought was so very dreadful.

"What care have I for your fate?" she asked fiercely. "Are you not my enemy, my tormentor, the man who ripped my world asunder?"

Or was he the benefactor who had held her demons and nightmares at bay when they chased her from sweet slumber?

Her confusion was an anxiety in itself, for she was in unfamiliar territory, beset by feelings and emotions that were far outside her experience. She wished he *had* been unkind, truly unkind, even horrid. How much easier it would be to hate him with a bitter venom, and in that hatred to find strength and even solace.

Raising her eyes to meet his, she wondered at the shadows that lurked there. They called to her, those shadows. With a painful, ringing clarity, understanding dawned, and she knew why she could not bear the thought of him swinging at the end of a rope.

He represented her dreams, this beautiful, flawed man, with his perfect face, his scarred soul, his undeniable appeal. There was no logic, no reason to attraction. Only pure and undiluted need. In some way, she thought his secret torments a match to her own. He was the fantasy prince of her unspoken childhood whimsy, transformed to a man with his own private demons and flaws. As she had demons and flaws, and guilt. The terrible, gnawing guilt. He had that, too. She could feel it, taste it.

Like to like.

If she could redeem him, perhaps it would be enough to redeem herself.

But to envision him dead as he described, his neck snapped by a hangman's rope, his body twitching . . .

She closed her eyes against such horror.

"I paid the piper before ever I did the crime. I see my current deeds as a balancing of the scale," he said.

Her lids flipped open. "I do not understand."

"I know." He smiled a little. "Besides, sweet, even if you turned me in, you would need proof of my crime, and that you will not find." He sounded both menacing and jovial.

A most unsettling combination.

Chapter 8

For the next two days Jane worked side by side with Wenna in the kitchen or the garden. She was glad for the tasks that were assigned her: kneading dough, chopping vegetables, familiar chores. With her hands busy, she focused on the day's work and did her best to thrust the uncertainties that clouded her tomorrows to the back of her mind. Despite the original stiffening of her manner when she first discovered Jane's identity, Wenna was friendly, and kind after a fashion. She seemed happy for feminine companionship and chatted amiably.

Mr. Warrick—Aidan, as he had bid Jane call him—rode out the first morning with Hawker. He gave indication of neither his destination nor his business, but he was very specific in his instruction to Jane that she was safe only by Wenna's side, and was not to stray far.

"Can you shoot a pistol?" he asked her, his gaze intent.

At her nod, he handed her a weapon, butt first, and warned her to have a care, for it was loaded. A week before, she would have shied away from

taking the thing. Now, she closed her hand around
it and was grateful.

She wondered how he knew that she would not
turn the barrel on *him.*

Her cousin Dolly had taught Jane to shoot after
her mother's death, never wanting her to be de-
fenseless again. Her father had agreed to the lessons. If she was honest, it was more because he
wanted her ready should anyone try to steal the
money from the pub, and less out of concern for
her safety.

The hours after Aidan's departure gave her no
cause to doubt his warnings. More than once, she
found the younger son, Digory, watching her with a
disturbing and calculating gleam in his eyes. She took
care to avoid both his company and his attention.

The second afternoon saw Aidan's return. Jane
felt a surge of pleasure when she saw him ride into
the yard, and she ran her dishrag over the plate in
her hand again and again, oblivious to the repeti-
tion. Suddenly, she stilled, appalled by her response, by the knowledge that she was so very glad
to see him. And yet, she could not bring herself to
look away.

Aidan slowly scanned the yard, the distant field,
the path that led to the shore, and then his gaze
swung to the window, unerringly landing on Jane.
She froze, her heart beating an erratic rhythm, and
she thought she saw his lips curve in the hint of a
smile.

No sooner had he dismounted than both Cadan
and Digory drew close. Pushing aside his greatcoat,
Aidan withdrew two bags, and tossed one to each of
them. His expression betrayed nothing of his emotion. The bags spun through the air, two rapid arcs.

Digory and Cadan caught them, the sharp jingle of coins distinctive and clear. Jane found the sound disturbing, and though the exchange was in no way furtive, she felt an ominous foreboding.

The bags were large enough to hold what might be a year's wages for some, and she could think of no legitimate work that would warrant such payment. She exhaled with a soft hiss. They were smugglers of a certain.

Watching as Digory bent his head and tugged his forelock in that oddly sardonic way he had, she felt a definite wariness, and she wondered what other murky deeds the Tubb family engaged in.

That night, as she lay tense and sleepless, the room dark as a cave, Jane heard men's voices raised in disagreement. She thought one voice was Digory's, but she was unsure of his companion. Some time later, the sound of a horse harnessed in the yard carried to her through the window, and later still, the sound of heavy footfall on the wooden floor of the hall outside her door.

Two men had argued, and she thought that one had gone and one had stayed, though identities and reasons were shrouded in mystery. She lay awake long after the footsteps receded, staring into the darkness, seeing only her own worst imaginings, specters that poked her and pricked her and did not let her rest.

She was glad for the dawn. The thin rays of early morning sun called to her. After tidying her chamber, Jane made her way to the yard. She stood listening to the sound of the ocean as it swelled over the earthen barrier that hid the path from any ship at sea. The air was crisp, and she wrapped her shawl tight about her shoulders as she walked beside the low hillock. She knew from years of experience that if she failed to work her ruined leg, it would seize and she would pay the price in stiffness and pain.

Mindful of Aidan's warning that she not stray far lest she come to harm, Jane meandered only a hundred paces or so, and then turned to retrace her steps on the path already taken. She knew his concern had little to do with the path itself, and more to do with those who might travel it.

"Fine morning."

With a gasp, she raised her head to find Digory slouching against the side of the house, watching her with surly temper. His shirt was buttoned in a mismatched manner, and his coat not at all, leaving Jane to wonder if he had dressed in haste, and if spying on her was his reason for being up and about this morning.

Was his careful watch at his own inclination, or Aidan's behest?

"Yes, it is a fine morning," she replied, studying him warily.

"Just out for a bit of air?" he asked, pushing his bulk away from the wall and sauntering closer until his shadow fell full across her.

"Yes." She met his gaze, unflinching. In her years serving at her father's pub, she had known men such as this, those who presented a jovial demeanor to their contemporaries, but took secret pleasure in bullying and browbeating. Any show of fear might induce him to leap upon her like a wild dog and tear her to shreds.

"And if you would be so kind as to step aside," she continued, carefully modulating her tone so it was calm and even, "I will conclude my promenade."

"Promenade. Well, la-dee-da," he sneered. "You

might find that staying close to the house is safer." He closed his fingers into a fist, his large fingers somehow gruesome in their brute strength. The movement made the joints crack and pop, the sound loud and disconcerting. "There's naught for you to see on that path, or in the gully, Jane Heatherington." Leaning close, he growled in menace. "A smart girl would keep to her room, and keep her eyes in her head."

Instinctively, Jane drew back.

"And where else would my eyes be but in my head?" Even as the words slid from her lips, her gaze snagged on the unmistakable shape of a knife hilt, tucked in the waist of Digory's grimy breeches.

Like a slap, an image struck her, a memory of the dead woman from the beach, empty eye sockets black and gaping. For the first time, Jane had the horrifying thought that 'twas not the fishes that had taken the woman's eyes, but a human scavenger.

With a sharp, broken inhalation, she fell back another step, pressing her fingers against her throat as Digory turned an oily smile on her. The smell of stale wine and old sweat carried on the shifting wind.

"Glad I am to see that you take my meaning." Digory's fingers strayed to the hilt of the knife, caressing it like a familiar pet. "Ginny. Her name was Ginny. She was a curious girl. And then she was a dead girl."

His words left her no doubt, no illusions. She felt sick and chilled to the bone. She had thought the woman drowned, fallen from a ship, or the victim of wreckers . . . terrible possibilities, all. But he suggested something far worse, murder of a specific and vicious intent.

"I know no one named Ginny," she breathed, a choking horror clawing at her.

"No?" He gave an ugly laugh. "Red-haired girl." He shrugged, and laughed again.

Fisting her hands in her skirt, Jane swayed. Her mouth was dry and her palms damp, her heart racing. She battled the urge to turn and flee. He would catch her in an instant. And maybe, just maybe, she was wrong. Maybe she had misunderstood.

She stared at Digory in wretched dismay. Ginny. The dead woman from the beach had been called Ginny. Had he gouged out her eyes, then held her beneath the water as she struggled and writhed, desperate to live? Or had he drowned her first, and then taken his blade to her?

Bitter bile stung the back of her throat.

Had Aidan bid him do such a brutal deed?

"Why—" Her voice cracked, and she paused, drawing a slow breath. "Why do you tell me this?"

"I know you've been poking around here and there, looking for things that have naught to do with you. You already cost a good man his life."

Davey. He spoke of Davey, and he blamed *her* for his death. Why? Why?

"I—" He looked beyond her and clamped his lips shut, then turned his head and spat on the ground.

A flash of movement on the path snagged Jane's attention. Heart racing, she swung her head to see Aidan striding toward them, still far in the distance.

Jane wrapped her arms about herself, her control tenuous, her voice betraying the revulsion and despair that swamped her. "Were you in Pentreath a week past? Was it you . . . ?"

"Women are ever flapping their mouths and asking questions." Digory's thick brows drew down, and he rubbed his palm along the dark hair on his jaw. "I know what you're getting at, girl, and I'll say it plain so even *your* simple mind can understand. If Mr. Warrick wanted killing done"—he let his gaze slide toward the path, toward Aidan's approaching figure, and then back to her—"he'd do the deed himself. Right handy with a knife is our Mr. Warrick."

Jane tried to still the trembling that took hold of her, leaving her a weak and pallid shadow of the woman she wanted to be. Strong. Brave. She must not show her terror. Brutes such as Digory Tubb fed on fear and weakness, taking in bleak emotion like the tastiest feast.

He drew close, the smell of him and the heat of his body thickening around her like a black cloud. Digory laughed, an ugly, rough sound.

"He takes pleasure in it," he whispered gutturally. "In the death struggle, in the hot well of blood wetting his fingers." He inhaled noisily. "Think on it. See it when you close your eyes. And never doubt that too much curiosity invites his blade—or mine—to turn on you."

The creak and groan of the coach played in synchrony to its lumbering sway. They left Wenna's house behind, time and miles stretching in an ever-lengthening swathe. Jane sat, hands folded in her lap, mind busy with all manner of terrible and frightening convolutions that twisted round and about until they left her cold and breathless.

"I instructed you to stay away from Digory." Aidan's softly spoken words carried a bite.

"So you did," Jane agreed, and turned her face to

the window, pretending interest in the view of the countryside. "But perhaps you neglected to provide him with instruction to stay away from me."

Aidan exhaled sharply, but she did not turn back to look at him.

The land on either side of the road was harsh and unplanted, with meager vegetation and few signs of habitation. Despite the sunshine, Jane's mood was gray and grim, Digory's forbidding words circling her thoughts like great black crows. Aidan's arrival had chased him off, but the maelstrom of revulsion his words and accusations had conjured remained.

He had meant to frighten her. Had he spoken the truth? Or was his vile allusion merely a game played for his own twisted pleasure?

"Jane." Aidan said only her name, but something in his tone caught at her heart.

She could feel the weight of his attention, measuring, waiting, and at last she looked at him, unable to do otherwise.

"If he had touched you, hurt you, I would have cut off his hand."

Yes, of course. That would have fixed everything. For an instant, she held her breath, and then words rushed out like bugs scuttling to the shadows. "Are you handy with a knife?"

He did not so much as blink.

"Extremely." One side of his mouth curved in a cynical smile. "And with a pistol, and with my fists. There have been times that my survival depended on more than my wits."

She nodded, aware that his admission brought them across some boundary, though uncertain exactly what it was. He made no pretense with her. No pretense that he was a coddled gentleman. No pretense that he was other than exactly who he was.

And exactly who and what was that?

Dipping her chin, she stared at her hands, at her fingers twined so tight they were white at the knuckles. Had he killed that woman at the beach, as Digory had intimated? Gouged her eyes from her skull because she had seen something she should not? Was he capable of such? She could not find it in herself to believe it.

Ridiculous, really, that she could not believe it of him. What cause had he given her to doubt his potential for brutality?

She recalled Aidan's words at the New Inn, when he said *she* had seen far more than he would have liked. Had he meant that as a threat? Dizzy with confusion, she jerked her head up.

"Do not look at me like that, Jane," he rasped, his voice like gravel. "I make apologies neither for what I was, nor what I am."

She held his gaze. The sun came in through the coach window, touching his hair, kissing the strands with lights of bright, burnished gold. His eyes, ever changeable, were now more the gray of a roiling sea than the blue of the sky. She thought she had put the mood upon him that turned their color dark and stormy.

What madness had taken hold of her? She was drawn to the very darkness that should send her fleeing far and away. And she was drawn to something else, some indescribable, intangible thing that made him the man he was: the man who had damned her to this uncertain existence as a bondswoman whose sole and unnerving task was to travel by his side; the man who had saved her from certain harm at

Davey's ruthless hands; the man who had chased off her secret demons in the long hours of the night and held her safe in his arms. The dichotomy was at once terrifying and reassuring, and the strange sort of kindness he had shown her made her wonder, made her want . . .

Air slid past her lips, a slow exhale. Lord, he was so pleasing to look upon, hard and male, his jaw rough with the night's growth of beard he had not bothered to shave, the shadow outlining the luscious curve of his lips.

It was dangerous, this sweet, dark ache that gnawed at her core and made her long to touch him, to breathe in the scent of him, to press her lips to his. She remembered how that had felt. And she remembered the sight of him at the inn, with his shirt hanging open and his muscled chest bared in the rich candlelight. Shocking thoughts gnawed at her, thoughts of touching him, running her tongue along his golden skin, sinking her teeth in to taste the forbidden pleasure of him.

He gave a low laugh that made a sharp sensation dart to her belly. "And do not look at me like *that*."

"Oh . . ." She shifted on the seat, looked away and back, feeling the hot flush of her embarrassment stain her cheeks. He read her so well. "Where will you sell the barrels you hid at Wenna's house?" she blurted. "I wonder why you left them there, so far from the beaten path."

"I do not intend to sell those particular barrels. They are intended for another purpose entirely," he replied with private amusement. "Two birds with one stone."

Jane frowned. What possible use could there be

for illegal barrels of brandy, other than selling them for a tidy profit?

There was no opportunity to question him, for the coach slowed and then rocked to a stop. Through the window Jane saw that two horses stood in the road, one riderless, the second carrying a man wearing a dusty greatcoat that appeared to have seen better days, and a black shovel hat that was pulled low on his brow. He was a stranger, she thought as she studied his form. Then he slouched lower in the saddle and turned his face away and, for an instant, something in the way he moved made Jane think that he seemed somehow familiar.

A wave of tension shimmered in the closed confines of the carriage. She looked at Aidan, and found him watching her, his gaze intent.

"You perplex me, Jane. And you make me feel . . . lighter." He continued to stare at her, his eyes dark and fathomless. She could not look away. "You are smart. Brave. And you make me laugh. Truly laugh. I had not expected that." One of the horses nickered and stamped its hooves restlessly against the road.

Some whisper of alarm tugged at her, and with it an *awareness* she could neither name nor explain. Instinctively, she swayed toward him, knowing she ought to shift away. And then it was too late as Aidan's lean fingers closed about her arm. He pulled her forward, dragging her against him with enough force that her breath flowed from her in a rush, and then he put his mouth on hers, open, hungry, the kiss hot and wet.

His tongue slid against hers in a way that made her gasp, his breath becoming hers. Sensation surged through her, crackling, sizzling, turning her skin hot and tight, turning her limbs boneless.

The pleasure of it, of his lips, his tongue, his fingers tangled in her hair, his breath blending with her own, she had never imagined the like, never known she could burn so hot and bright.

Hunger coiled deep inside her and spread like poured honey. She moaned, the sound spilling out of her, taken into his mouth.

Breathing heavily, he drew back, and this thing that reared between them was written in the hard lines of his face. His aching, his yearning, his wanting, all there, so unmistakable, a matched set to the tumultuous cravings that gnawed at her.

She wanted to fist her hand in his coat and drag him back. She wanted to shove open the coach door and feel the cold wind on her fevered skin.

And she wanted to cry.

She felt a rare and unusual anger that he had brought her to this, and a terrible, contradictory urge to hold him close.

His brow furrowed, and he rubbed the knuckles of his right hand against his breastbone, up and down, as though seeking to ease some unspoken pain.

"You—" He shook his head. "Hawker is armed, and he's a damned fine shot. You'll be safe. Be sure of that." Raising one brow, he studied her. "And you have the pistol I gave you."

She nodded.

He pushed open the door and stepped into the road.

When will I see you next? She knew better than to ask, and tried to convince herself she did not care. A fool's errand, that. A blast of winter air swirled through the coach, wrapping Jane in its chilly embrace as she leaned forward to watch him in a clamor of confusion, her heart and body still singing from his touch.

His chest expanded on a deep breath, and then he turned his face and met her gaze. At length, he spoke, his voice low and harsh. "I thought I had forgotten how to laugh."

He closed the carriage door with a firm push and crossed to the waiting horse where he swung into the saddle with easy grace. The great black beast pawed and snorted, sending tufts of white steam through the air. Then the two men turned their mounts and cantered off down Bodmin Road.

Jane watched Aidan's retreating figure until he disappeared over the horizon. The coach lurched into motion once more. Wrapping her arms about herself to ward off the chill, she wondered where he went, and then she wondered why she should care.

The connection between them was far more dangerous than any corporeal threat.

Hours passed. Listlessly, she watched the unchanging scenery. She picked through the basket that Wenna had packed for them, and ate a portion of the food, though her appetite was less than hearty. As she rearranged the cloth over the top of the remaining food, she could not help the pang of concern for Aidan's welfare and his hunger.

Unsettled, she tried to think of other things, but such attempts invariably brought her to ponderings of murder and motive and truth wound tight with lies.

Finally, lulled by the monotony of movement as the carriage swayed, she dozed, and when she awoke it was to find that a deep and heavy darkness had descended. Scooting forward on the bench seat, she looked out the window.

They were on the high ground of the open moor. A constant angry current of air buffeted the vehicle to and fro, for there was no tree, no hill to break the wind's harsh breath. Through the carriage window Jane could see the dark expanse of sky. Now and again, the clouds shifted, allowing a clear view of the star-speckled heavens, then shifted again, leaving only unbroken gray to fill the narrow expanse of the window.

This was not a night to travel alone on the Bodmin Road. Pulling back into the corner of the carriage, Jane wished that her solitude were not so complete. Nay, in truth, it was not mere solitude that unsettled her, it was the ill-conceived wish that Aidan Warrick's solid and comforting form was yet beside her. She knew such fancy was poorly placed. He was no sweet savior, and despite the wicked lure he presented, he was still her enemy.

She took a deep breath and reminded herself that she was not alone, for Hawker was with her, driving the coach. Still, a current of unease swelled within her until it threatened to overcome her common sense. She pulled her cloak tighter about her shoulders, her hand sliding into her pocket, there to grasp the rounded shape of the button she had found beside Davey's stiff and lifeless body.

A choking laugh escaped her as she realized that she sought comfort from a token that might well implicate Aidan as a murderer. Though he had denied it, she wondered if she should place her trust so easily in his words.

Suddenly, a shot rang out, and through the walls of the carriage she thought she heard a muffled cry. Apprehension surged, a cold, crashing tide. Instinctively, Jane leaned forward and peered out into

the night, preferring to know the face of danger
rather than cower from it.

She could hear the sound of men shouting in the
road, and Hawker's bellow as the horses shied and
whinnied their distress. The carriage rocked on its
high wheels, faster and faster still, and coming
down the road Jane saw the shadowy forms of three
men on horseback.

She wanted her pistol. Snapping the sash closed,
Jane reached to the bottom of Wenna's basket and
closing her hand around the weapon, she pulled it
free. She would not go lightly to whatever ghastly
fate might be foremost on the minds of these men.
She would kick and claw and bite, and she would
survive. Of that, she was certain.

The carriage jerked to a sharp stop. Immediately,
there was a cry and then a heavy thud, as though a
large sac had been tossed to the ground. Jane's
breath came fast and harsh as she wondered if they
had killed Hawker and thrown his body in the road-
way. Fear and horror tightened sharply, a band
about her chest, and she could not breathe, could
not think, so great was the panic that assaulted her.

Closing the fingers of her left hand about her
right wrist, she steadied her aim, the pistol pointed
at the carriage door. An instant later, the door flew
open with enough force to send it crashing against
the side wall. The light of a lantern filled the gloomy
interior, momentarily blinding her.

Rough laughter tumbled through the coach's interior as a grimy hand reached in to close talon-like
fingers about her wrist. A sharp twist, and her fingers numbed, the pistol falling from her grip.

She realized her mistake. She should have shot

the second the door flew open, rather than waiting to identify the intruder.

"Look at her," came a coarse voice, and she thought she might retch at the horrific familiarity of the sound.

Gaby. The man who had been Davey's cohort that first night she had arrived at the New Inn. Had she escaped then only to fall prey to him now? Bitter bile churned inside of her, and the metallic tang of fear was sharp on her tongue as he yanked hard on her arm, dragging her from the interior of the coach.

"Not so high and mighty now, eh? Looking at Davey and me like so much dirt. You've come down a mite now that you haven't got Mr. High-and-Fancy Warrick to protect you. And isn't that just a right laughable thing? You think he's better 'n us, cause he has such a face, but if you only knew where he's been, what he's done . . ."

Jane struggled against the iron grasp that encircled her wrist. She glanced about at the faces of Gaby's companions, then cast her sights farther into the darkness, desperate to know what had become of Hawker. She could only pray that he was unharmed.

One of Gaby's cohorts, a large man with a vacuous expression, shook his head from side to side as though clearing it of cobwebs. "Don't say now that we've gone and stopped His Lordship's coach." He moaned softly. "No, don't say you've led us to such a foolishness."

"You promised us a bounty," the second man whined. "You never said we'd pay for it in blood."

Gaby spun toward him, dragging Jane sharply against his chest, pressing the barrel of a pistol to the underside of her jaw. He was not tall, not overly large, but there was a wiry strength to his frame and an evil purpose that surrounded him like the stink of a well-used chamber pot. She realized that he must have a second gun at his waist, for she could feel its distinctive shape pressing against her back.

Fear sharpened her senses, making the air seem colder, the night darker. The pounding of her heart boomed like a drum.

Jane tried to pull away from him, but he only laughed and held her tighter, his hands rough and brutal. The need to struggle, to scream, nearly overwhelmed her. Sinking her teeth into her lower lip, she stifled the urge, thinking that she might have only a single chance, an instant of inattention, and she must use it to her advantage.

Both of Gaby's companions were shaking their heads now, and the larger man stuffed his pistol in the waistband of his breeches, holding his hands palms forward in front of him.

"If'n you'd told me who we was going against, I never would have come, Gaby. I'm an idiot, right an true, but you're a bigger fool that don't deserve to live if you think he'll let this pass." He glanced at his companion. "Jacko an' me want no part of this, Gaby. We'll be on our way, an' if you have any smarts at all, you'll leave her here in the road and be away yourself, an' on the next ship bound for the colonies. Else he'll find you Gaby, and kill you sure."

With that, he turned and lumbered along the road, his companion following close at his heels. Both men caught the reins of their mounts as they passed, and swung up. In an instant, they were cantering back the way they had come.

Jane gasped as Gaby twisted her arm and

doubled it behind her back, his fingers a solid vice about her wrist.

"Go ahead and scream," he whispered against her ear. "There's no one to hear you."

Terror swathed her like a shroud, and she stood, trembling, refusing to cry out. At her silence, he grunted his disapproval and gave her arm a sharp yank until she thought it would surely wrench from her shoulder.

"Why?" She gasped against the pain. "Why do you do this?"

"Why?" he snarled. "Because me an' Davey go all the way back to when we was in nappies. He was like a brother to me . . . a brother . . . an' you, *you* made me kill him."

"What? I never—"

"Shut your yammering maw! You set a fire in his blood and he had to have you. Had to stay, there at the New Inn. Had to wait for the night, for your light to go dark. He was going to steal you away from His Lordship. Talked about giving you pretty lace an' a trinket or two." Gaby grabbed the flesh of her arm and twisted cruelly. "Me, I see nothing to go after. Scrawny, crippled bitch, and I told him so. But no, he was bound and determined."

The clouds had moved off, leaving the moon full and bright. From the corner of her eye, Jane saw a large shadowy bulk next to the ditch twitch ever so slightly.

Not dead. Hawker was not dead.

A flicker of hope unfurled.

"Bound and determined to do what?" she asked, shuffling an awkward circle in the hopes that Gaby would follow, thus removing Hawker from his line of sight.

He turned her in his grasp so their faces were close, and she could smell the stink of rotting teeth and unwashed flesh.

"Bound and determined to swive you, you stupid bitch!" He let out a low hiss. "I never meant him to die. We argued, we did . . . I just thought I'd prick him enough to make him weak, and we'd leave the New Inn. But then you came to the window and he lurched back to get a better look, and, well, he fell on my knife and was done for." He was silent for a minute, breathing hard.

Jane fought to maintain her composure, though her desperation was a thick and choking fog.

"You killed him same as if you held the knife," Gaby said, menace heavy in his tone. "And so I'll kill you."

Hawker was sitting now, his gaze sharp, pistol leveled at Gaby's back. They would have only one chance—

Suddenly, Gaby spun about, and Jane found herself between him and Hawker's pistol. She felt the tensing of her captor's body as he recognized the situation. A flood of misery turned her blood to ice.

Hawker would not save her.

Gaby fired, his gun belching smoke and flame. To Jane's horror, the pistol dropped from Hawker's hand, and he clapped the other hand to his upper arm.

She felt Gaby's grip slacken, and then tighten, and in that instant she realized that Hawker had fired as well. With all her strength, she twisted, lifting her damaged knee. The impact shook her as her limb connected somewhere on Gaby's body. Pain ricocheted through her. She cried out and her ruined leg gave way, making her stumble. Gaby's breath left him in a whoosh. His grip on her wrist slackened.

Forcing her mind to focus only on her task, Jane wrenched her hand free and snatched his second gun from the waistband of his breeches as she moved. She staggered back, frantically clinging to balance, willing herself not to fall. Leveling the barrel at him, she gulped air and fought the nausea that threatened to overcome her.

There was blood on his face. Hawker's ball had grazed the side of his skull.

"Well now, girlie," he said, backing away slowly. "Don't be hasty now."

Jane followed his movements, never letting him out of her sight. She was dimly aware of thunder rolling in the distance, growing closer. He continued to move away, toward Hawker, who scrambled awkwardly along the ground with hand outstretched.

Hawker's pistol. Dear heaven.

With unexpected speed and agility, Gaby dropped and rolled, a second faster than Hawker. Jane's heart lurched as he came up with the fallen pistol in his hand.

Hawker lurched to his feet, swaying unsteadily, his gaze fixed on Gaby, his fists clenched.

Take all the time you need, Janie. You have all the time in the world. Her cousin Dolly's voice echoed in her mind.

She thought her whole body shook with fear, yet the pistol was steady before her, held in a grip she had practiced so many times under the watchful eye of her cousin and, on occasion, her father. Something changed in Gaby's expression, a tension around his mouth, his eyes, and Jane knew her time had run out.

It seemed that the seconds spun an endless skein as the clouds moved from the face of the moon and she imagined his finger tightening on the trigger. Instinctively, Jane tightened her own.

The thunder grew louder, pounding in her ears, mingling with the frantic thumping of her heart.

All the time in the world.

Jane aimed high on his right shoulder and squeezed the trigger. The recoil knocked her back, and she stumbled on her weak leg, collapsing to the ground. With a shuddering breath, she tossed away the now-empty pistol, hands shaking, stomach heaving. Gaby lay on the ground, unmoving.

She had a shot a man. *Shot* him. Had she killed him? The possibility made her skin crawl. She had meant only to wound him.

Her gaze flew to Hawker and she scrambled to her feet, only to find herself caught about the waist and pulled against a tall, honed form. She knew even before she turned, not thunder, but the pounding of hooves on the gravel road. Aidan Warrick had returned.

"My God, Jane!" There was urgency in his tone as he ran his hands over her shoulders and arms, then pushed her back, his gaze roaming her body. "Are you hurt?"

She shook her head, her gaze straying to Gaby's motionless form. A trembling overcame her and she shook uncontrollably, barely able to remain standing as the horror of the past moments overtook her.

"D-d-d-did I kill him?" she stammered, her hands clutching Aidan's forearms for support as she swayed dizzily. "I aimed only to wound him. To save Hawker and myself."

Aidan's gaze locked with hers, cold and hard and

flat. Merciless. Here was a man who was capable of anything.

"You aimed to wound, sweet Jane. But he still had a loaded pistol. Even wounded he could have shot you, put a ball through your innocent, brave heart."

"So . . . I killed him?" The possibility made her sick.

Aidan's mouth tightened, and he pulled her against his chest, his strong arms wrapping her in safety. She felt his lips move against her hair.

"You aimed to wound, and your aim was true," came his rough whisper. "But *I* aimed to kill."

Chapter 9

Aidan doffed his greatcoat and wrapped it around Jane's trembling form. He withdrew at once, not touching her more than he must, and she felt a sweeping regret that he offered no succor. Her wish that he pull her close, embrace her and comfort her no doubt would have surprised him as much as it did her.

As she stood, swaying slightly, she could sense his fury, a cold and vast rage, held under such rigid control. She wondered that he did not crack apart like the surface of a frozen lake, leaving broken shards to float atop the deep and fathomless cold.

The events of the night had put the darkest of moods on him, and the way he looked at her . . . it was the danger to her person that ate at him. He had killed Gaby to protect her. Those facts should make her cringe with horror. She was more than a little terrified to find that they did not, to find instead that they made her feel safe.

All her life she had spun fantasy and built imaginary walls in an effort to feel safe. And here, on this desolate stretch of road, with the scent of blood carried on the wind and the stink of gunpowder staining her clothes, she finally found security. Because she had managed to defend herself.

And because, again, Aidan Warrick had not let the nightmare take her.

She felt many things. Relief that she had not killed a man. Immense gratitude that Aidan had come when he did. And wariness. His words, and his tone, played over and over in her thoughts. *But I aimed to kill.*

A terrifying truth, and a marker of previous deeds. Gaby was dead, his spirit gone to walk with other nameless, faceless ghosts.

How many men had Aidan killed in his lifetime?

Slipping her hand into her pocket, Jane closed her fingers around the hard shape of the button from Aidan's waistcoat. A talisman, of sorts. So Aidan's word proved true. He had not killed Davey. She knew that now, but could find no doubt that there *were* others. Men. Perhaps women. A shudder took her and she wrapped her arms tight about her waist, thinking of Ginny, pulled from the ocean, and of Digory Tubb's vicious implications.

Aidan's gaze scanned the road and came to rest on Hawker, who stood unsteady, his face a stark white oval. He had shucked his coat—Jane took it as a good sign that he had strength enough to do that—and his fingers pressed against his arm. Wet blood glistened in the moonlight.

"Wait in the coach, Jane." The words were bitten out in sharp precision. "I will deal with Hawker."

The thought of sitting in the dark coach, alone with her fears and the memory of Gaby spinning with the force of the shot, then falling to the ground with a dull thud . . . She did not think she could bear the solitude. Too, she worried at Aidan's harsh mood and the possibility that he might blame the driver. He had said that Hawker would keep her safe but, in the end, that had proven untrue. And Hawker had left her once before, the first night at the New Inn. What price would the youth be forced to pay for this second failure?

She shook her head. "Let me stay with you," she said, catching at Aidan's arm to substantiate her plea.

His gaze met hers, his features a cold, cold mask, but his eyes blazing. For an alarming moment, she thought he would decline, and then he nodded and carefully pulled his arm from her grasp, as though that small contact was beyond his ability to tolerate.

"I'm sorry," she mumbled, dropping her hands. She caught the lapels of his greatcoat, and shifted the bulky weight across her shoulders, masking the trembling of her hands. Her heart twisted at his rebuff but she held his gaze. Her pride demanded it.

His icy façade cracked. Something flared in his eyes, something dark and primitive, a raw emotion that made her breath catch and her pulse race.

He made a sound, low in his throat, almost a groan. "I keep my civility by the thinnest thread, Jane. Touch me again, and you free the beast."

Uncertain of his meaning, she studied him, her pulse hammering. And then she was very certain. He spoke of feral nature and primitive instinct. Base need.

On a slow sigh, her breath escaped her. She leaned in, closer, closer, uncaring that she was foolish, a moth skirting too close to the flame. She wanted his strength, his heat, his power.

A noise at her back, a short, rasping cough, made her freeze.

Dragging out the tail of his linen shirt, Aidan looked away, toward Hawker who stood clutching his hand to his bloody shoulder. As he strode to Hawker's side, he tore a strip of cloth from his hem and folded it into a thick square. Jane followed behind. She drew a jagged little breath, horrified that she had forgotten everything, the pistol, the body, Hawker's wound, mortified that for an endless moment there had been only Aidan.

"I'm sorry." Hawker swallowed. "I'm a sorry excuse for a guard."

He ducked his head, yet his posture did not bespeak fear. In that instant Jane realized he was not afraid of reprimand or reprisal. He was ashamed.

"I'm a sore disappointment again. To you, sir. To myself," Hawker whispered.

Jaw tight, Aidan stepped closer and examined the wound.

"You'll live," he said, and then he pressed the square of linen to the gash. The breath left Hawker on a pained hiss. "The ball went through the flesh, but not the bone. You'll be keeping all your limbs." He turned to Jane and said, "Press this here."

Stepping forward to lay her hands against the square of cloth, she saw the deep runnel gouged in Hawker's flesh.

"Fault and blame, they matter not," she said softly, struggling to keep her tone steady. Though she had borne little enough of his cruelty, she suspected Aidan was capable of such. Could he harm this boy in a cold fury for failing to meet his exacting standard? The thought frightened her. "We are alive, and that is both a gift and a blessing."

Aidan made a low sound, and she thought perhaps he would refute her statement. Instead, he tore a second strip from his shirt and tied it tightly around Hawker's arm.

"Can you handle the reins?" he asked him.

Opening her mouth to protest, Jane choked back the words as Hawker stood a little straighter, ready to meet his employer's request, somehow redeemed in his own self-worth. *Men.* She closed her mouth and watched him shuffle carefully toward the coach.

Her gaze skidded along the road to the body, and she quickly looked away.

"What will you do with him?" she asked.

"Do?" Aidan shrugged, vibrating tension as he watched Hawker bend with slow care to lift the dragging reins from the ground. "Why, I'll tie him to the back of the coach."

She sucked in a sharp breath, horrified by the thought that he meant to punish Hawker by tying him to the back of the coach and dragging—

"Christ, Jane. You *do* think me a monster." Aidan's breath hissed between his teeth. "Gaby's corpse. I'll tie the body to the back of the coach and see him buried when we reach Pentreath."

Her gaze shot to his, and she saw . . . what? Bruised feelings? His mouth thinned.

"Go on." He gently nudged her in the direction of the carriage door. "I'll join you in a moment."

"What will you do to Hawker?" she persisted.

A stillness crept over him, fearsome and remote.

"What would you have me do? Maim him? Whip him?" he rasped. "For a fault not his own? *I* failed to foresee this circumstance. *I* bear the burden of guilt. Perhaps I should hand *you* the whip to take to my flesh for leaving you in such danger."

Flayed by his words, Jane jerked back and shook her head from side to side, wishing she had not pressed him, wishing she had been quicker to comprehend. Suddenly, she understood the target of his fury. Not aimed at Hawker, but at *himself*. Still, she was shocked by the vehemence, the strength of his assertion.

"Your self castigation is misplaced," she said firmly. "*Gaby* chose to pursue some twisted vengeance. Surely you see you are not responsible for his actions. Surely—"

He stepped close, looming over her, eyes narrowed. "You are *mine*, Jane. *Mine to keep safe.* I'll not live with the knowledge that all I've done to spare you—" He clenched his jaw.

"Spare me?" she blurted in confusion. "What do you mean?"

He looked away, staring up the gray ribbon of road. "Go to the carriage now."

A bitter wind swirled, biting deep, and Jane realized that while she was warm with Aidan's greatcoat wrapped about her, he stood in shirtsleeves and waistcoat. Thinking how cold he must be, she reached up and tugged on the collar, but as she began to slide the padded coat from her shoulders, he caught her wrist.

"Keep it," he said. "I want you warm."

His tone invited no discussion. Pressing her lips together, she studied him, the sculpted planes of his face, taut now with tension, the line of his mouth drawn rigid. Finally, with a small sigh, she turned and made her way to the coach. Hawker opened the door for her and she climbed inside. After an instant, the carriage creaked and dipped as Hawker clambered to the driver's bench.

Jane sat rigid, her fingers twined tightly together. She heard a grunt and then a thud, accompanied by the groan of springs and rods. She shuddered, unable to chase off the image of Aidan heaving the dead man onto the back of the coach and tying him in place.

Joining her moments later in the small, dark space, Aidan lowered his tall frame onto the opposite seat. His expression was unreadable as they lurched into motion. Moonlight came through the window, and she watched as he peeled off his black leather gloves. The sight of them chilled her; he must have put them on to handle the body.

"Are you well?" he asked, his eyes glittering.

"Yes." The word was little more than a whisper, her answer true enough. She was neither physically harmed nor dead, which meant she was not *unwell.* If her heart yet pounded a little too hard, and her stomach tightened and heaved with nerves, she was still far better off than she might have been.

Distressed was vastly superior to dead.

He leaned forward, eyes downcast, lashes forming crescent shadows on his cheeks. Jane held her breath as he reached into the pocket of his greatcoat, which was still wrapped about her, and drew forth a small, round tin. With precise movements he pried off the lid and held the tin out to Jane. She stared at it in confusion. The smell of peppermint tickled her nose.

"When I was"—he clenched his jaw, his lips drawn down at the corners, and then he continued— "when I was a child, my mother kept a tin of sweets. She always gave me one when I skinned a knee or came up bruised. She said candy was good for small hurts, that if I had something sweet, I would not be sour." He blew out a sharp breath and said no more.

Jane stared at him in the moonlight, feeling as though his admission had cost him some secret forfeit, as though it had pained him to say those words. Carefully, she took a peppermint and popped it in her mouth, grateful for the strange sort of comfort he offered.

Watching him steadily, she wondered that he shared this bit of himself with her, and wondered, too, what he had looked like as a boy. Golden-haired and gray-eyed. She tried to picture him laughing and running and chasing after a ball, and was saddened to realize she could not see him so, could not imagine him young and carefree.

They rode in silence and through the carriage window she saw the great dark saucer of sky, the scattered glitter of stars flung there as though by a careless hand. She sucked in a breath as she saw the familiar crenellated tower of Pentreath's church in the distance, a black shadow against a black sky. Soon they would pass within calling distance of her father's inn. A bittersweet sadness stole over her.

She shifted to better see her surroundings and her knee brushed Aidan's. He tensed, but did not move away. Sending him a sidelong glance, she found him watching her intently.

"Please," she said softly. "Let me stop and tell him all is well. Let me put his heart and mind at ease . . ." Her voice trailed away as Aidan shook his head.

"Do you imagine he spares a thought for you?"

Jane gasped at the harsh words, struck by their cruelty.

"I do," she said vehemently. "And I wish to reassure him."

"For endless months and years I dreamed of stealing Gideon Heatherington's ease, yet now you ask me to give him succor." He drummed his fingers on his thigh, a slow and steady beat. "I *cannot.* I am a man of dogged intent, sweet Jane."

"Yes, I believe that." Implacable. Relentless. Even cruel. Yet, he had been strangely kind to her as well. "But even a man of dogged intent may choose to alter his path."

His answer was slow in coming, and he turned his face from her as he spoke. "For two decades I have walked a wild and oft times treacherous course, yet always have I held sight of my clear and ever-present goal."

She knew his goal. She was certain he yearned for her father's destruction, perhaps even his death, but only if it was slow and terrible.

"What is it that you think my father did to you? He is a decent man. A good father . . ."

Her voice trailed away as he shot her a look of undiluted incredulity, and she bit back the codicil that decency and goodness were matters of opinion. No benefit could come of adding fuel to Aidan's smoldering anger.

"Tell me why you hate him so," she said softly. "A heavy weight is easier when shared."

"I beg to differ. Some burdens cannot be made easier." He leaned back against the seat, closing his eyes, pinching his thumb and forefinger over the bridge of his nose. With a sigh, he dropped his hand, but his head remained tipped back, baring the strong column of his throat. "You confound me. Your innocence, your goodness. Your bravery." A soft rumble escaped him. "I had not expected to like you."

He had not expected to like her? She had expected to hate him. So where did that leave them?

The moonlight filtered through the window, bathing the interior of the coach in gentle luminosity. He lifted his head, opened his eyes, and she thought she had never seen such a heartrending lack of emotion. His expression was as barren as a frozen and fallow field.

"You threaten my goal, sweet Jane, make me lose sight of where I must go. If you distill my vengeance, then I am lost. It is my northern star, my compass in the storm. It is all that I am, all that I can ever be. There is nothing else left for me but my burning hatred."

His words pummeled her already bruised heart. *I would be your compass.*

The thought winged its way toward her lips, only to catch in her throat, clogged by her heartbreak. She wanted to demand answers to the questions that haunted her, but though he applauded her bravery, she found herself too cowardly to press him.

"Please," she whispered. "I need not speak with him. Send Mr. Hawker to bear news of my well-being."

Through the window she could see the shape of the Crown Inn just a short way up the road, and the lantern that glowed at the entrance. She thought of her father, serving at the bar. Was he laughing with his cronies, or was his mood soured by worry and an overabundance of drink? She had to believe he thought of her, worried for her.

"If he had killed me . . . that man, Gaby . . . would you have left my father to wonder at my fate, to

spend month after endless month waiting for some
news, some word, or would you have told him—"
She choked on the words.

"'Tis neither more nor less than he deserves." He
laughed darkly. "What perfect and convoluted justice that fate should grant him the reality he bestowed on another."

She could find no meaning in his words, and as
she studied him, his tense jaw and his balled fists, she
thought they would drive past the Crown Inn, for his
expression seemed set in stone. Her heart sank.

Suddenly, he reached up and rapped sharply on
the roof of the carriage. The vehicle lurched to a
stop and after a moment, Mr. Hawker jerked open
the door.

"Give him some trinket, Jane. A handkerchief.
Something. And a message, though I caution you,
be brief," Aidan rasped, sinking back into the shadows. It seemed the words caused him pain, that he
sacrificed a part of himself with this concession.

Jane's heart leaped with joy. That he had softened
enough to allow this small thing—this most monu-
mental thing, if truth be told—gave her hope that
she might somehow dissuade him from whatever terrible course he was set upon. And she wanted to dissuade him. *Needed* to. Not only to save her father, but
to save Aidan, as well. Though she knew not what
eventuality he contemplated as his final vengeance,
the certainty that his chosen course would destroy
him gnawed at her.

He wanted her father to suffer dreadfully, yet he
yielded to her in this plea. He was a contrary, contradictory man, and she could not understand him.
Still, she could not deny the gratitude she felt that
he gave her this opportunity.

"Thank you." On impulse she reached across the space that separated them and closing her fingers round his much larger ones, she squeezed gently. He glanced up, bafflement and wariness gracing his features before he looked away once more.

Frantically, Jane dug through the pocket of her cloak, searching for her handkerchief. It was not there. Her fingers closed round the button from Aidan's waistcoat. She had naught else to send, yet it seemed supremely inappropriate to use the button from her captor's waistcoat as balm for her father's worry.

Besides, there was a secret corner of her heart that was loathe to part with this physical reminder of Aidan Warrick, a corner that wanted to hold the button close. She dared not examine that malapropos emotion too thoroughly.

In the end she decided to send only words of comfort. "Tell my father that I am well," she instructed Hawker. "Tell him that I have not been treated unkindly—" She shot a glance at Aidan's profile. He sat still as could be, barely appearing to breathe. "Nay, tell him I have been treated *kindly*. Yes. That is better. As proof to the veracity of my words, tell him that you bear witness in lieu of the sheet I was to hang that first night."

Hawker sent a startled look in Aidan's direction.

"Go." Aidan growled. "Do as she asks."

"Aye, sir." Hawker closed the carriage door and strode toward the inn.

Aidan looked at her then, his eyes narrowed in contemplation.

"I do this for you, sweet Jane, and I am at a loss to explain the why of it." His expression hardened, and she thought he must have read the hope in her gaze. "Oh, do not misconstrue my intent. Gideon Heatherington will know days and nights of torment. He will know true suffering of body and mind. He will live in the hell that is his due. But not today. Today, swayed by your blameless and honest plea, I offer him a small reprieve."

Jane nodded, not daring to speak, choosing instead to savor this sweet concession and not press for more than he could bear to give.

Moments later, Hawker returned and the coach heaved into motion once more. Jane perched on the edge of the seat, leaning close to the window. With a heavy heart she saw her father lumber into the yard. He stood staring after them, and then he turned his face and she thought he spat on the ground.

Troubled, she wrapped her arms about herself and watched the shape of the Crown Inn grow smaller and smaller as they left her father's hostelry behind.

It was not long before the great shadow of Trevisham House loomed before her, alone and barren, with the vast ocean so black around it. She smelled the salt, heard the crashing surf and massive waves, and the sigh of the wind.

Or perhaps it was the souls of ages past, crying out to her in warning.

Chapter 10

Standing in the shadow of Trevisham House nearly a week later, Jane stared out at the ocean. As far as the eye could see it stretched, a vast expanse of rippling gray silk. But beneath the surface lay the promise of a treacherous swell. It *would* come. She had only to wait for it.

She turned in a slow circle and studied the coast. Directly across the stretch of water that separated Trevisham from the mainland were the fishermen's cottages, stacked in three stories so the fishing gear could be stored below. Pretty, they were, with white walls and thatch or slate roofs. These things were so known and familiar to her.

Shivering, she drew her shawl tight, and thought that she should have brought her cloak. The temperature had been deceptive when first she embarked on her stroll. Soon, the cold clime would chase her indoors.

With a step and a half-turn to her left, she faced the curve of the cliffs. In the far distance she saw a tiny dark shape. She could not discern any great detail, but she knew it was the outline of the engine house that lodged the tin mine pump. A hard-won living that, underground in the tin mine. Still, no harder than tending the wind-swept farms up top, or braving the merciless Atlantic in a small fishing boat. Hard work, all, for an honest living.

'Twas what she missed . . . the work. The busy hands. She was used to serving ale until well past the chime of midnight, and used to cooking and tending the garden and washing the stairs.

Her mother had been a squire's daughter raised for a genteel life. She had tutored Jane in manners and letters, but life's reality had determined Jane's daily custom. She was no lady of quality reared to paint and play the pianoforte. Despite her mother's tutelage on the fine art of pouring tea and the skill of delicate conversation, Jane knew exactly who she was: an innkeeper's daughter, used to hard work.

Aidan had robbed her of that, and she was of a mind to fight for what he had taken.

A full week now she had done naught but walk and worry. She did not know what to make of her employer, her puzzling, infuriating, maddening employer. He had brought her to Trevisham, deposited her in an enormous chamber fit for a princess, and then stalked out without another word. She had not been invited into his presence since, though he clearly was in residence, for she saw him from afar as he rode across the causeway or strode through the garden. Once, she had hurried down the stairs upon hearing his voice, only to find him gone by the time she arrived in the front entry hall.

He had ripped her from her very full, if somewhat mundane, life but had failed to provide her with a purpose, a task with which to fill her *new* life. She had expected to be his servant. Instead, she was in a limbo of uncertainty, left without place or goal. It was a cruelty of diabolic nature.

She could not spend another idle day like the last without threat to her sanity.

Perhaps that was Aidan's intent.

Setting her hands on her hips, Jane glanced at the house. The army of servants he employed had been brought all the way from London, and their rank and order were clearly defined. All and sundry seemed to know their place, from the aloof butler, Coldwater, to the unctuous housekeeper, Mrs. Francis, to the scullery maid who whispered that her name was Penny when Jane pressed her.

There were workmen, too, set to restoring the crumbling part of the house that had fallen to ruin after so many years vacant.

Everyone had a station, a duty.

Except for Jane.

Her first morning at Trevisham, she had descended endless stairs and wandered through a maze of corridors until she had finally found the kitchen. The staff had been aghast that she had encroached upon their territory, and a footman quickly escorted her to the enormous dining room, where a feast was laid out. She had dined alone and, when she mentioned that she found the dining room somewhat forbidding, the footman, whose name she learned was Giles, had appeared flustered.

"Mr. Warrick instructed that miss's comfort was of utmost importance. Perhaps miss would prefer the breakfast room for future meals," he had intoned solemnly.

Thereafter, the venue had changed, but her restlessness had remained.

Now, a sigh escaped her as she acknowledged that

in their time together Aidan's presence had grown
on her. To her mortification, she realized that she
missed him. She wandered closer to the path that
led a steep decline to the pebbled beach. The way
seemed treacherous given her unstable knee. Wary,
she decided against the descent, though a new
exploration would surely be a fine distraction.

Startled by a sound behind her, she spun, flinging out her arms to steady herself as she came face
to face with the exact perverse, uncooperative man
she sought.

The sight of him both soothed her lonely heart
and exacerbated her feeling of neglect.

"Trying to frighten me into an early grave, are
you?" she asked.

"You are far too courageous for that." He shared
a small smile. "In high temper, Jane?" His gaze
raked her. "Angry over my absence, or my arrival?"

Her pulse raced, in equal measure frustration
and pleasure.

"Have you been avoiding me?"

His brows rose. He shrugged. "After a fashion."

"And here I had thought you fearless," she
muttered.

He laughed, and she remembered what he had
said to her that night on the Bodmin Road. That
she made him laugh.

She felt filled by the warm sound of his amusement.

Fawn-colored breeches and a tweed coat hugged
his tall frame, and over his arm was draped a beautiful cloak of the finest blue wool, the hood lined in
silk, and the rest lined in soft ermine. She eyed him
uncertainly as he held the garment up for her to
put on.

With a shake of her head, she protested. "The cloak is lovely, but it is not mine."

"It is now." Aidan met her gaze, his amusement gone, replaced by a faint tension.

Stunned, Jane half raised her hand, then let it drop. Something flickered in Aidan's eyes, and for a single instant she had the ridiculous notion that he was somehow vulnerable.

"If you do not like it, you need not wear it." He shrugged and began to fold the material over his arm once more.

She had bruised his feelings. The possibility seemed absurd.

"No. I . . . I do . . . That is, I—" She hesitated, unsure of the appropriate etiquette. She should not accept such a costly thing from him. Surely such an offering did not come without payment of some sort.

Hesitantly, she reached out and touched her fingers to the material, marveling at the quality. "You are most kind," she whispered. "I just do not understand—"

He cut her off. "Do not try to understand. Just enjoy. Let me give you this."

The words he did not say hung between them. *Let me give you this because I have taken so much.* His lips curved in a tight smile. "And, for a moment, let us both pretend that I am kind."

The steady beat of her heart marked the passing seconds. "I neither understand *you,* nor your twisted logic," she said, blunt. "You have only to say the word, and I will have my life back exactly as it was. *There* would be a kindness."

"Would it?" Gray-blue fire, like the heart of a flame. She was caught in his regard, plumbed by it and warmed by it, and left flushed and confused.

That *was* what she wanted . . . was it not? To return to her father's pub and forget that she had ever met Aidan Warrick?

As Aidan settled the cloak about her shoulders, Jane studied him with a sidelong glance, aware that she could not pretend indifference, or even dislike. The bare truth was that she did *not* wish that she had never met him, only that they had met under a different circumstance.

Such ridiculous notions, for had there been no need for him to claim her as bondswoman in payment for her father's debt, then she likely never would have met him at all.

"Walk with me," Aidan ordered, offering her his arm.

"A prettily worded invitation," she murmured. He shot her a questioning glance. With a sigh, she felt the last vestiges of her annoyance slip away and she gingerly rested her hand on his forearm, the tweed of his coat scratchy beneath her palm. He led her in the direction of the path that would bring them to the sea.

Alone, she had not dared to attempt the sharp descent, but with Aidan by her side, she braved the risk.

The terrain was uneven, strewn with small rocks and pitted in places. She picked her way with care, even as she thought that she must apply the same caution to her anticipated discourse with her employer.

Jane dragged a deep breath and then spoke. "Aidan, when you purchased my services, what exactly did you intend for me to do?"

The muscles tensed in his arm, and though he said nothing, she knew he had heard her quite clearly.

In a rush, she forged on. "There must be something, some task you would assign to my attention. I must have *something* to occupy my days, some purpose to my life. I cannot simply stare out the window at the sky and the sea. My needlework is abysmal and my skill at watercolor even worse, though Mama did try to teach me."

The memory made her pause, and she thought of how she missed visiting her mother's grave. She cast Aidan a sidelong glance. This battle would be won one skirmish at a time.

"I am accustomed to hard work, to cutting and chopping and serving . . . In fact, I *like* to work. Such idleness is a torment for me—"

Jane broke off as her foot slid on a rock and her leg twisted beneath her. She dug her fingers into Aidan's arm, and his free hand jerked forward, as though to catch her should she fall.

Holding her breath, she rested her weight on him for an instant as she fought to right herself, and won. With her lips pressed together, she gathered her composure before taking another step, and when she did, she could feel his eyes upon her, studying her gait. She forced herself to walk on, to pretend that his intent perusal did not unsettle her.

"Is it stiff?" he asked.

Her gaze shot to his.

"At times," she said. "But the greater concern is the weakness. I will walk a step, or ten, or two hundred, and then without warning, the limb simply melts away beneath me."

She cleared her throat, appalled by her verbosity. 'Twas the most she had ever talked on the subject of her ruined limb to anyone other than the doctor from Launceston. *His* sound advice has been lim-

ited to a strong admonition that she walk as little as
possible, and dose on laudanum as often as possible.

"Two doctors, one from Launceston and Doctor
Barker in London, have said there is nothing to be
done."

"Doctor Barker," Aidan repeated.

She nodded. She herself had found his name by
chance when a guest at the Crown Inn left an array
of pamphlets from the Royal Society behind. Ex-
cited by the information she read, and the sketches
of splints drawn there, she had badgered her father
until he agreed to write the man. Though Jane had
had no direct contact with him at all, her father
had sent a detailed description of the situation. Dr.
Barker's opinion had been clear enough.

The look Aidan leveled on her was far too intense for her comfort. She could not imagine why
she had told him these things, could not imagine
why he had asked. Suddenly, she remembered the
terrible words her father had hurled at her in
Aidan's presence, calling her a crippled gel. Mortified, she tipped her head to look at the sky.

"We're in for rain," she said in a rush. The smell
of sea and salt was rich in the air, and as they came
full upon the beach, she looked to the horizon. Lapping at the rock-strewn shore, the water from this
vantage looked like a rippling sheet of dark glass
that blended with the pewter sky far in the distance.

Aidan stopped abruptly and turned to face her, his
raised brows suggesting that he was well aware she
avoided the topic of her ruined limb. He scrubbed
his hand over his jaw. "See to the goddamned menus,
Jane. The gardens, the servants. Choose what task
amuses you, what task pleases you."

For a long moment she could only stare at him in

confusion, and then, as his meaning dawned, in astonishment.

"Those are the duties of the lady of the house," she demurred. "They are not the sorts of things a bondswoman is assigned."

He raised one brow. "Have you much experience at the assignments of a bondswoman?"

"You know I have not."

"Well, I have as much, or as little, familiarity with the matter as you." A ray of sunlight broke through the clouds, gilding his hair and his skin. He smiled, dangerous, rakish, so alluring. Her heart skittered in her breast. "So do as you damn well please, Jane. Perhaps if you work at your watercolors, your talent will improve." He gave a single chuff of low laughter. "Whatever makes you happy."

"Happy?" she parroted. "You want me to be happy?"

Slowly, gently, he reached out and brushed a stray hair from her cheek. She could not think, could not breathe; her entire being centered on his touch. "Aye, Jane. I find that that is exactly what I want."

She closed her eyes, her pulse leaping wildly and her thoughts crashing back to the times he had kissed her. Was *that* happiness, that wild, tumultuous feeling that heated her blood and made her long to taste him and touch him and bring her body close to his?

Her lids flipped open once more as he dropped his hand and stepped away.

"You may come and go as you will, Jane. You are no servant to me." His gaze narrowed. "Only have a care that you do not tarry at The Crown Inn."

Ah, well, she had expected *that* edict. "No servant to you? What am I then, if not your bondswoman?"

"You are not—" He broke off in clear frustration, and the skin around his eyes and lips tightened. "Fine. Then I assign you your duty. You are to play the role of my guest."

"Do not rumble at *me*, Aidan Warrick. This mad situation is entirely *your* doing." She had said the wrong thing. She knew as soon as the words left her mouth.

"Not entirely," he said shortly, and turned his face away to stare out at the swelling waves and encroaching clouds. She thought she saw a longing there as he looked to the ocean.

"I may visit my mother's grave?" Jane asked tentatively after a long moment had passed.

"Daily, if such is your wish." Still he did not look at her.

"And my cousin Dolly?"

He shrugged. "Invite her to tea. Invite the entire damned village." He did not need to state that the invitation did not include her father. "Take the coach to Launceston and visit the shops. I shall make certain you have adequate coin. Do what you will, sweet, whatever it is that women do."

"Women do many things," she said softly, trying to tread with care. "They bake and sew and knit and read. They laugh. They visit with their families . . ." Her words trailed away as he speared her with a sharp glance. She made a gesture of frustration. "You do not describe the duties of a bondswoman, Aidan."

"Nor do you, sweet. Nor do you." They stood thus for a time, the cry of the ocean birds fanning out above them, and then Aidan sighed. "What is it you want of me, Jane?"

The blunt question, spoken in his gravelly tone,

made her uneasy. What *did* she want of him? She *should* want her freedom, a return to her old life.

A breeze caught his thick honey-gold hair, blowing it back from his face. His eyes were purely stunning, more blue than gray today, deeper than mystery, and she realized with a near painful pang that she wanted him to touch her, to kiss her the way he had that night at the New Inn and again in the coach.

So here was the bald truth of it, if she was brave enough to face it. She had *not* yearned to confront him this morning and demand a chore, a purpose. She had yearned just to *be* with him, to drink in the sight of his harsh splendor, to breathe in the scent of his soap and his skin, to brush her fingers against the muscled strength of his forearm.

Shamed by that realization, she looked away.

With an oath, Aidan caught her chin and turned her face to his.

"I thought to stay away," he rasped. "To grant myself freedom from this chain you cast about me. But a week stretched like three months, each moment a cruelty. I found my thoughts consumed with you." A harsh laugh escaped his lips. "Madness it might be, but your presence brings me peace even as it destroys my peace of mind." Dropping his hand, he clenched his fingers and stepped back.

Tears pricked her eyes. "'Tis not my intent." She sucked in a breath. "And I will not bear the burden of blame that is yours, and yours alone. *You* are the creator of this situation. Your actions and choices have led us both here."

"Ah, there's my brave girl, speaking the truth even if I have no wish to hear it. Does anything make you afraid?"

Too many things.

Everything.

Unless he was by her side, and then her fears and torments seemed less than they could be. But that she would not tell him.

"You are the daughter of my enemy." The assertion pained her, ground glass scraping tender flesh. "You should hate me. You *see* the beast in me, yet you are not afraid. Why, Jane? Why are you not afraid? You know what I am."

Yes, yes, yes, she knew.

"I see no beast. You are a man." Jane closed the distance between them and laid her palm against his cheek, desperate to understand, to heal the great gaping hole that threatened to suck away his humanity. She could feel it, feel his agony, though she could not fathom its source.

"The truth of your words rings clear," she said. "I *should* hate you." The last was spoken with uncharacteristic vehemence, the syllables echoing hollowly among the rocks.

There was pain in his gaze, and despair, and then . . . nothing.

"I *will* destroy your father." His tone was flat.

"And will you destroy me? Kill me? Cast me from your highest tower? Your vengeance fills your heart. But when you are done with it, will it be enough?" Her pulse raced, and her cheeks felt hot with emotion.

She flung one arm toward Trevisham House where it sat high atop the mount that they had just descended. "Do you know, once, long ago, I swam for my life against the waves, believing that if I could only reach *this* island, *this* shore, I would be safe. I heard Trevisham calling to me that day, heard the lost souls of a hundred years crying above the storm, guiding my path. The rocks took a price from me, in pain and blood and heartbreak. But, in the end, my life was saved. Do you think I fear this place now, that I fear you?"

"You should." He touched her, a brush of his knuckles against her cheek, and she nearly moaned at the hot, sweet current that invaded her blood. "Be wise, Jane. Find that fear and hold fast to it."

"I have known what it is to suffer, Aidan, and now you would add to it. Whatever his limits and flaws, my father is all that is left to me. You will destroy him." She dragged in a breath before she whispered, "And that will destroy me."

She turned away, blinking back tears, remembering her mother's oft-spoken words to her. *Watch out for your father.* All through her childhood, her mother had repeated the refrain. *Watch out for your father. Do you understand, Jane?* She had done that. All these years, she had done that, but the guilt and the loss did not ease.

"He is not worthy of your loyalty." He stood so close, coiled tension and raw power. "Jane, I cannot change what I am. What Gideon Heatherington made me."

"No. Your words are a fallacy. My father did not make you. A man makes himself, chooses his own path. You *can* thrust aside this wicked obsession."

"You *dare* ask me?" He closed his hands around her shoulders, spinning her to face him.

"Yes," she whispered.

"I cannot—" In his eyes, she read his determination, his dominance, his need. "Any more than I can set aside this madness, this burning need to bind you to me and make you mine." Leaning close, he touched his face to her neck, breathed deeply.

Wild emotion careened through her, leaving her trembling.

With a cry, she stepped away, her back colliding with a large, rough boulder. He advanced, pressing the palms of his hands to the rock on either side of her, trapping her between a wall of cold stone and hot, muscled man. She breathed the scent of him, citrus and spice, and she wanted to press her nose to his skin and breathe in until she was filled with him.

A smoldering spark flared and roared through her, burning away common sense, leaving a trail of molten need in its wake. Should she let him, he would consume her. His name escaped her lips on a sigh. "Aidan."

"*This* is why I meant to stay away." His eyes darkened to the shade of the sky in the moment before dusk, and he thrust his fingers into her hair, loosening the coil she had secured at her nape. She was breathless, remembering the way he had kissed her before, the feel of his mouth and the taste of him, and the mad, pounding thrill he had roused in her.

Arching her body, she raised her face to him, beguiled, mesmerized, wanting him so badly that her limbs trembled, and the world spun dizzily. With a low groan, he leaned in, pressing his open mouth to hers. The tip of his tongue traced her lips then thrust inside, licking her, tasting her.

With a groan, he shifted full against her, granite-hewn muscle, the thrust of his hips pressed tight to her own. Her blood ran hot and thick, and a heavy ache pulsed in the pit of her belly, sultry and pleasing.

She closed her eyes, rushing on a sizzling current of awareness, attuned to the taste of his hot mouth on hers, the rough scrape of his callused fingers on the tender skin at her nape, the iron bands of his arms wrapped tight about her.

Her breasts felt heavy, full, the juncture of her thighs liquid and achy in a strange and unfamiliar way. The intensity was harsh, almost frightening, but, oh, she *liked* these feelings, wanted them to go on and on. With a low, inarticulate sound, she shifted her hips against his, closer, tighter, feeling the hard press of him.

The stroke of his hand along her waist ensnared her, higher, higher. She held her breath, arching into his touch until his hand closed over her breast, stroking, caressing, the tips of his fingers teasing the sensitive peak, sending sharp shafts of wanting radiating through her limbs. With a strangled moan, Jane curved her body to his, reckless in her need to get closer to him.

Thrusting her hands through the open front of his coat, she pulled at his shirt, goaded by a frantic urge to free the cloth and push her hand beneath to touch the warmth of his skin. As her palms brushed his naked waist, she moaned, and pushed deeper, wanting to feel the broad expanse of his back.

He tore away with a low oath, and stood, panting, his head lowered, his eyes dark and fathomless as he stared at her. He looked fierce and primitive, and she ached to press herself against him, and tug his head down until she could taste him again.

Through the haze of her rampant desire, she became aware that he shook, as though holding himself back by sheer force of will. He raised his hands, looking at them with an expression of distaste, turning them palms up and palms down, and

finally clenching them into fists and letting them
fall to his sides.

"I have killed men." A harsh scrape of words. He
lowered his head, drew a breath, and another, and
when he raised his head once more, his eyes were
bleak. "Not just with a pistol or a knife, Jane. I have
taken a man's head in my hands and twisted until
the sharp crack of death filled me with satisfaction."

Oh, God. The horror he described assaulted her,
a cold and frightening blow. Whatever tender emotion he roused in her breast, Aidan Warrick was a
stranger to her, a man of secrecy, cast in shadows
and darkness even when he stood in the light.

She had been a breath away from letting him
take her, here, on the pebbled beach, in plain view
of any who might pass.

Letting him take her? Nay, in a moment she would
have *pleaded* with him to do the deed. She fell
against the boulder at her back, struggling to still
the trembling that overtook her.

He raised his fists. "You deserve better. Better
than these hands on you. Better than what I can
give you. I am filled with venom and hate." He tore
his gaze away and looked out to the water, as
though the sight of her was more than he could
bear. "And you deserve better. Far better."

"You do not mean these things," she whispered
brokenly. "You cannot. There *is* good in you, there
is kindness and affection—"

"Do not weave a web of fantasy," he broke in
sharply. "What emotion do you imagine in me,
Jane? Hate? Vengeance? They are the only emotions I know."

Feeling sick, she stared at him. He wanted her.
Yet he denied himself. Why? She stared at the rigid

line of his jaw, and conviction coalesced with the clarity of a cold winter's dawn.

"Honor," she said, knowing with certainty that it was a trait he valued. He had told her so that night at the New Inn. "I imagine honor in you. Nay, not imagine. I *know* it is there."

She stared at him for a long moment, feeling as though a heavy veil was pulled from her eyes. "*That* is why you made me your bondswoman, isn't it? Not because you meant to hurt my father by taking me. You do not believe he has enough care for me to *be* hurt. No, it was because your honor forbid you from seeing an innocent harmed, so you took me into your care so I would not suffer when you destroyed my father."

The sound of her own heart thrummed wildly in her breast as she waited for his reply. Finally, she could not stand the silence.

"Look at me!" she cried, shocked when he did just that, his gaze stark and severe. Tears poured down her cheeks, and she swiped at them with the back of her hand.

"You are a tool I use to wound the man I hate with bitterly honed precision," he said, his tone dull.

She nodded, her lips pressed tight together, and then the breath exploded from her. "Lie to yourself, Aidan, if you must."

He opened his mouth. Closed it. Opened it once more and a sound escaped him, not quite a laugh.

"I am a poor liar. A dangerous lack in a smuggler and thief." He shook his head. "Jane, I would protect you from any who would do you harm. Including myself." A deep inhalation expanded his broad chest. "Most especially myself."

He stood before her, rigid in his self-imposed denial, each breath measured, controlled.

"I will send Hawker to see you safely back to the house." His eyes narrowed. "Do not leave this beach or try to climb that path without his escort."

Her throat clogged with heartbreak, Jane could only nod in reply. She tore her gaze from him as he stalked off, and stared instead at the waves that now crashed against the shore, angry, turbulent, mirroring the maelstrom in her soul.

Chapter 11

There was fog the next morning, smokey gray and thick, curling cold, damp tendrils about Jane's frame, making her shiver. Aidan had agreed that she might go anywhere save the Crown Inn and so, released from her captivity to some small degree, Jane walked toward the church. The way was achingly familiar and she was glad for the tiny bit of ease she found in the comfort of habit. She paused at the road that led to the village, wondering if she dared walk past the Crown Inn, not to tarry there, but only to look upon its known and comforting façade.

How would he know, her enigmatic and unfathomable master? Had he set a watchdog to mark her every move? For an instant, she thought perhaps he had.

The fog swirled around her, and the hairs at her nape prickled and rose. Unease crawled through her.

Slowly, she turned a full circle, aware of the unshakeable sensation that she was not alone, that unseen eyes spied upon her, and unspoken threat dogged her steps. She could see no one, but she

sensed he was there, a watcher hidden from her
sight. She had felt this way before, the day that
Ginny's body had been dragged from the ocean.
The day that Aidan Warrick had come for her.

That day she had been firm in her conviction
that someone watched her, first from the shadows
and then from the cliffs, and she was equally certain of it now. She had assumed that it had been
Aidan on the cliffs that first morning; he had ad-
mitted his presence there. But she did not think he
followed her today, or that he sent one of his min-
ions. There was something cold and dark in the
sensations that dogged her.

Who, then?

Tensing, she glanced about once more, anxious,
wary, searching for unseen menace. She found
none, and that left her wondering if perhaps her
distress was confounding her rationality, nervous
apprehension conjuring danger where there was
none in truth.

She was tired and irritable, her emotions in turmoil. The long hours of the night had been a torment, restless and fraught, with the wind whispering
through crack and crevice to taunt her and chill her,
body and soul. She had huddled beneath her blankets, the horror of Aidan's words crawling about in
her thoughts until at last exhaustion had carried
her away. She had found no easy rest.

*I have taken a man's head in my hands and twisted
until the sharp crack of death filled me with satisfaction.*

She had dreamed of that, the dreadfulness of it.

And she had dreamed of Aidan's eyes, burning,
tormented, as though despite his avowal of satisfaction, he had in truth found none.

Shaking off the remembrance, she sent a last longing glance at the road to the village and then turned instead to the graveyard. The fog draped the landscape, obscuring her surroundings. She glanced over her shoulder, unable to expunge the certainty that someone stalked her, unseen, unheard.

With a determined edge, she quickened her pace, her gaze fixed on the path. Her heart was heavy with the knowledge that she had taken Aidan's wretchedness into herself, allowing both his gruesome confession and his suffering to haunt her. There were depths to his character—and his torment—that she could not hope to understand.

She would give him ease if she could, even to her own detriment. The realization was frightening. A tangled skein of questions and dismay were her lingering companions, and though she knew that his ghosts were not her own, she could not seem to muster the will to chase them off.

Reaching her mother's grave, Jane lowered herself to the ground at the base of the stone. She bent her strong leg beneath her to bear her weight while her ruined limb poked out at an angle. A pile of curled and desiccated leaves had accumulated in the shadow of the granite headstone, and as she brushed them aside they crackled and crumbled beneath her fingers.

Though her thoughts were in disorder, her actions were rote, habitual, and she took some comfort in setting things to rights. With the grave now free of debris, Jane was about to rise when she spotted a small pink shell half buried in the dirt. She dug it from the ground and brushed the loose earth from its smooth surface.

The shell was the one she had brought from the beach days past. Recollections of that morning spun through her mind, images of Ginny's white-green face, the snaking tendrils of her red, red hair and her limbs dragging deep grooves in the wet sand as Jem and Robert towed her from the ocean's embrace.

Pushing herself to her feet, Jane rested her hand on the headstone as she scanned the graveyard. Her breath eased out in a soft hiss. In the far corner, beneath the dead elm was the dark, turned earth of a fresh grave. Was Gaby buried there?

Or Ginny? Alone, in a pauper's grave with no one to care?

Alone. Alone.

Tears stung her eyes, and she swiped at them with the back of her hand. Strange that she felt such empathy and sadness for a woman she had not known.

Jane swallowed against the tightness that closed her throat. She knew nothing of Ginny's remains, and that lack hammered at her. She felt so isolated, so displaced. For most of her life she had been party to any seed of news or gossip that blossomed in the pub, snatches of talk that reached her as she smiled and served up another tankard of ale. In her old life, she had been a good listener; she would have known if that grave was Ginny's. But now, she had no one, no human connection, for she could find no place among the servants at Trevisham. She was a woman accustomed to conversation and friendly association. Her new circumstance had left her robbed of both.

A forlorn ache settled deep inside her, a feeling of sadness and loneliness. She hoped that was *not* Ginny's grave. She hoped that family had come to claim the dead woman's remains, that she had had prayers said for her and someone to mourn her passing.

In a rush, Jane resolved that speculation was not enough, that she must *know* for certain what had become of Ginny. The need to know was suddenly fiercely important.

Dolly, she thought. Dolly would have news of Ginny's remains.

Wonderful, familiar Dolly, with her acerbic humor and cackling laugh.

Yes, that was exactly what she needed. A visit and a hot cup of tea with her cousin, a few moments to pretend her life was just as it always had been.

"I am sorry that I was away so long, Mama," Jane whispered. She dragged her fingers along the glass that fronted her mother's miniature. Suddenly, she froze. The glass was no longer cracked, but unmarked and intact. Someone had seen to its replacement in the days since she had been here last.

Not her father. He lacked the means.

Aidan.

One more inexplicable kindness that deepened the mystery of him and accented her confusion.

Frustration edged her actions as she snapped her skirt smartly to shake off the last of the leaves that yet clung to the hem. She must not think of Aidan, must not revisit his kindnesses again and again until they magnified and took on such proportion that they masked his cruelties.

Since coming to Trevisham, she had slept poorly, tossing in her cold, lonely bed, missing the warmth of him and the scent of his skin and the even cadence of his breathing. Lying beside him in the bed at the New Inn, she had felt secure, protected, safe, things she had not truly felt in more than a decade. He had held the nightmares at bay.

She thought of the way he had looked the previous morning, the wind catching his hair and the sun turning it the color of good ale. The curve of his handsome mouth. The shadow of stubble that darkened his jaw. How many times in the past week, alone in the night, had she closed her eyes and *felt* the touch of his hand, the lush caress of his lips, felt his heat and his need as though he was pressed full against her in truth?

She was quickly becoming ensnared in a fantasy of her own weaving, one that was dangerous in so many ways. Aidan had told her exactly what he was.

A monster.

A man who professed satisfaction at twisting another man's neck until he was dead.

Dead, dead, dead.

Like Ginny was dead. Had Aidan killed her? Was that the truth of Digory's ugly insinuations? She could not think it. Could not bear it.

She wanted to wish it away.

She longed for him, ached for him.

His own admissions cast him as the villain. *But I aimed to kill.* When wounding Gaby might have been enough.

Oh, there was no benefit to this endless quarrel she fought with herself.

Dragging in a deep breath, she proceeded between the headstones, determined to seek out Dolly's company, and equally determined to leave her frightening fascination with Aidan Warrick buried deep. She limped from the graveyard, closing the gate behind her. The hinge squealed in protest, and she paused, her hand yet resting on the cold metal, the chill leaching through her glove.

She snatched her hand away. How was it that the rusted hinges of the gate were exactly as they had been days ago, still in need of oiling? The intervening time had seen her entire *life* torn to bits and scattered on the wind.

A shiver prickled across her skin, like the legs of a thousand centipedes. Her head snapped up, and her gaze shifted to the dead elm, an eerie sight with the fog twisting around it like a shroud and its canopy of blackened branches reaching clawed fingers over the stone wall.

There was a dull scrape, and the crunch of dead leaves. Her breath came in rough little gasps.

Did something move behind the thick trunk?

A sharp snap, a twig broken.

Three steps she took to her right, until she could see round to the far side of the blackened tree. Her heart thudded in her chest and she wrapped her arms tight about herself.

The cry of a raven pierced the air.

On a sharp exhale, she bowed her head, feeling foolish.

There was no one there.

The fog enveloped her, a heavy, damp blanket, pressing in. Pulse racing, she began to walk, slowly, then faster, with her awkward gait, her foot scraping the ground with a distinct dragging rasp. Pressing her palm to her thigh, she reinforced each step, praying that her knee would not choose this moment to give way.

A sigh escaped her as she reached Dolly's cottage. The building was small, the walls washed white, and off to one side was a strip of turned soil

that Dolly used for her vegetables. A thin stream
of smoke coiled from the squat little chimney. Jane
smiled, touched by relief, glad to think that Dolly
was at home.

She found the door ajar.

"Dolly," she called, pushing the portal the rest
of the way open. "Hello?"

When there was no answer, she called again, and
then limped around back, thinking that perhaps
Dolly had stepped outside. She was not there. Odd.
Jane walked to the front of the cottage once more.
The open door and hint of chimney smoke were
both good indicators that Dolly was likely to return
very shortly. Knowing she was always welcome in
her cousin's home, Jane went inside.

The simple square room was tidy as could be,
neat and clean, the stone floor swept. A peat fire
smoldered in the open fireplace and the rich smell
of mutton stew flavored the air. On the table were
a single plate and an empty cup, set as though for
ready use.

Briefly, Jane considered boiling the water for tea.
Deciding instead to wait for Dolly, she sat down in
one of the two roughly hewn chairs and prepared
to wait. Moments passed, and she glanced at the
dishes on the table.

Pretty.

The flowers made her think of the warm sun and
summer. She ran her finger along the smooth edge
of the plate.

The flowers . . .

Jane cocked her head to one side, foreboding
nipping at her with sharp little teeth.

Thrusting herself away from the table with such
force that the chair overbalanced and clattered to

the floor, she stood, breathing fast and heavy. She could not name the source of her dismay, she only knew the sensation as it slithered through her. She wrapped her hands tight around the table's edge, certain that there was something wrong here, very wrong.

She spun and stumbled to the door. Suddenly, she did not want to be in this dark little room with the stink of mutton turned greasy now and repulsive. Confused by her change of heart, frightened by it, she wrenched the door open and raised her head to find a tall shadow blocking her way.

Alarm twisted a cold lump in her chest and she cried out. Blinking, she pressed her hand to the hollow of her throat as recognition dawned.

"Mister Hawker," she said on a gasp. "Oh, you startled me."

There was wariness in his eyes as they met hers and then slid away. He looked equally surprised, she realized, as though he had not thought to find her here.

He stammered his apologies, and Jane heard his words without really listening, her thoughts spinning.

When she had first recognized him framed in the doorway, she had thought him sent by Aidan, instructed to follow her and act as warden as he had at the New Inn. But looking at him now, with a certain caginess in his gaze that she had never seen there before, she acknowledged the error of that impression.

Mr. Hawker had held *no* expectation of finding her here.

"What are you doing here?" she asked. "Do you know my cousin Dolly?"

His gaze slid past her to the dim interior of the cottage, shifty in a way she could not truly explain, and she was left with a feeling of suspicion as the silence lengthened.

"Why, I've come to fetch you," he said at last with bluff good humor.

He lied.

The realization was shocking.

With it came the recollection that Hawker had failed in his assigned task not once, but twice, failed to watch her and protect her as Aidan had bid. Was there some hidden import in that, or was she simply spinning tales where none existed in truth?

Drawing a deep breath, she kept her eyes downcast, lest Hawker read her growing mistrust, and then she noticed the leaves that clung to his booted feet. Like the leaves she had found at the graveyard.

With a shake of her head, Jane silently chided herself. There were dead leaves all about. Stepping from her cousin's cottage, she pulled the door closed behind her.

As she walked with Hawker back toward Trevisham, she pondered all the possibilities that might have precipitated his lie.

And she failed to conjure even one that was not disturbing.

Jane returned to Trevisham in time to stand on the front step and watch Aidan leave. She had not spoken with him since their encounter on the beach when he had kissed her and touched her and roused such feelings in her heart that she was left trembling just thinking of them. Hands clasped tight before her, she watched him pause and turn and search her out, his gaze burning into her even from such a distance.

Where did he go?

She dared not wonder, had no right to wonder.

Such tangled, twisted things were the caverns of her heart.

She stood on the step long after he was swallowed by the fog, and Hawker with him. Only when she turned to go inside did she wonder if she might have been wrong, if in truth Hawker *had* been sent to fetch her back to Trevisham.

The following morning found Jane desperate to fill her hours with some useful task, having spent the remainder of the previous day with nothing to occupy her save her distressing reflections. She sought out the housekeeper, Mrs. Francis, and proposed the cleaning and airing of the uninhabited west wing, though, in truth, she expected the woman to present some opposition to her suggestion. She was surprised to find that despite a certain reserve, Mrs. Francis claimed she was glad for Jane's help, and assigned the scullery maid, Penny, to accompany her.

"Thank you, Mrs. Francis," Jane said. "I appreciate this."

The housekeeper turned her nose up just a little and replied, "Mr. Warrick was most clear in his instruction. You must do as you please, Miss Heatherington. *Exactly* as you please."

And so Jane had her explanation, one touched with an edge of irony, for she suspected that if her pleasure led her to the Crown Inn, there would be someone to stop her.

Moving from room to room, Jane and Penny chatted as they worked, and Jane felt a rising of her spirits as the hours passed and Penny's reserve gave way to genuine camaraderie. Late afternoon found them in a dusty chamber on the third floor with thick cobwebs hanging in the corners and the smell of disuse coloring the air.

Jane pummeled the velvet draperies and then the cushions of the settee. Her thoughts wandered to Hawker's strange behavior the previous day. Questions assaulted her and she mulled over possibilities, in one moment assigning Hawker the role of villain and in the next finding herself unable to believe ill of him. With a sharp exhale she landed a solid slap on the settee cushion, and the cloud of dust made her choke and cough.

"I wish you would let me fetch Patience and Clarey, miss," Penny said, watching Jane with a frown. "You could tell them what you want done."

"No," Jane replied, for what she thought might be the hundredth time. "I have no intention of sitting and watching while others work. I need to be busy, Penny."

"Yes, miss." The maid turned away to dust the washstand, but her dissatisfaction was clear. "Pretty bowl," she said after a moment. "I like the flowers."

She dipped her cloth and wrung it out, then dropped it in the murky pail with a grimace. "I'll just fetch fresh water. This lot's too dirty to do any good."

"And some fresh cloths." Jane crossed to the washstand and dropped her filthy rags in the bucket. Her gaze snagged on the bowl with its painted flowers. She reached out, almost touching the bowl, almost . . .

Jerking her hand back with a quick inhalation, she froze. Her vision narrowed, as though a dark tunnel was closing in on her, and all she could think of were Dolly's plate and cup, certain she had seen the pattern before on china far too fine for a simple kitchen.

Wenna's plates had borne the same flowered pattern as Dolly's.

"Miss! Are you all right, miss?" Penny asked, her tone high and frightened. "You're white as parchment!"

"No . . . yes . . . I—" With a shake of her head, Jane tried to find the connection between her own cousin Dolly and Wenna Tubb. The china was identical, the pattern one she had never before seen on Dolly's table. With a sick dread she battled the obvious association.

Digory Tubb, with his sullen demeanor and his threats and his knife. By his own implication, he had been in Pentreath around the time poor Ginny had washed ashore. The day Dolly had whispered of seeing a wrecker's light to the north.

Was that how Wenna got her china? Had her son Digory lured a ship to the rocks and then murdered all survivors in a terrible orgy of thievery and evil?

The possibility was ghastly.

Cornishmen believed that what the sea gave up from a ship taken by storm or mishap rightfully belonged to them, but a ship downed by wreckers, by cruel and purposeful intent, was a different matter entirely. To take profit from such a despicable deed was loathsome.

Horror nested in her, a wriggling, writhing mass of desperation and fear. How had Dolly come to have such plates in her possession? Where had they come from? Blood roaring in her ears, Jane stared at Penny in sick dismay.

"Come sit. Come sit." Penny tugged at her arm and tried to drag her to the settee.

Jane looked to the window, forcing her lips into a smile. "I just need a bit of air, Penny."

The maid looked dubious.

"Truly, I am fine." To prove her point, Jane crossed to the window and shoved it open, breathing deeply of the cold air.

She stared out, thinking, brooding. The earlier sunshine had faded with the lateness of the hour. A thickening blanket of darkening clouds moved inland, pewter edged with bruised purple and blue. Clammy, cold air enveloped her and made her shiver. The mizzling rain and brooding sky promised worse to come.

Penny hovered at her elbow making small sounds of distress. Turning, Jane laid her hand on the girl's shoulder.

"Go and fetch the water, Penny. You see I am quite well. It was the dust, nothing more. Just the dust."

The maid stared at her for a long moment and then nodded. "I'll be bringing Clarey with me when I return," she said. "And I'll not hear another word about it."

Desperate to be alone with her thoughts, Jane nodded and turned back to the window. She heard the slosh of water as Penny lifted the bucket, and the sound of her feet tapping a rhythm as she walked away.

The shadows lengthened as Jane held her place, staring out at the increasingly agitated ocean, a reflection of the chaos that scattered her composure. As the sky grew darker and darker still, so did her thoughts of men dead, and a woman with her eyes gouged from her skull, and ships and wrecks, and

at the center of it all, Aidan Warrick. The eye of
the storm.

Jane was about to turn away from the window
when a tiny flicker caught her eye, on the coast far
to the north. It winked and blinked and then disappeared, and she wondered if she had truly seen
anything at all.

She looked again to the ocean. The wildness of
the waves increased and they rose high before
crashing against the rocks. And then she gasped
and jerked forward, splaying her fingers against the
glass, for there in the midst of the furor she *did* see
a light, bobbing and weaving like a drunken man,
tossed hither and yon by the churning water.

Squinting against the growing darkness, she felt
certainty grow. There, against the gray and foaming
sea, she saw the shadowed outline of a hull, the
dark masts reaching to the heavens and the tiny
light lurching with each swell. Caught in the storm,
a ship was rapidly being forced closer and closer to
the treacherous coast.

Her gaze swung back to the north. *Had* she seen
a light there on the shore, a wicked, treacherous,
false light? A wrecker's light? Was it the storm or
human perfidy that lured this ship to its doom?

The expanse of shore that stretched away from the
village and the sharp outline of jagged rocks that
peppered the bay were blanketed by the thickening
darkness, but she knew they were there. The teeth of
the beast, ready to grind any that ventured close.

Her pulse galloped. She spun and rushed from
the room in an awkward, listing lope, desperate to
find help, to send up a hue and cry. That ship was
bound for the rocks, bound for destruction.

They would die. They would all die, taken by the frigid, sucking depths.

"Oh, dear God." For an instant, she thought her leg would buckle. *Not now. Not now.* She hurried forward with great, lurching steps that sent shards of agony shooting from her knee.

Calling for help, Jane slid clumsily down the long flights of stairs, her fingers scrabbling at the balustrade. More than once she thought she would fall. As she careened onto the landing, she staggered, crying out. Strong arms closed about her, steadying her.

She found herself held in Aidan's sure grasp. His hair was damp, the strands darkened by the rain. He must have just now returned from whatever business had taken him away.

"Are you hurt?" he demanded with harsh urgency. He pegged her with a hard stare, his fingers tight about her arms.

Short little huffs of air pumped in and out as, gasping for breath, she stumbled over her words.

"A ship—" Her chest felt tight, as though bound by iron rings, like a keg of ale. "I saw it from the window. I think—I think it will break upon the rocks!"

Aidan's eyes darkened, the pupils dilating, and his jaw tensed. "Are you steady now?" he asked, easing his grasp on her arms.

She nodded.

He dropped his hands. "I've sent Hawker to the village to sound an alarm."

Already? How had he known?

The wrecker's light she thought she had seen on the north coast . . . Had there been enough time for him to carry that light and still be here now? No. No. Surely not. And how could she think it?

His expression was coldly determined, so controlled

she thought he might crack. He looked down at her, his eyes gray as the stormy waves.

Her stomach clenched.

She had never seen a ship break apart, but she had heard the heartrending stories. The *Johnkeer Meester* had gone down in inky darkness somewhere off the Mullion cliffs. At dawn, the bodies of the sailors had washed ashore, and two women, and a newborn baby. The *Abigail* had foundered between Lizard and Gunwalloe, in full sight of a score of men who tied themselves together and struggled to reach her. All were lost, including nine rescuers who were there battling the waves one moment, and simply gone the next.

Aidan was going out there, to save those he could. Dear God, he might never come back.

Knowing too well the aching emptiness of loss, of regrets and wishes for just a single moment more, she did not hesitate. She rose on her toes and pressed her mouth to his, uncaring of any who might stand watching.

"Come back," she whispered as she drew away. Come back *to me*.

Something dark and deep flickered in his gaze, something she could not fully interpret. Touching his fingers to her lips, he studied her with fierce concentration and then he nodded once. He turned and sprinted across the hall, and soon, Aidan and a contingent of servants were heading out into the storm, into the night, to try to save those lucky few who might survive the wreck.

Chapter 12

Unable to stand by and do nothing, Jane bid the maids gather blankets and baskets of food.

"I'm sorry, miss," Penny cried tearfully. "Sorry it took me so long to get back. I was looking for Clarey, and she was nowhere to be found. She—"

"Hush now, Penny. 'Tis of no matter. But can you run and fetch my cloak, my old scarlet one from my chamber?" Jane glanced at her feet. "You will be faster than I."

Penny hurried off and as soon as she returned they rushed from the house and heaved themselves into the last wagon leaving Trevisham, loaded with blankets and baskets hastily packed by the cook. The way was treacherous, great waves crashing over the causeway as they passed. The rain and sleet pelted down upon them, soaking them in a matter of moments.

They rode on until they reached the start of a narrow path where the cliff descended sharply to the shore. Here they stopped, climbed from the wagon, and then made their way to the stretch of beach. The sound of the breakers was a terrible roar that slapped the night with fury.

Around her, Jane could see the men of Pentreath scrambling down the cliff path. Careless in their haste, they sent pebbles and loose earth tumbling before them. She turned her gaze to the ocean, to the great crashing fists of water that snatched up the ship then cast it about like a child's toy. Unable to look away, she watched in appalled fascination as one wave, larger than the others, caught the dark hull and flipped it effortlessly on its side against the jagged teeth of the rocks that hid beneath the churning foam.

The wretched squeal of splintering wood and the crack of timber tearing asunder carried across the water. Then the foundering bulk rose high on the crest of another wave, and for a single shining moment, Jane thought it would right itself, would roll upright with its long thin masts pointing to the sky.

A noxious queasiness came upon her as, with a dreadful noise, the ship simply crumbled to pieces like a house of cards. She pressed her forearm against her belly, her horror nearly sending her to her knees. Above the howl of the wind she thought she heard the terrified cries of those who were thrown into the water. She saw them, tiny specks, clinging desperately to the splintered wood. They floated and sank, then popped up like apples in a bobbing tub at the Launceston fair.

Minutes crawled with infinite slowness.

"Save those you can!" Aidan's gravelly voice carried above the storm. "Tie yourselves together and reach those you can. No man goes into the water without a rope about his waist."

She whirled and watched him stalk along the beach. It appeared he was assigning groups to work together at set tasks, donning the mantle of leadership as easily as he might don his coat. Lengths of rope appeared and men looped themselves together in groups of eight or nine. A lifeboat rowed out, but it was no match for the tempest's rage and was quickly hurled back against the shore.

Again and again they tried, and after a long while, Jane saw the specks floating closer. The same waves that bashed at the lifeboat were carrying people who clung on to scraps of wood closer, and closer still.

Aidan stood waist deep in the pounding surf, and others waded into the surging tide after him. Careless of the danger to himself, Aidan took a step deeper into the churning water, reaching for the form of a man sprawled across a jagged shard of wood. Catching him by one arm, Aidan dragged the survivor to safety, handing him off to those closer to the shore.

So it went for hours, sodden fragments of wood bobbing and dipping with the whim of the sea, one or two carrying a battered sailor, but most washing up on the beach barren of both burden and hope.

A horse nickered, and Jane turned her head to see a wagon rolling toward the beach, coming from the north. It carried a lamp, the yellow glow a moving beacon. She found the sight odd and strangely disturbing, conjuring memories of the light she had thought she saw hours past, and of Dolly and her insistence that weeks ago she had seen a light to north, an evil light, a wrecker's light.

Jane stared at the wagon. Two men sat on the bench, but the distance was too great for her to see more than that. She wondered who they were, and why their pace was so easy and slow. 'Twas almost as though they were watchers of this terrible scene, making no effort to speed their way to the beach and help in the rescue. All her earlier suppositions and unease clamored and clanged as she thought of Dolly and Wenna and Digory Tubb, and too-fine china and ships and wrecks.

She shuddered and her gaze swung back to the dying ship. Surely *this* wreck was no work of wicked men, but a terrible accident of nature.

The rain eased and finally stopped, and some of the men managed to build a large fire in the center of the sandy stretch of beach, bringing dry peat and some wood down from the cottages. They hauled the survivors closer to the flames, where Jane and Mary—the barmaid from the Crown Inn—and some other women set to warming them with borrowed blankets and words of encouragement. Jane tucked a blanket around a pale and shivering man, and spoke with him for a time, wishing she had news of those he asked after.

"Would you like to go up to my cottage?" Mary offered. "The distance is not terribly far. You can be warm and dry"—her gaze flicked to the horizon, and back—"and away from here. They'll come and tell you the way of things, you can be sure."

Hollow-eyed, the sailor shook his head and murmured a polite refusal.

"I'm m-m-meant to stay," he said, huddling beneath the blanket. "At l-l-least to pray, if I can do naught else."

To pray, yes, for those who washed ashore, both living and dead, Jane thought. And for those whose lives were at risk. Her gaze raked the waves searching for Aidan. He was there, chest deep, a step farther than any of the others, and the sight of him eased her heart some small bit.

Suddenly, a hand clamped on her shoulder and

she spun to find her father standing at her back.
With a cry, she flung herself against him, and if he
did not cling to her, well, displays of great affection
had never been his way. She breathed in the familiar smell of ale and tobacco, and then stepped back.

"You look well, Janie girl." He sounded . . . angry.

"I am well." She studied him, noting that his coat
was damp from the earlier rain, but his breeches
were dry. He had not been in the sea with the
others. "Do not fear for me, Father. Aidan Warrick
is no cruel master. In truth, he treats me more as
guest than servant."

Gideon's face turned cruel. "Aye, I heard exactly
how you've been treated." He spat on the ground
near her feet. "Joss Gossin had a word or two to
share."

She felt all color drain from her face in a cold
wash, and then a slap of heat as she flushed. Her
father thought her Aidan Warrick's whore. She
opened her mouth to protest, to explain, but a
loud cry made her turn.

Another man was pulled, alive and spluttering
from the white, frothing tongues of water that
sucked at him. Jane turned back to her father with
a smile, buoyed despite her distress, only to find
that he had walked off and left her standing alone.
She swallowed the lump that swelled in her throat.
What were her petty hurts and hardships in the face
of this night's horrific loss? There would be time
enough for her to feel sorry for herself later, and to
feel sorry for the venom spread by rumor.

Frowning, she wondered when her father had
had occasion to speak with Mr. Gossin. The New
Inn was a goodly distance away. Something nagged
at her, some unheeded oddity, but she could not
place it. Arms wrapped about her waist, she let the

thought go and stood watching the men fight the waves and the cold.

A large slat of wood drifted toward shore, a distance away from the rescuers. Clinging to it was a white-faced woman, her dark hair streaming wild and loose down her back. She clutched a bundle beneath one arm.

Dear heaven, a child.

Jane stumbled forward, hand outstretched as she watched the woman struggle to keep hold of both her precious bundle and the lifesaving timber. Suddenly, the child slipped from her grasp, and she gave a desperate cry, her face contorted into a mask of horror as the child sank below the waves.

A mother. A child. The crashing waves. For an instant Jane was carried back on a serpentine wave of memory.

"No!" she yelled. She almost dove into the surf herself, but knew that she was no match for this storm. Raising her arms, she waved and called out, desperate to catch the attention of one of the men in the water.

As though attuned to her cry, Aidan turned toward her. His eyes met hers, and he followed her gaze to the foundering woman who pitched this way and that and slapped at the water in a growing frenzy. Her mouth worked, again and again, but the ocean stole her cries.

Aidan bent low into the waves, and the water crashed over his head. Heart pounding, Jane held her breath until he surfaced once more. Something flashed in his hand, catching the flicker of the flames on the beach. His knife, the one he wore always in a sheath on his leg.

With movements sure and quick Aidan sliced the lifesaving rope that held him to the others. Terror made Jane sway as she watched him fight the thundering breakers, holding his balance against their wrath as he slogged forward. She wondered that he made any headway at all in the face of the water's hammering strength. Then, as he reached the woman's makeshift raft, he disappeared beneath the frothing sea. Jane's heart pounded a frenzied tattoo, her gaze riveted to the place he had been.

Come back. Come back to me.

He had nodded in reply, in tacit agreement both to the words she said aloud, and those that stayed locked in her heart. Oh dear heaven, do not let him break his word.

Do not let him leave her.

Come back. Come back to me.

She was dimly aware of the villagers who dragged the desperate woman from the sea, holding her back from flinging herself into the waves in search of her child.

Too long. Aidan and the child both had been under far too long. Jane's heart lurched with a pain sharp and pure, a fear so great she thought she would fly apart from the terrible honed edge of it.

OhGodOhGodOhPleaseGod. As though in answer to her prayer, Aidan surged from beneath the waves, a tiny bundle clutched in his arms. The child made no sound, no movement. Jane shuddered, her frame wracked by a trembling that came from the cold and the fear and the horror, and she wanted to rail and weep at the death of an innocent. Tears snaked down her cheeks, of grief and despair, and of a secret swell of joyous relief at the sight of Aidan, wet, bedraggled. Alive.

He dragged through the water and others stepped forward with arms outstretched to take the drowned child. He shook his head, and turned his shoulder to them. The mother was wailing now as her legs gave way beneath her, a high-pitched keening that tore at the ragged edges of Jane's own control.

Turning the child face down over one arm, Aidan wrapped him in what appeared to be a tight hug. With a sharp jerk, Aidan squeezed the child's chest, then released, repeating the movement again and again. The mother's cries grew ever more frenzied, a howling pain that carried out to be swallowed by the roar of the waves.

And then the child coughed, spewing water in a high arc through the air.

The mother's wailing stopped abruptly, as though someone had plugged a spigot.

"Oh, may God bless and keep you!" the woman cried. She struggled to her feet, fell, and then rose again to heave herself across the sand. "May God bless you!"

She fell at Aidan's feet, wrapping her arms first around his legs, and finally about her squalling, coughing child as Aidan lowered him into her arms. Others came forward with blankets, and Aidan faded back, watching from the edges of the crowd.

Pushing wet hanks of hair back from his face, he turned first to his right, then his left. His gaze shifted, impersonal, assessing, and finally lit on Jane. He smiled, a narrow half-curve of his lips, his eyes burning with a fierce light.

He shook terribly, she saw. Snatching up a blanket, she scrambled across the sand, her leg dragging a deep gutter behind her.

"You are safe," she whispered. With a snap of the folded blanket she freed it and tossed it up about his shoulders. She fell against him, uncaring that he was soaked through and that he soaked her. "I feared—" Her voice broke and she shook her head. "You are safe."

He was cold as ice, shaking so badly she marveled that he could even stand. His strong arms closed about her, holding her tight against him. With one cheek pressed to his broad chest, the frenzied beat of his heart keeping time with her own, she closed her eyes and wondered for an instant if he bolstered her, or she bolstered him, or perhaps they buttressed each other, each doomed to fall if either let go.

Aidan let Jane feed him warm tea and drag him near the fire for only a few moments. Once the worst of his shaking subsided, he insisted on tying himself back into line, looping the rough hemp about his waist and taking his place among the others as they battled the waves.

In nightmarish misery, the minutes dragged past and, in the end, there was no one left to save, no hope left to stoke. The child had been the last living creature given up by the sea. After that, only the dead washed ashore, and finally, only fragments of the raw wooden skeleton of the ship, tossed on the sand.

Weary to the bone, the villagers began to coax those few they had managed to save away from the beach, packed in wagons, or walking with blankets draped about their shoulders. Exhaustion marked them all, and a deep gnawing sadness for what they had seen and suffered.

Such horrific loss. Of life. Of possessions. Of dreams.

Finally, to Jane's secret joy and relief, Aidan slogged from the water. She snatched a blanket from the dwindled pile and with every muscle in her body screaming in protest of the damp chill that crept into sinew and bone, she went to him, dragging her crippled limb along like a twisted branch. Her foot gouged a trail in the sand with each lurching step.

He met her partway, and her heart thudded at the sight of him, wet clothes clinging to his tall frame, shadows of fatigue forming dark crescents beneath his eyes. Despite the weariness that etched his features, he was so very magnificent to her.

With shaking hands, he went for the buttons of his waistcoat, but she brushed him aside and undid the fastenings herself, uncaring who might see her tending to him. The cloth clung stubbornly as he shrugged out of the dripping garment, and she curled her fingers into the collar and tugged with all her might. His skin was so cold. With renewed vigor she pulled until the waistcoat came free. She reached for the lacings of his shirt, but he caught her wrists, leaving her wondering at his strange modesty. Snatching the blanket from where she had dropped it, she wrapped him in the thick wool to ward off the chill.

"The dawn must come soon," Jane said, aching to fill the void of silence with human sound.

"For us, the dawn will come." His voice was rough gravel.

Snatches of conversation drifted along the beach, and the song of the ocean, far tamer now than it had been hours past. The length of her arm was pressed to his and she felt the shaking of his muscles as his body instinctively sought to warm itself.

She wanted to warm him, to press her mouth to his and breath heat into him, from her body, from her soul, from the deep, dark longing that burned hot at her core.

"Your lips are blue with cold," she said. "Let me fetch you another blanket before you catch your death."

He closed his hand about her arm as she made to turn away, long fingers, strong, pale against the dark red cloth of her old cloak.

"I have been far colder than this. Tonight's paltry chill is a balmy breeze." Aidan laughed, a hard sound tinged with bitterness. "As to catching my death . . ." He turned to her, his eyes burning, and his hand fell away. "Would you mourn me, Jane?"

Until my dying breath. She caught her lower lip between her teeth, making prisoners of the words, for once they spilled forth, there would be no calling them back.

"Don't answer." He pressed a finger to her lips, his touch brief, his skin cold as ice.

Brave and strong and true, he had battled for every life this night, willing to sacrifice his own. But what of other nights?

The mystery of him tormented her.

"How many men have you killed?" she asked, the words soft and hard at once.

He stilled, then offered a rakish smile, laced with menace, designed to hide much. "More than one, so why bother with the tally?" The smile dropped away. "It's what I am, Jane. What I was molded to be."

Was there ever justification for such a foul and evil deed? Wetting her lips, she recalled the feel of the pistol in her hand, the recoil as the shot flew and found its mark in Gaby's flesh. She had shot him because he would have killed her. Was that justification?

"Would you have me beg a pretty pardon of you, Jane?" Aidan rasped. "Ask forgiveness when I am not sorry in the least?"

With her gaze locked on his, she battled her perplexity, her dismay, the turmoil in her heart that
pummeled her with vicious blows. How could
Aidan be both the villain and the hero?

She thought of another cold dawn, another day,
a woman dead at the far end of this very beach, and
she saw at least one clear certainty. "You did not kill
her. Ginny. You did *not* kill her."

"Do you ask me, or tell me?" He did not look at
her, instead staring out to the horizon, but she
heard the tension in his tone.

"Tell you," she said, and his breath hissed from
between his teeth. She studied the clean, handsome
line of his profile and felt a cool assurance. "I am
certain of it. Whatever, whoever, decided Ginny's
miserable fate, 'twas not you."

She slipped her hand into his. He did nothing
for a long moment, and then, finally, his fingers
closed tight about hers.

"It matters not, Jane." He sounded infinitely
tired. "I am still exactly the man I was before you
reached that conclusion. My soul is still muddied,
my heart shriveled and black as coal."

Yes, she knew that.

And still she held her fingers laced with his.

Jane could not say how or when they returned to
Trevisham. The journey was a great blur of chattering teeth and shivering muscles. Having offered his
coach and the wagons as transport for the servants
and the survivors, Aidan pulled Jane up before him
on a great black beast that tossed its head and
pawed the ground impatiently. And then they were
away, riding through the bitter night, her back

pressed to his chest and the both of them wrapped in a dry blanket.

She could not imagine how he found the strength to hold himself astride, but he did, his body a hard wall at her back.

At Trevisham, he tossed the reins to a groom, and helped Jane down from the horse's back. She had taken only three halting, agonized steps, her aching limb threatening to dissolve out from under her, when he muttered a soft oath. Sweeping her into his arms, he strode through the house to her chamber and bellowed for a hot bath to be brought straight away.

He lit candles and stoked the flame in the hearth until it crackled and roared with blessed warmth, the lord of the manner doing the tasks of a servant. He appeared indifferent to the oddity.

In a short time, two young lads with sleep-tousled hair and bleary eyes brought the copper tub and poured steaming water from wooden buckets. Jane sidled closer to the fire, and stared longingly at the water, knowing it would go far toward easing the ache in her leg. The servants withdrew. She waited for Aidan to go as well, and then sucked in a startled breath as he stepped toward her.

Nervously, she worried her lower lip between her teeth, far too aware of the width of his shoulders, the height of him as he towered over her. His waistcoat was gone, shucked at the beach and never retrieved. He stood before her in shirtsleeves stiffened by salt and brine, dried by the wind. She could smell the ocean on him, though she must surely carry the scent as well.

Tipping her head back, she looked up at his face, at the hard planes kissed by firelight. His long hair fell in unkempt snarls, darkened by the touch of salt and sea. A fine gold stubble glinted on his jaw.

Exhaustion did nothing to dull his allure—not the shadows beneath his eyes, or the lines etched to bracket his mouth. He was elegant, sculpted lines, gilded gold.

He was unbearably beautiful.

"The tub is huge," she murmured, then glanced away, wondering if perhaps she might have chosen a different topic of conversation.

"I had it made that way. A reminder of my fortunate end." There was sarcasm there, a faint ugly edge.

"I do not understand."

"There was a time when I was lucky for a splash of salt water on my skin. I vowed that if I ever had the good fortune of success, I would commission a tub as large as the one that lives in the memories of my childhood." He gave a careless shrug. "Of course, to a small child, a tub appears far larger than it truly is."

For a moment, she said nothing, overwhelmed by the information he had shared. Those frugal sentences revealed so much. A privileged childhood. A harsh youth. What exactly had made him into Aidan Warrick, the man?

The only sound was the tick of the mantel clock counting the seconds. Grasping the edges of her cloak, he undid the frogs that held it closed, his movements spare and intent. She trembled, her breath catching.

"Jane." Her name was a command, bidding her to draw near.

"Go," she whispered raggedly, raising her eyes to his as he dropped her cloak to the ground. She sensed that his actions held a particular meaning. "You must go and take off your own damp things before you catch the ague."

He stood mere inches from her. She could feel

the tightly leashed energy that coursed through him despite the trials and tribulations of the night.

His hard mouth curved in a half smile. "I will take them off here, sweet Jane. Or you may peel them from me, if that is your preference."

She gasped at the image conjured by his softly spoken words, at the touch of his hands as he cupped her face and leaned in until his lips brushed her mouth. She stopped breathing, wanting to press herself full against him and open her mouth and take his tongue as he had taught her. His fingers stroked her jaw, her throat, before coming to rest on her collarbone, leaving a trail of tingling awareness.

"Unless you bid me go." His gaze locked with hers. "And Jane, know that if you send me away, I *will* leave. The choice is yours."

Choice. Once before, he had reminded her that the choice to accompany him had been hers. Now, he left the decision of intimacy to her. On a night saturated with death, he offered her a moment to taste life.

"You have only to stand close to me, and my blood begins to sing," she whispered, her breathing swift and uneven. "Where is the choice in that?"

His pupils dilated, dark pools surrounded by a bright band of gray and blue, glittering in the firelight. Sinking his fingers into her hair, he tilted her head, and when his lips met hers once more it was no tender kiss, but an open-mouthed claiming that sucked her into a vortex of need with uncompromising speed. She moaned as his tongue swept into her mouth, tasting her, stroking her, fulfilling the secret wish of her heart. He kissed her with intensity, with focus, and she felt as though she was his entire world in that one hot, wild moment.

"My God. You make me want to feast on you, taste every sweet inch of your body," he rasped.

He captured her mouth once more. Her skin was awash in shimmering sensitivity, every stroke of his palm, every touch of his fingers making her weak with an aching desire that clenched low in her belly and shot through her limbs with near painful force. His fingers moved to the buttons of her dress, undoing them one by one.

Her breasts seemed to swell against the cloth, to strain for his touch.

Curving her hands about his hard shoulders, she reveled in the feel of his powerful frame, strong and solid. She leaned into him, the movement bringing her weight onto her damaged leg. A terrible wrenching pain shot from her knee to her thigh, and with a cry, she stumbled, crumbling to the floor, one hand clutched to her now gaping bodice.

A dreadful realization stole over her. Whatever his reason for wanting her, she did not doubt the sincerity of it. But she doubted the likelihood that his passion would withstand the sight of her misshapen limb. Tears pricked her eyes as he hunkered down next to her, his expression one of concern.

"Your leg, sweet? Here, let me work the stiffness from the joint." His fingers grasped the hem of her dress, and he began to pull it up.

The thought that he would look upon her flawed limb was too much for her, he whose face and form surpassed perfection. Insecurity gnawed at her, her emotions strummed to a knife-edged volatility, and she knew that she would not survive the look of repugnance that would surely twist his features when he saw the ugliness beneath her skirt. Tears trickled down her cheeks as she frantically pushed at his hands, desperate to stop him from seeing her secret horror.

"Jane!" He rocked back on his heels, withdrawing his hands, his expression one of confusion. "Did I hurt you?"

She scuttled away from him, shaking her head wildly from side to side. "No," she whispered.

There was hurt and perplexity in his gaze, and she was stunned to realize that her rejection caused him pain.

With fluid grace, he rose to his feet, giving a sharp nod. "Very well. I promised to go, and go I shall." He strode toward the door, then paused and spoke without facing her, his voice low and rough. "Once again I must ask that you forgive my trespass."

Jane's heart fractured at his words. She had wounded him without meaning to, but how to explain—

"Wait!" she cried. "There is no trespass to forgive!" Dragging in a fortifying breath, she continued, "The fault is mine."

Slowly, he turned to face her. The candlelight cast his face in a flickering glow, highlighting cheeks and brow and jaw, accentuating his rugged beauty. He studied her with a cool and distant smile, in control now, his mask firmly in place. All this Jane saw, and it only served to convince her that he would surely find her lacking.

Odd, that she had never before thought of herself as a woman of insecurity, never considered herself so faint of heart. Now, faced with the burning desire of this man, her dark prince of shadows for all his golden beauty, she had never regretted her imperfection more, for he would surely find her defect repugnant.

He took one step toward her, hands fisted at his

sides, and the mask slipped just a little. "Tell me why you bid me go when your eyes plead that I stay."

Tears clogged her throat, but she refused to let them force her silence. Better to end this now, end her foolish fantasies and tell him the truth. Lord, could he not see, did he not know that her limping gait was caused by some terrible anatomic flaw?

"I am not perfect." The words came out flat and hard.

He blinked. "And?"

She stared at him for an endless moment while the fire crackled in the hearth and the wind rattled the windowpanes. "And you are. Perfect." She looked away. "I will surely repulse you."

In an instant he closed the distance between them, hunkering down before her once more. "Look at me, Jane," he commanded.

As she turned her face to him, he stroked her cheek.

"Listen to me, sweet." Slowly, he raised his fingers to the lacings of his shirt, but the knots had dried tight. With a snarl, he grasped the edges and tore through the lot, so the cloth hung open revealing the elegant planes of his chest, the ridges of his belly.

She stared at the smooth expanse of skin, and the thin line of hair that arrowed down his taut abdomen to disappear into the waistband of his breeches.

"Listen to me, Jane," he said again. "You think me perfect. Me? I stole you from your home, dragged you into danger not once, but twice, nearly costing your life." With an impatient gesture, he raked the snarled strands of hair back from his face. "I offer no excuse for what I am—smuggler, privateer, pirate—name me what you will. And you dare call me perfect?"

Her breath came fast and harsh, for in his gaze she yet read his desire, the sharply honed lust that he made no effort to conceal.

"You think I will find you repugnant?" He gave a strangled laugh. "Hardly that. You are strong and brave and beautiful, my Jane."

She shook her head.

"No one is perfect." He rose to his feet, towering over her, and she could not take her eyes from him as he drew his ruined shirt first from one shoulder, then the other, before letting it slide from his fingers with a soft swish to puddle on the floor. "Everyone bears scars, some more noticeable than others." A strange, sad half-smile curved his lips. And then he turned his back to her.

She cried out at the sight of him, unable to stop herself. His back was a hideous meshwork of scars, raised ridges of angry puckered skin that crisscrossed with ruthless precision, as though someone had flayed the flesh from his back, right down to the bone, then shoved it back in place with cruel and uncaring hands.

The flickering light of the candles only accentuated the shadows and hollows. She could not imagine the pain he had endured.

A fresh surge of horror buffeted her as she realized that the scars were long healed, that this torture had been carried out many years ago, that some unspeakably evil soul had inflicted this cruelty on a child.

"Who did this to you?" She could barely breathe, so great was her rage, so intense her anger at the perpetrator of such a heinous crime. "*Who did this to you?*"

He turned to face her then, and in his eyes she read her answer.

"No," she moaned, wrapping her arms about herself. Not her father. Not *her father.*

Aidan met her gaze, and when he spoke, his voice was cold and flat as the stone face of Kilmar Tor. "It was another's hand that wielded the whip upon my back, but your father placed these marks upon my soul. Gideon Heatherington condemned me to hell, and like as not, he wishes I had extended my visit there and stayed to act as right hand to the devil."

A sob caught in her throat. If he truly believed what he said, then there was no mystery in his grave hatred of her father, no secret to his enmity. The mystery was his kindness to *her*, his enemy's daughter.

She stared up at him where he towered over her, reading so much in his bleak expression, even as she read nothing. The light of the candles haloed him, touching his hair, his skin.

"How can you look at me?" she whispered. "How can you bear to even be near me?"

"You are not him," he said simply, without the slightest hesitation. "You are . . . *you*. Bright light to my darkness. The promise of dawn in my endless night."

Jane stared up at him, the pain in her heart so great, she wondered how she might survive it. He opened his mouth and she thought he would say more. Instead, with a soft oath, he bent and pulled her to her feet, quickly divesting her of her damp dress, tearing it in his haste.

Her protest drew a snarl. "I will buy you a dozen to replace it. A score."

Shivering, clothed in only her shift, she watched him warily as he tossed her shredded garment aside.

"The bath grows cold," he muttered. Scooping her unceremoniously into his arms, he deposited her in the tub, shift and all. The water cocooned her in steaming warmth, a luxury that made her moan softly.

As he made to draw away, she closed her fingers around the sinew and strength of his forearm. Their gazes met and held, his cool and distant, hers, she knew, relaying every emotion that surged in her breast, giving clear view of her confusion and pain. Her empathy. Perhaps even her love.

Oh, God, no. Not that. Could she have fallen in love with Aidan Warrick, the pirate, the smuggler, the man whose every breath was taken solely so that he could achieve the vengeance he craved? Aidan Warrick, the man who doffed his coat and wrapped her in its warm folds on a cold night . . . who dove into the gray morass of the sucking tide to drag a child from the embrace of death itself?

He had killed to keep her safe.

He looked at her with heated desire, never seeing her as a woman defined by her twisted limb.

No friend could be as true as this man, her enemy. Dear God, was there no ease to her confusion?

The candlelight licked the hard planes of his chest, the ridged terrain of his firm belly. She knew now the physical scars he bore, and suspected what marks he carried on his soul, yet, to her, he was unutterably magnificent. Not flawed in her eyes. Perfect. She saw only his splendor, and the affection and esteem he had shown her. And for the first time since that long ago evening when she had tarried too long and walked home too late, when a stranger had stolen her youth, her naivete, left her lame and motherless, she saw herself as whole and strong and brave.

For that was how Aidan saw her, and through his eyes, she had glimpsed the truth. She had been shaped by her past, but she was not defined by it. Now, if she could only help him to understand that same thing.

"Ah, Jane, 'tis best I go," he rasped, taking a step back.

"No. 'Tis best you stay. Here. With me." The words were out before she could think to stop them, and once they were free, she could find no will to call them back.

His gaze locked on hers, he nodded slowly. "Be certain, sweet. There is no going back." Bracing his hands on either side of the tub, he leaned close, studying her, his expression taut, and then he let his gaze roam lower, to her body so barely covered by the clinging wet cloth of her shift.

His slow regard left molten heat each place it rested.

"No going back," she whispered, reaching up to cup his cheeks. "Only forward, Aidan." *My love. My love.* "We go forward."

Arching up, she pressed her mouth to his.

Chapter 13

Jane kissed him with all the emotion in her heart, and all the passion that had built through so many days of heated looks and fleeting touches. Aidan's response was immediate, his arms like living metal, banding her, half lifting her from the tub as his mouth opened over hers and his tongue stroked and tasted, a low masculine sound of pleasure coming from deep in his throat.

"This tub will hold two," she whispered, unsure where the thought came from, but certain that she wanted him there in the warm, scented water, skin to wet skin, rubbing against her. The image made a tight coil of heat twist deep inside her.

Where had her exhaustion gone? She felt alive and awake, her body strummed to heightened awareness.

He laughed, the sound rich with promise, curling around her and through her and coming to rest at the juncture of her thighs in a steady pulse.

She looked away as his hands went to the waistband of his breeches then, seduced by curiosity, she looked back to find him naked, tall and lean, muscled and beautiful. Her gaze lingered on the jutting fullness of him, thick, long, and she wet her lips, half fascinated, half cautious.

"Scoot forward, sweet," he instructed, his voice mellow and sure.

Jane did as he bid, closing her eyes as she felt him step into the tub behind her. The hairs of his legs brushed the skin of her shoulders, and she shivered at the touch. Water sloshed up and over the sides of the tub, crested over the peaks of her breasts, lapping at her skin and leaving her painfully aware of her body and of the aching need deep inside. As he settled behind her, she moved in the warm water, leaning back, rubbing slowly against the solid wall of his chest.

"This shift must go," he said, and ran his finger along the edge of her wet chemise. "I would have you naked in my arms." The low words were a bare warning. He twined his strong fingers through the cloth and tore it sharply, his movements sending the water sloshing once more.

She made a murmured sound of protest, but he wrapped one arm around her and lay his hand flat to span her collarbone. He trailed his fingers to the pulse that beat a hard rhythm in her neck, and finally up to her lips. The pleasure of his touch rippled through her. "I'll buy you a dozen shifts," he whispered, his breath warm against her shoulder. "Nay, two dozen. Three. Gowns. Jewels. Anything and everything your heart desires."

"I do not need that." *I need only you. You are my heart's desire.*

She moved her head back and forth, rubbing her mouth on his finger, opening her lips to run her tongue along the length of it, nipping, sucking, driven by instinct and pure undiluted wanting, driven to suck and bite, and to rock back against the hard prod of him that pushed insistently against her buttocks. He was goading her to madness with each slow swipe of his fingertip across her lower lip, and with the feel of him, hard and thick and full against the small of her back.

She shivered as he took up the soap and began to wash her, his hands strong and sure, his breath warm on the back of her neck. For a moment she felt terribly uncertain, inexperience leaving her lost in the pulsing tide of her escalating desire. He nipped her shoulder and lost the soap when she jumped, leaving them both laughing as he searched for his slippery prey, and then leaving her gasping while his soapy hands caressed her breasts, lightly, then a little harder, her nipples between his fingers as he coaxed and pinched. Her head rolled from side to side, and small gasping moans escaped her lips.

A low chuckle rumbled in his chest. He skimmed her waist, the column of her neck. She curved into his touch, nearly crying out in frustration as his hands moved to her shoulders, her arms in soap-slick caress. And then he slid his fingers lower to tease her beneath the water with a lush stroke to parts of her that felt hot and full with need, building her desire to a sharp-edged pleasure that bordered on pain.

Her breath stopped. Her heart stopped. He moved his hand away and she moaned and rolled her hips, a sinuous undulation.

"Touch me there. Again." She arched her back, wanting his hands between her legs and on her breasts once more.

Perverse man, gliding his fingers along her waist when all she wanted was for him to touch her swollen nipples, to stroke them and pinch them, and to caress her between her thighs as he had a moment past. He washed her hair, her skin, all parts of her except for those that throbbed with a frantic ache. His every action was a sweet torment as he teased her and stoked her fevered sensibility with clear and finely honed intent, drawing the circle of her pleasure ever tighter, ever stronger with his slow seduction.

She was left shaking with the power of her yearning.

Squirming, she managed to turn within the tub, and then sucked in a sharp breath as a pang wrenched her twisted limb.

"Wait," Aidan whispered, grasping her hips and settling her more comfortably, until she faced him with her thighs spread across his, her crippled leg cushioned on his own.

He bared his teeth, a smile that was not a smile, hard, rapacious. Yanking her closer, he opened his mouth on hers. Oh, God, the taste of him, the feel of his tongue twining and taking, his teeth grazing her, biting the full flesh of her lower lip, spiraling her to madness. She followed his tutelage and did the same to him, rewarded with the rough sound of his pleasure.

The pounding of his heart and the harshness of each breath gave him away. His control was hard won, his body taut with feral need. She did that to him. Dragged him to the brink.

Taking up the soap, she did for him as he had done for her, lathering the hard planes of him, teasing, tormenting. His chest. His taut belly, and lower, letting her fingers close around the thick, smooth length of his arousal as she followed instinct and imagination, stroking and touching, changing her speed and pressure as a sharp hiss of pleasure or a harsh groan guided her touch.

With a growl, he closed his arms around her and rose from the tub, water rolling from them both in a thick curtain.

He brought her tight against his chest and dropped them both to the bed, his body coming hard atop her.

Whispered words of heat and need, she knew she spoke, but for the life of her she knew not what she said. Set aflame, set free, she turned her face into his neck, licking and biting and sucking until he hissed and pulled back and claimed her with wet, open-mouthed caresses, working his way down her neck, her collarbone, her breast, to close his mouth around her nipple and draw deep.

"Oh-h-h-h!" The breathy cry was no release, for the tug of his mouth on the sensitive peak—more than pleasure, not quite pain—drew her deeper into the dizzying spiral. She moved her hips, wriggling, pumping, straining without conscious thought to bring him closer still. He laughed, a dark sound of sensual abandon.

Positioning himself between her thighs, he rubbed the head of his shaft against her, wide and hot, sliding into her and pulling back, shallow pulses, stretching her. With each thrust she felt a burning, slick glide that was light and dark, sore and not. The careful rhythm and depth were not enough. With instinct born of femininity she angled her hips toward him, wanting more, wanting all of him deep inside her.

One thrust, strong and sure, and he took what she offered, breaching the last barriers of her body and her heart. She cried out in surprise, but not true pain, for it was a momentary twist, a pinch, nothing more.

Full, so full. She was nothing but keen sensation and blazing agitation, wanting, needing.

He reared back, watched her, moved just a little, and she clenched her fingers in the muscles of his buttocks as pleasure scored her.

No wonder he had wanted this, had watched her with heated gaze and sharp-edged lust.

Reaching between them, he stroked her, drawing a gasp of surprise, a moan of delight. He began to move, a little rough, until she thought she would die of it, this tense ecstasy that made her gasp and cry out. Faster, deeper he went, and Jane surged to meet each thrust, reveling in the feel of sinew and strength as he flexed above her.

The harsh rasp of his breath inflamed her.

The tension inside her coiled tighter on itself, and she writhed and gasped, breathless, if she could just—

Teeth bared, he came into her, again, again. He lowered his head, took her nipple in his mouth, sucking on her with terse, strong tugs and he pushed himself deeper than she had thought possible.

He nipped her and she splintered apart, bright light and swirling heat.

He withdrew, thrust deep, and she felt him throbbing inside her, with her, his body motionless now above her, his head thrown back. The surge of sensation stole her breath, her mind, her sanity, and every part of her pulsed in perfect synchrony with him for a frozen moment when all and everything was only jagged hot delight, her release and his melding to one.

Finally, finally, she tumbled down a long and sloping hill to reach the ground once more. She curled her fingers into the muscled expanse of his back, felt the ridged scars beneath her fingers.

He was what life had made him, forged in fires of pain and grief and secret tragedy, dragged through by the pure strength of his will.

And he was hers, she thought fiercely.

Hers.

Jane came awake to the feel of warm, hard man draped around her body. Sunlight streamed through the window, painting the walls and floor with a bright glow. She thought it must be well past noon. Closing her eyes, she searched her soul for purity of emotion. There was no pang of shame or guilt. She smiled, feeling at peace with herself, wondering how that could be so. She had breached all bounds of propriety, all bounds of good sense. ✿

She had found joy. Love. She froze, that realization sending her heart tripping at an erratic pace and denial coursing through her. What value love, if it was felt by only one? What danger love, if unrequited? She knew better than to love him.

"A frown, sweet?" Aidan nuzzled her neck, the rough scrape of his stubbled jaw making her laugh. "Better," he said. "Better your laughter than your frown. I would hear your laughter always."

She rolled to her side, staring deep into his eyes. "Only a fool laughs all the time."

Catching a wisp of her dark hair, he smoothed it back from her face. "You are no fool, Jane."

Such a strange undercurrent to his words, perhaps concern, or a guarded caution. "Am I not?" she whispered. "Am I not the greatest fool for thinking—" She pressed her lips together, holding fast to the words before they tumbled free.

He waited for her to continue, his changeable eyes narrowed in thought, and when she said nothing more he frowned. "Regrets already, love?"

Love. He called her love. A carelessly tossed word with no true meaning.

"No regrets." That much was true. She would never regret the hours of pure and true beauty she had found in his arms, the delight he had given her, the gift she had bestowed on him, her innocence, such that it was. "No, Aidan, I have no regrets."

He smiled then, and when he did, she realized how taut his lips had been, recognized the easing of the tension that had etched fine lines to bracket eyes and mouth. Her answer had mattered greatly. The insight startled her, and warmed her, and filled her heart with hope.

"You were wonderful last night," she whispered.

Surprise flashed in his eyes. "Why, thank you, sweet."

"Oh, dear." She gasped, suddenly aware of how he had construed her remark. "No. Not that! I meant on the beach. When you saved that child. All those people. I never meant your lovemaking—"

"My lovemaking was not wonderful?" His lips twitched, the whisper of a smile. "I am desolate . . . Here, let me try again. . . ."

Lighthearted. She had not thought it possible for him to be so.

With a shift of his weight, he rolled her beneath him, his hand skimming lightly along the curve of her waist, the flare of her hip.

He was laughing now. She could feel his body shaking against hers with his mirth.

"Insufferable," she whispered, but she knew her tone lacked conviction. She was so very glad to see him smile, to hear him laugh. Unbidden came the memory of him on the Bodmin Road, when he had told her that he thought he had forgotten how to laugh. She had brought him this.

"Aidan, you are a true hero. You saved so many lives."

With a sigh, he shook his head and gently stroked her cheek. "Do not color me with a wash of light and glory, Jane. If I could truly wear the badge of honor you would give me, I would be a far better man than the one I am."

"You risked your life for others," she pointed out.

"But nothing can erase the sins of my past, sweet, or make up for the lives I have taken." Dark words, spoken in toneless litany. Terrible words. "Nor can it erase the fact that I lack any remorse."

A sudden chill crawled across her skin. She knew he had killed, knew he had shot Gaby on the Bodmin Road. But that had been in defense of her life. She had not wanted to think about his reasons for killing others. How many others? She wanted to believe that however many he had killed, he had had no choice, had harmed no innocents.

"I know you dream, Jane. No sweet slumber, restful and kind, but a dark and tormented pit that yawns wide beneath you." A statement, not a question. She made no reply, and certainly no denial. Yes, he knew the demons that chased her in the night. He had held her close as she faced them down.

"I, too, have dreams, love," he continued in his smoke and brandy voice. "I wake with sweat pouring down my back, and I remember. Not just the bite of the lash, or his terrible laughter as he wielded it. I remember the feel of my hands around his throat, the crack of breaking bone, and the dreadful surge of satisfaction when he finally stopped thrashing. Nay, not remember. I live it again and again, and, Jane, I cannot force myself to feel regret for it."

"Aidan." Her every emotion laced that one whispered word. What she would not give to erase his pain.

Something flickered in his gaze, perhaps recognition of the feelings she could barely bring herself to acknowledge. When he spoke at last, his voice was low and dull, little more than a whisper. "They are there, waiting for me, their eyes dark, endless caverns, their souls, if ever they had such, long departed." He looked at his hands. "Did you think Gaby was the first?"

She made an inarticulate sound of sympathy. With a snarl, Aidan rolled away from her and surged to his feet, naked, feral. Crossing to the far side of the room, he pressed one palm against the wall, back bowed, head hanging forward. His shoulders fell, then lifted as he blew out a rapid breath and then dragged air to his heaving lungs. Tears pricked her eyes for she longed to go to him, to soothe his pain.

But she knew not how.

"What torture is this that I should want the daughter of my enemy?" He glanced at her, a quick, desperate look. "That I am called to choose between my vengeance—that which kept me alive through years and trials that few would even wish to survive—and you, Jane. You soothe my raging heart." He paused then, and the silence stretched. Finally, he said in a voice laced with torment, "You offer me the first peace I can recall."

"Aidan," she whispered again, rising to cross the space that separated them, careful in each step for her leg was stiff and aching. She laid her cheek against his scarred back, pressing the palm of one hand to his warm skin. He smelled of the sun and the sea, of the soap from their bath, and of man, pure and clean.

He turned, wrapping her in his embrace, closing strong arms about her as though to protect her even from himself. Burying his face in the curve of her neck, he ran his nose along her throat and inhaled deeply.

"I was eleven years old," he began, his voice low and rough, "sailing on a ship much like the one that sank here last night. Only the ship I traveled on was not the victim of a storm, but rather the prey of wreckers."

The word made Jane's stomach churn. Wreckers. She swallowed, thinking of the twinkling lantern light she thought she had spied on the shore last evening. She could not see how to tell him, not now.

"I remember the shuddering groan of twisting, breaking timber, and the sick heave of the ship as it rolled. My mother gripped my hand so tight. I can still recall the way my bones pressed together sharply under her grasp. Of my father there was no sign. We were thrown into the waves, clinging like barnacles to a ragged splinter of wood that barely held us afloat. The shore came into sight, and on it was a fire. Its bright flame gave us hope."

Jane's thoughts turned to the fire they had built on the beach last night, the flames meant to provide life-giving heat to the survivors. But even before he said the words, she knew that the fire in

Aidan's memories had been meant for a different purpose.

"Then came the shapes of men running in the frothing surf," Aidan continued. "We were close upon them, my mother calling feebly for help, exhausted now, her teeth chattering with the cold . . . I remember the instant she realized they did not come to our rescue. My mother moved to shield me, begged them as they pried her hands from the wood and watched her struggle against the waves."

"Oh, God, Aidan." Jane clutched him about the waist, fearful that if she loosed her hold, she would also lose her control, and would sink to the ground, overcome by his suffering. He stroked her hair absently, his large hand moving in a gentle rhythm along the sleep-tangled tresses.

"She sank quite quickly, the black water closing over her head. I still did not understand that they had killed her." His tenor did not change, the cadence of his words flat and even, but inside, oh, inside, she knew his heart was battered by the memory. How could it not be when her own heart was near torn asunder by the image of the small boy alone in the frigid water, watching his mother taken by death?

She held that same memory, her own mother draped across the rocks, and later, her body, bloated and frightening, being dragged from the surf. A trembling took her.

"You are cold." With a frown, Aidan drew her back to the bed. "Let me wrap you in the blanket, sweet, before you catch a chill."

Even now, as he spoke of this terrible memory, his thoughts were for her. Her comfort. Her safety. She did not protest as he drew the thick quilts from the bed and set them about her shoulders, sinking with her onto the mattress and drawing her into the shelter of his embrace.

"How did you survive?" She could not imagine it, a little boy, battered and desolate, alone in the storm.

"One of the men caught me by the back of my shirt, lifted me from the water like a wet puppy. He dragged me up the cliff, to the very edge. I remember his size, a big man, and brawny. His face is lost to me, but I will never forget his voice. 'Do you swim, boy?' he asked." Aidan tightened his grip on her, and she felt his cheek against the top of her head.

"And then?" she whispered.

"I lied. The one time in my life I lied well. My mother's spirit governed my lips. 'No, sir' I said, and he threw me far out into the ocean as though I weighed no more than a feather. I remember the tug of the tide and the brutal waves. The cold ugly fear." He laughed, a harsh, dark sound devoid of mirth. "I was soon to learn that I knew not the meaning of fear."

She wanted to take it away, the pain, the horror. She would gladly suffer the bite of that fear herself, if only she could take away his agony. And in that moment, she knew, her heart swelling inside of her, her depth of emotion increased with each word he spoke, any hope of denial cast aside. She *did* love Aidan Warrick, smuggler, pirate, little boy lost. Loved him with a fierce and true strength that terrified her, for only tragedy could come of loving a man so dangerous, so certain and cruel in his intent. He would hurt her without meaning to.

And, without meaning to, she would let him.

"I cannot forfeit my vengeance, Jane." His assertion gave voice to her thoughts, her fears.

"You speak of vengeance, yet your story holds nothing of a reason for your hatred of my father." Clutching the quilts tight about her, she sat back and studied him, determined to hear the whole of it, nurturing the seed of hope that she might yet turn aside his singular purpose.

He hesitated. "Why must you know?"

Incredulous, she stared at him. "Why? You mean to destroy my father, my only family, and you ask why I would know the reason?"

"I would spare you this knowledge."

"Then spare my father," she whispered, knowing the futility of her request but hoping, hoping, that he might relent.

His expression hardened. "I was plucked from the waves by a passing ship, one that ran French brandy and pilfered silk, and within a day, the excise men arrested all those aboard. The captain told the very truth, that I was a lad pulled half-drowned from the waves. But there was a revenue man determined to believe what he would. In his mind I was cabin-boy to a pirate, and he would hear no other possibility."

Jane stared at him, mute with dismay. She had known her father was not always an innkeeper, and suddenly, now she knew what he had done in the time before. Her father had been the excise man Aidan spoke of.

"He saw me sent to the hulks," Aidan said.

The hulks. Prison ships that adult men barely survived. She knew the rumors of what they did to men on the hulks, and she knew that those who sur-

vived often came back with their will broken and
their wits gone.

Her father had condemned a child to hell. A
child, who had grown to become *this* man, filled with
anger and hate. Dear Lord, she could not bear the
weight of it.

"I twined my hand in his coat, begging him on my
knees, and he kicked me aside like a dog. 'Twas the
last I begged of any man." He ran his hand along the
tangled length of her hair, a gentle stroke that left
her feeling bereft and confused, his tenderness at
terrible odds with his icy tone and the story he told.
"And suddenly I knew his voice, that excise man; I
heard it in my nightmares. Some nights, I still do."

He was silent for a moment, and she could feel
her heart slamming against her ribs. Each beat
prefaced the next, harder, stronger, and she could
not breathe, could not move. She knew, oh, God,
she knew—

His gaze locked with hers. "That voice asking if I
knew how to swim."

The pain was terrible, sharp-taloned and deep,
as though a blade stabbed to her core, twisting to
the right and the left. *Her father. Her father.* Memories assaulted her, recollections of his drunken
ramblings, words that suddenly fit this horror
when pieced together in an unbroken chain, and
the endless excuses she had built in her mind. But
this . . . this . . .

Salty tears welled in her eyes. "My God, what you
suffered . . . because of my father . . ." She stared at
him in utter desolation, a deep, dark anguish pressing on her heart. "I thought he was a good man. A
good father . . ." She said the words and tried to

mean them, yet she no longer doubted that Aidan had known a different man, hated a different man.

She felt battered, bruised, dizzy with the strength of her devastation, and yes, her anger.

"A good father . . ." He nodded. "Let me tell you of such a one. My father survived the wreck and spent his life searching for me, traveling from country to country in pursuit of a phantom, the son he refused to believe was lost to him. His lungs were weak, I learned, and he hacked and coughed until his life slipped away. He died still dreaming that he would find me."

Something ominous and sinister whispered through her, and she knew his tale was yet to end. There was worse to come, and she held up one hand, half wishing that he would spare her, though in truth she would not rest until she knew the whole of it.

"My father died the day before my feet touched English soil, one day before I made my way to his door. The twenty-fifth of July, 1802. I survived that damned prison ship and then a pirate's sloop for endless, stinking years only to be damned to a different hell on my return. My father died without ever seeing my face again, and as I looked upon him, cold in death, with his one hope unrequited, I swore there was no forgiveness in my soul. I vowed on my father's corpse, on my mother's memory, that Gideon Heatherington would pay for the marks on my back and the hate in my heart, and then pay double for my father's wasted life."

There. The end of the tale, and an ending more terrible and tragic than ever she could have imagined. She was too horrified to cry, though she thought that her heart wept tears of blood and pain for what he had suffered. He could be barely more than thirty, and he had lived enough torment to weigh down ten lifetimes.

Reason had no part in her actions then. Had she the will to deny her heart, logic dictated that she run far and away from this man before he tore her soul to shreds. Instead, she reached for him, resting her palms on either side of his beard-shadowed jaw and pressing her mouth to the hard, unyielding line of his lips.

"Mine," she whispered. "Your pain is mine. The boy you were, the man you are, I take all into my heart."

He jerked back and caught her wrists, his eyes shadowed and dangerous as he stared down at her. "I will not yield in this, Jane."

"And I will not cease my efforts to sway you." Oddly, she felt no fear. He would never hurt her apurpose; that she knew as a certainty. Nay, he would hurt her without distinct intent, an offshoot in small part of the harm he would cause her father, and in greater part, the harm he would cause himself.

She *knew* that his success would not earn him peace. He could kill her father in a dozen different ways, and still it would not grant him peace.

Just as the smuggler's death here in Pentreath those many years ago had not eased her own torment. So he had died. Drowned. His death had changed nothing, given her back none of the things he had stolen. There had been no comfort in it.

Aidan's gaze shifted to her mouth, and she saw the flare of heat and need in his eyes. He loosed his hold on her wrists, and she let her hands fall to her lap.

"This was never my intent, to catch you up in my

hate. I meant only to take you from harm's path, to see you—the only innocent in this sordid play—safe from the consequences of your father's actions, safe here in my home." He shook his head. "I should set you free, send you away." But he did not move.

Free. How long had she dreamed of being free, flying like the raven or running like the ponies that pounded across the moor? Somehow, she could not imagine leaving Aidan Warrick as any sort of freedom.

"Send me away, Aidan? Send me from you because you wish me gone, because you have done the deed and have no further use of me? Or because you fear your resolve will weaken?"

"My resolve will never weaken, sweet. It was hewn in a stinking pit, forged with my blood." He moved his hand with a sharp gesture of frustration.

She knew not what end there would be to this path she chose. Likely she would find naught save heartbreak and pain. Yet, in truth, she could not take any other road.

Wetting her lips, she spoke. "If one of us is to go, Aidan, it must be you who chooses to leave." She tried for a smile. "For you see, we are in *my* chamber."

With a sound part laugh, part groan, he caught her hand and pressed his lips to her palm. She could feel his small smile against her skin. "On this road lies madness."

She lifted her eyes and met his gaze. "A fine pairing, then. If we are both mad, neither shall notice the malady in the other."

Chapter 14

Aidan took her to the moor. Not to the deepest, most barren part of it, but to the edge, not so very far from Pentreath. He drove the carriage himself, so it was just the two of them, sitting shoulder-to-shoulder high on the driver's bench. Jane turned her face to the winter sun and the wind. With the beautiful cloak Aidan had given her about her shoulders and a blanket wrapped over her legs, she was warm. Happy.

Their pace was unhurried. He held the reins with ease and comfort, and she wondered at that.

"You are a puzzle," she said, watching the movement of his gloved hands, remembering the way he had touched her with those hands, stroked her, teased her. She blew out a quick breath.

"A puzzle? Why is that?"

"The way you are with horses. I would think it strange for a man of the sea." She glanced at him, at the hard masculine profile, softened only by dark gold-tipped lashes.

"I like to do things well," he said lazily. The smile he sent her was predatory, and yes, she believed he liked to do things well. That he demanded it of himself, in fact.

"Look." He pulled the carriage to a stop. Jane held the side of the seat as they rocked forward and back.

She followed his gaze and the line of his outstretched arm. There were wild ponies, almost a dozen, grazing in the distance. Two broke off from the rest and gamboled about in a wide circle. The sight made a lightness well up inside her and she laughed, easy and carefree.

Turning her head, she found Aidan watching her, his blue-gray eyes sparking with heat. "Your laughter. It fills me," he said.

"Fills you?" she asked playfully. "Like porridge?"

His brows rose, and then he nodded. "Yes, exactly."

A startled snort escaped her. She had not expected him to give quite that reply.

"Truly." He studied her, solemn now, intent. "When I was on the hulks, there was no food. If I was lucky, I caught a rat." She gasped, but he kept talking in that same calm, even tone. "I used to dream of porridge. Hot and warm, with sugar sprinkled overtop and a thick dollop of creamy yellow butter melting into a puddle." He lowered his lashes and tipped his face up to the sun. "I would have given anything for a bowl of that porridge, anything to taste it on my tongue and feel it warm my belly."

The lump that formed in her throat was hard and thick, and she blinked against the sting of tears. "I have never heard porridge made so appetizing."

"Exactly." He slanted her a half-lidded glance that made her breathe just a little faster.

"Do you still dream of porridge?" she asked.

In slow perusal his gaze slid to her lips, her breasts, and finally back to her eyes.

She swayed toward him.

"Ah, temptation." His chest expanded on a deep breath, and then he exhaled. "I want to show you something. But if you look at me like that, the only thing you will see is the inside of the carriage."

For a moment, she wondered at that.

"So that I might take a taste of you," he clarified.

"Oh." Heat unfurled in her veins.

"Yes, oh." His smile was purely wicked, dispelling any melancholy his earlier story had evoked.

"Come," he said, and swung lithely from the high seat before turning to stare up at her.

Jane scooted forward on the driver's bench until she was at the very edge. Climbing up had been an interesting experience. She wondered how she might get down.

"I will catch you."

For an instant she felt dizzy and the distance to the ground suddenly seemed very far. She looked up. The sun shone bright, a glowing disc against the undisturbed expanse of blue sky, warm on her face.

"Shall I trust you?" She looked down once more, breathless, the words coming in a rush, meaning far more than she had intended them to.

Silent, solid, he just stood there with his face upturned and his arms outstretched, waiting, waiting.

"Then catch me," she said, and let herself fall from the seat.

He did catch her, high against his chest, and then he turned her and let her slide the length of him. His palms skimmed along her arms. They were so close together, she could feel the steady beat of his heart. She tipped her head back, her gaze locked on his. One beat, two. A part of her was amazed that she had found the courage to suppose that he would not let her fall.

Was she terribly brave or terribly foolish to trust him so?

Lacing the fingers of one hand with hers, he drew her over, opened the door of the carriage, and reached in. When he turned back to her he held a leather device that looked a little like a horse's bridle, but not quite, with two leather hoops, one larger, one smaller, joined by thick leather bands and buckles, and soft red felt lining the whole of it.

"Here, this is what I wanted to show you." He shook the thing lightly so the buckles jangled. "Put it on."

She stared at him, completely confused. "Put it . . . on?" She shook her head. "On what?"

"On you." He smiled a little.

"I beg your pardon?" She glanced to the front of the carriage, at the horses' bridles and reins, and then she looked back at Aidan, appalled.

Reading her expression, he threw back his head and laughed. She loved the sound of that, and the knowledge that he thought it her gift to him.

"'Tis a splint, Jane. You told me that your leg gives way, that it folds out from beneath you. This will work, I think." He loosed his hold on her and spread the leather loops vertically with both his hands, so the larger circle was on top and the smaller on the bottom. "I wrote to London—to your Doctor Barker, in fact—when first I saw you. Oddly, he was unfamiliar with your case, but open with his advice once I explained what I could. I took his suggestions and added some modifications of my own."

Something in what he said puzzled her, something odd, but she couldn't place it, and her attention was riveted by the peculiar contraption he held.

"Do you see?" He shook the harness again. "I lined the leather with felt so your skin will not chafe, and here"—he poked at the bands connecting the two circles—"I reinforced the bands at the sides. Six layers of leather. Sturdy, yet flexible. I can add if needs must."

He lifted his head and caught her staring. She could only imagine how wide her eyes, how high her brows. Astonishment was too mild a term to call the emotion that surged through her. His smile began to fade.

"I believe it *will* work, Jane."

She stood there, trying to understand what he had done. For *her*. With his own two hands. Such a creation took time. Planning. Craftsmanship. He had begun it when first he *saw* her, before they had even met. She felt hot and cold as she reached out tentatively, her hand trembling, and took the harness from him.

"You made this—but how? When?" She turned it this way and that.

"Amazing, the skills I have learned in my lifetime. By necessity, I am deft with a needle"—he shrugged—"among other things."

Right handy with a knife is our Mr. Warrick. Digory Tubb's voice was clear in her mind.

Refusing to let such thoughts dim the day's sunshine, she walked to a low boulder, sat, and rucked up her skirt. She could feel Aidan watching her as she slid the strange harness around her leg and

buckled first the larger top ring about her thigh
and then the smaller bottom one about her calf.

"Like this?" she asked, raising her head.

At his nod, she went back to the fastenings, ad-
justing them until they were neither too tight nor
too loose. It felt strange—like two belts wrapped
about her leg—and a little stiff. Dropping her hem,
she rose.

"Can you bend your knee?" He leaned down and
touched the back of her thigh through her skirt,
running his fingers along the outline of the harness.
Even through the cloth, she felt the heat of him.

"Yes, I think so." She took a tentative step, then
another, stretching and working her damaged leg,
amazed that despite the oddness of the sensation,
the harness neither pinched her nor hampered her
movements. Instead, she felt a small confidence in
her own stability. With a startled laugh, she turned
a slow circle, head back, arms stretched wide.

Coming all the way around, she stopped and
watched as Aidan doffed his gloves and his greatcoat and tossed them in the carriage. His broad-
shouldered form was accentuated by the loose folds
of his fine lawn shirt and the trim outline of his
waistcoat. He took her cloak and folded it atop his
coat, leaving her with only her shawl about her
shoulders.

From the corner of her eye she saw a blur of
movement. Looking up, she found the herd of wild
ponies tearing across the moor, their short sturdy
legs churning the ground, their brown bodies glis-
tening in the sunlight.

*Do you dream of running free on the moors, Miss
Heatherington? Like the wild ponies?* Aidan's words

from what seemed a lifetime ago rang in her ears. Her gaze flew to his.

He had done this. Made this harness so she could run. *Run.* She was lightheaded with the enormity of it. "I thought it an impossible dream."

One corner of his mouth curved up. Slowly, he held out his hand. She stared at the broad palm, the strong fingers, desperately wanting to believe. Terrified to believe.

"Take my hand, love," he said, the rough texture of his voice sliding over her. "Run with the ponies as you do in your dreams. I will not let you fall."

She felt as though the world tilted on its side. The thunder of the horses' hooves pounded in her ears, mating with the wild thrumming of her blood. She wanted to do this so very desperately, to run wild and free for the first time in more than a decade, to feel the wind whip her hair and her lungs scream for breath.

"Yes." She wove her fingers firmly through his.

He smiled at her, a reckless grin that held nothing back. The sun caught the brightest glint in the thick strands of his hair, and the clear blue of the sky reflected in his eyes. Dazzled, she could only stare as the smile took years and cares from him, turning time back and making him the youth he must once have been.

Tightening his grasp, he began to walk—drawing her with him—then run, slowly at first, as she stumbled and struggled to find her rhythm, and faster, his firm grip giving her strength and balance, until he was no longer dragging her, but loping beside her, gifting her with an unbearably sweet taste of freedom.

Freedom.

Her lungs heaved and burned, her legs ached with unfamiliar strain, and oh, how she loved it. She knew that she was not graceful, that her gait was uneven, tortured, but she could not bring herself to care. They ran parallel to the herd, and she was released from her chains, flying like the raven as she had only in her fantasies and dreams.

The ponies quickly disappeared in the distance, and with their departure, Jane felt her strength wane. She slowed her pace, and finally stopped, her chest heaving, her heart banging against her breastbone like a drum.

Leaning forward, she rested her hands on her thighs as she dragged great gasps of air into her belabored lungs. Finally, the frantic rhythm of her heart slowed, the painful gasps fell into a smooth pattern. Breathe in, breathe out.

She dropped her arms to her sides and straightened, noting that Aidan was not winded; his chest rose and fell at a slow, steady pace.

"Walk it off, Jane," he said, and drew her back the way they had come. "Else you will cramp."

She did as he bid for a bit. As they approached the carriage, she stopped and stared at the man who stood watching her in silence.

"Oh, look what you did for me, Aidan!" she cried. "Look what you did. You cannot know . . ." Her voice trailed away at his expression.

"But I do know, Jane," he said, his gravelly voice flowing with an odd, almost melancholy cadence. "I do know what it is to dream of running free." He paused, looked away, and then let his gaze slide back to rest on her once more. "I would see your dreams come true, sweet."

Words tumbled against each other, twining in a

coiled jumble. With an inarticulate sound, she spun closer to frame his face with her palms, feeling his skin and the rough stubble of his jaw. She looked into his eyes, his beautiful gray-blue eyes, bright now with satisfaction, and she kissed him soundly on the mouth before spinning away with a laugh. Then she stood there looking at him, smiling, feeling as though he had gifted her with the moon and the stars.

"Pretty, pretty girl," he murmured. "With your cheeks flushed and your eyes sparkling." He stepped closer, his expression changing. "I like the way you look at me, as though I made the sun rise and set. Will you always look at me like that, Jane?"

Yes, yes, yes.

Another step, and another, he crowded her, all grace and lithe power. On instinct she retreated, feeling the air shimmer with a new tension. Her back bumped against the side of the carriage and it rocked lightly on its high wheels. She felt hot and flushed and giddy, though whether from the unfamiliar exertion or the heat of Aidan's heavy-lidded gaze, she could not say.

Catching her arm, he pulled her to him and sealed his mouth over hers, no sweet kiss, but a hard and open-mouthed taking. His lips were cold from the wind, and her own as well, but his tongue was hot, and the taste of him made her moan. She twisted the fabric of his shirt in her hands; the sculpted mass of his shoulders shifted beneath her fingers.

A shuffling step, in tandem they moved, and then his weight came upon her, pressing her back to the carriage. The kiss became darker, more demanding, and the wild thrum of her pulse grew apace. She felt as though she was running again, dizzy with it, the urgency of his touch driving her. Her dress came undone under his deft fingers; her bodice gaped.

He shifted, moving his lips to the column of her neck. The wet trace of his tongue made her shiver, lower, lower. Tugging the cloth aside, he closed his mouth around her nipple, sucking gently, then harder, a swirl of tongue, the nip of his teeth, until she was panting, her hands tangled in his hair, her back arched to offer herself more freely.

Need streaked through her, finding a home deep inside, gathering at the juncture of her thighs, throbbing and tense. She moaned as he dragged her skirt up, his palm sliding along the skin of her thigh and higher, finding the moist, hot folds of her sex, probing, stroking.

She shifted her hips, an undulating rhythm, her head falling back again the side of the carriage, her limbs trembling.

"We cannot—" She sucked in a sharp breath as his fingers slid over the most sensitive part of her.

"We are alone." His tongue traced up her neck, and she felt him free himself from his breeches, a hard jutting ridge, so tempting as he swayed against her.

She knew him now, knew the scent of his skin, and the taste of him, the honey-brown hair on his chest and the line that traced down his belly to nest at the base of his thick shaft. She knew the secrets of his pain, the sounds he made in ecstasy. That knowing made her want him all the more.

Wild, delicious anticipation and the pulsing heat of desire spun in a tight coil, so intense it took her breath. His kiss was potent, deep and wet.

Beneath her hand she could feel the flex of

muscle, the coiled tension, the strength of him, power and barely leashed hunger. She wanted to sever the last of his control, to make him lose himself in the wanting as she was lost. Closing her hand about his shaft, she followed the smooth contours, the thick head, the silky skin, her caress eager and a little rough. He sucked in a short breath and froze against her.

She wanted this, wanted to feel him inside her. Here, under the sky and sun, fierce, untamed.

With a growl, he yanked her skirt higher to bunch at her waist, and pushed his fingers up into her, stretching her, the heel of his palm pressing her until she moaned and squirmed, one hand tight around the hot length of him, the other clutching his shoulder, her fingers biting deep.

He was not civilized or careful. He was raw. Uncouth.

And she was mindless with the thrill of it, the feral, staggering hunger.

Moving her mouth to the base of his neck, she closed her teeth on skin and muscle, hard enough to make him grunt, hard enough to fracture the last of his restraint.

He swept her up, her back against the carriage, her legs wrapped about his waist. With one hand beneath her buttocks, and the other supporting her bad leg, he angled until the broad head of him was at her opening.

She cried out as he thrust up and in, filling her, a slick, hot glide. With rough, deep strokes he took her, and she tilted her hips forward, the hard carriage at her back lending her purchase. Deeper, she wanted him deeper, and faster, and—"Oh, yes. Like that." She panted, words stolen from her lips as he did as she bid.

There was no civility in this, only pounding fervor, untrammeled, unrestrained.

Clutching at his shoulder, her head thrown back against the carriage, she shook with the force of her passion. He gave a rich, low groan of pleasure, the sound coiling through her, pulling her senses even tighter.

He kissed her neck, licked her. Bit her. A jagged cry ripped from her throat. She shattered, throbbing around him as he drove in hard, his body rigid, his teeth on her skin, his release pumping through him, through her, and the ragged, hoarse sound of his breathing mixed with her own.

She was suspended above the ground, his strong arms her only support as her shivers subsided and her heart slowed.

I love you. Words without breath or sound, they swirled through her mind, through her heart. *I love you.*

She had not imagined that love would be so wonderful, so awful, so magnificent and terrifying at once. Emotion tugged at her, vast in scope and depth; it left her reeling. A sound escaped her, half laugh, half sob.

Aidan tensed, and then a shudder shook him. He slid from her, leaving her open and moist, a little bereft. With care, he set her back on her feet, holding her as she found her balance, her skirt sliding slowly along her legs, coming to rest in rumpled folds. Finally, he drew back and stared down at her, his expression grave.

"No frowns," she whispered, and pressed the flat of her fingers to his lips.

Her time with him was a gift. She should take it and hold it to her breast and treasure it for the greatest he could give. Because to hope for more was to invite devastation. She was not such a fool.

He was a creature of darkness, of hate and vengeance, claimed as such both by his own words and by all she had seen. But he *did* hold some kind regard for her.

It would have to be enough.

It was not enough.

She would love him, vast and endless and with all her heart, until her dying breath. But damaged as he was, he did not know how to love her even a little.

There it was, the truth, naked and stark. She had known that he would hurt her without meaning to, and that without meaning to, she would let him.

Through the open carriage door, the sun slanted in a slash of yellow ocher across the velvet seat and one half of Jane's skirt. She could hear Aidan murmuring to the horses, and she wondered how he knew that she had wanted a moment to gather her wits and her thoughts.

Such passion. Such emotion. She pressed her lips together and took a long slow breath.

She unfastened the brace and carefully placed it to the side. Her fingers lingered on the supple leather, and her heart was both light and heavy.

So many things to ponder and fret over and scrutinize, but one coalesced, certainty nipping her as she stared at the brace.

Her father had lied.

I wrote to London—to your Doctor Barker, in fact—when first I saw you. Oddly, he was unfamiliar with your case . . . Aidan's words condemned Gideon Heatherington for a charlatan, the niggling unease she had felt earlier coming to roost as she slid the bits of the puzzle together. All these years, her father had claimed that he had sent to London to Doctor Barker, the renowned scholar in his field, and that the good doctor had pronounced her a helpless cripple. And, oh, how her father had moaned and fussed that the consult had pushed him to penury.

Lies. Lies. Lies upon lies. And what was the truth?

Would she even recognize the truth if it struck her across the face?

Swallowing, she wrapped her arms about herself. The truth was that she had known it all along. She had seen how unwilling her father was to part with even the small payment for the doctor at Launceston. In her heart of hearts, she had always known he would not buy another opinion. So Doctor Barker had been a fantasy.

Until now.

She shuddered. Did she know her father at all?

Carefully, she climbed down from inside the coach, holding her skirt above her ankles. Turning, she looked at the brace where it lay on the velvet seat. Aidan had done this for her, spent hours and hours planning and conceiving, cutting leather, stitching, piecing the thing together. With his own hands.

The thought was staggering.

There was no sound to warn her of his coming, but she knew. The light shifted, a long shadow falling across her and the carriage seat both. Aidan stepped up behind her. Wordlessly, he reached past her and drew out her cloak, then draped it over her shoulders. Closing his hands about her upper arms, he turned her to face him.

Still reeling from the untamed pleasure of their lovemaking, the emotion of it, she lowered her lashes, inexplicably shy.

"The brace . . . when must I wear it?" She raised her gaze to his.

"Not all the time. Doctor Barker was clear in his opinion that too frequent use would weaken the muscles." He was frowning a little, studying her, but he did not press any questions. She was glad for that. She could not bear to explain her new realization of what her father had done, to provide Aidan with yet another confirmation of Gideon Heatherington's perfidy. Nor could she bear to explain that despite all, he was her father, and though she reviled what she now knew of him, a part of her loved him.

"Are you hungry?" Aidan asked.

"Famished."

"All that fresh air and exertion?" His expression was only polite interest, but in his tone she heard a smile. She could not help but smile in return, and a light shiver touched her frame as she thought of exactly what exertion he described.

"Are you cold, sweet? Do you wish to ride in the carriage?"

"No." She wanted to sit beside him, and look upon his face, and press the length of her thigh to his. She wanted to hear his voice, and talk with him.

Taking her hand in his, he raised her fingers to his lips. His eyes sparkled, blue and pewter. "Then off we go. We shall raid the kitchen at Trevisham."

For an instant, she imagined the look on the butler's face, his mouth pinched in disapproval.

More likely, they would end up in the enormous dining room, separated by endless feet of gleaming mahogany table. She did not have the heart to tell him so.

With care he helped her to the driver's perch, and then clambered up beside her with easy grace.

As they rode back toward Pentreath, their shoulders brushing as the carriage dipped and swayed, Jane said, "Tell me why Hawker refers to you as His Lordship."

Aidan cast her sidelong glance. "Because I am."

"Excuse me?" She laughed, certain that he teased her.

"A lord. I am one. Though I can never claim the title for, with my father dead, where is my proof? Who would name me the rightful heir, the drowned son returned from the depths of the ocean? Would the new heir gladly hand off his inheritance without significant evidence? Somehow, I think not."

She wriggled sideways and stared at him, staggered when certainty coalesced. He was perfectly serious. "But . . . that is not fair!"

Her exclamation drew a startled laugh from him. "What in life is fair, sweet Jane?" His shoulders rose and fell in a shrug. "It matters not. There is no coin. Only a title and a moldering country house, entailed, with crumbling walls and the family silver sold long ago."

His tone belied his casual dismissal, and his words made her sad. "How terrible."

"Do you think so? I thought it as well, and so I paid the new lord's debts. Bequeathed a reasonable sum, in the guise of an ancient cousin who had died without issue. 'Twas my noble effort on behalf of the person I once was."

Honorable. He was always so honorable.

"You do not sound happy about it," she observed.

"I was very happy to give the money. Less happy when the fool went to his club and gambled the lot on a single hand of faro. Ten thousand pounds. I left him to his despair then. There are limits to my largesse. But I did manage to purchase my father's unentailed townhouse for a very good price."

Ten thousand pounds. Dear sweet heaven. "You are wealthy." She had supposed he was, but what he described was far greater than she could have imagined.

His smile was a flash of white teeth against golden skin. "Beyond your wildest dreams, sweet."

"Oh!" She weighed the bounds of polite inquiry, and then stepped far beyond acceptable limits to ask, "How?"

The smile faded. "The man whose neck I snapped, the captain of a pirate vessel"—he paused, sent her a quick look beneath his lashes—"he fancied his whip and his cat-o'-nine. Almost as much as he cherished his bounty. He was a frugal bastard, and when I killed him, all that was his became mine. It was an easy matter to build on his fortune."

She took a slow breath, appalled by his talk of whips and cats. "By piracy?"

"Actually, no. Well . . . a bit."

"You told me that you are a smuggler."

"I am. I enjoy the excitement of a run across the channel." He looked positively wicked as he said, "There is a certain charm in evading the excise men, or running a narrow passage in the reef to escape a revenue cutter."

"So your fortune is built on smuggled goods."

"No. You could call that more of an . . . entertainment. My worth came by legal trade. I am now a very boring businessman. It was an avenue I had an uncanny knack for. Every cargo I invested in came to shore safe and sound, regardless of the odds. Every warehouse I purchased filled with an item in high demand. My ships weathered every storm." He was silent for a moment, holding the reins easily in his hands, and then said darkly, "It seems that once I turned to murder, my luck turned to the better."

Her breath slid from her in a hiss. "Do not say that."

"What? That my luck turned?" He sent her a side-long glance. "Or that I turned to murder?"

He was mocking her, his tone mordant.

Pressing her lips together, she measured her response and could think of none fitting.

"Do you love me less now, Jane?" he asked softly, the words heavy with cynicism.

Ah. So that was the crux of it. Suddenly, she felt afraid, cast into unfamiliar territory. How was she to lead him through this maze when she was so very lost herself? And how was she to answer without revealing her heart?

"Love has no conditions, Aidan," she said, careful.

"*Do* you love me then, Jane?" The question was so low it was almost lost to the creak of the carriage and the steady clomp of the horses' hooves. "'Twould be unwise."

The pain in her heart was swift and terrible. He knew it, of course. She could not imagine he did not. But to *tell* him, to *say* the words, knowing that he was incapable of loving her in return. . . . She stared into the far distance wondering where this could lead, and how she would survive the journey.

"I would be a fool to tell you if I did," she whispered.

"And you are no fool." For a long while he said nothing more, and then, "I have killed only men, and each of them in self-defense. Their lives or mine. I chose to survive." His charm and easy banter were gone now.

She sat frozen, her heart pounding, knowing that his words were a strange sort of concession, answers he had refused to give before but shared now in a convoluted expression of his regard for her.

"Never a woman. Never a child. Never one weaker or unarmed. A man with a whip was the first, my hands slick from my own blood running down my back and arms, my body weak but my will bolstered by my burning hate." He flicked the reins as the horses lagged. "Once, a man who held a knife to my throat in a rather rude awakening from my slumber. There were more. Many more." He looked at her obliquely. His lips flattened. "Once, on a moonlit road, a man who froze my blood and stopped my heart because he held a pistol to one I—"

One I love. She willed him to say it, certain he spoke of the night he had shot Gaby to save her life.

"—had no wish to lose."

She had not known she was holding her breath until this very instant when it burst free.

They continued in silence then. The rocking of the coach lulled her, and feeling drained, she relaxed her body against his, their movements matching the pitch and sway.

A deep rut jarred both the carriage and her concentration, and Jane realized they had reached the main road of Pentreath, that they drew abreast of the Crown Inn.

Suddenly, her skin prickled and the fine hairs at

her nape rose. She stared hard at the building as they rolled past. The sign above the door swung forward and back, caught by the wind, and the strident creak carried to her across the yard, above the scrape of the carriage wheels on the road and the jingle of the harness.

She shuddered.

Someone watched her. Someone . . .

There, the door of the inn was open, a dark silhouette filling the space. A man slouched against the wooden jamb. She could feel his eyes upon her.

From beneath her lashes she glanced at Aidan and found him staring ahead, his jaw set. She inched closer to press tight against him, and turned her head as the carriage moved on, unable to dispel the feeling that whoever stood in the shadows, his presence here in Pentreath boded ill.

As a cloud moved across the sun, the man stepped out from her father's hostelry, from shadow into shade. He stood in the yard, watching, and she swallowed a gasp.

The man was Digory Tubb.

Chapter 15

It had always seemed to Jane that dusk on a rainy day was an eerie thing, painted in bruised shades of smoke and pewter. She stood at the window in the library of Trevisham House, watching the sky slowly turn to darkest gray, and then blue-black. With the wind rattling the windowpanes, the heavy clouds hanging low and Aidan away from the house, gone on horseback an hour past, she felt anything but easy.

There had been something in his manner, something *wrong*. She had not asked his destination. Perhaps she had not wanted to know.

A strange melancholy dogged her, leaving her anxious and skittish. Turning from the window she went to sit in a chair by the hearth and took up a book of poetry, letting it fall open across her lap. The light from a single lamp played across the pages. She found she could not read, and in the end she sat thinking on what a strange and peculiar thing her life had become.

She knew her mood, recognized it for the self-indulgent moroseness it was, and so she thought her imagination played tricks upon her as, from the very

walls of the library, there came an eerie, echoing
sound, a dull scraping, like stone against stone. Her
head jerked up and she froze.

The book of poetry in her hand fell shut, and she
inched to the edge of the gold brocade chair. A
shiver crawled across her skin.

The noise came again. *Scrape. Scrape.*

Only a very large rat, indeed, could scrabble so.

Placing the book on the table, she glanced about,
wondering if she ought summon a servant or simply
remove herself to another room.

The sound ebbed and flowed. Jane rose and
turned a slow circle. From the corner of her eye,
she saw the glow of the dying fire in the hearth,
almost completely ash now. She stood for a long
while, listening, her muscles tense, and she imagined the echo took on the tone and character of
footsteps at a distance, disembodied and ghostly.

Drawing her shawl tighter about her shoulders,
she paced out the perimeter of the room. Here,
next to the desk, she could hear almost nothing.
Here, next to the fireplace, the sound was keener,
and here next to the bookcase it was louder still.
She pressed the flat of her palm to the wooden
shelf, and her ear to the wall. It came again, the
sound distant, echoing.

Mysterious passages, ghosts and fiends: she had
the alarming recollection of the novel Aidan had
given her to read at the New Inn. The impression
of it was suddenly unutterably strong in her mind.
Almost in jest, she tapped the wall and pulled on
the sconces. In truth, she had little expectation of
discovering a panel that would swing open to reveal
a dark corridor, damp and mildewed, festooned

with cobwebs. She laughed nervously at her own improbable thoughts.

With a shake of her head, she turned away, and then there it was. Not a secret or hidden door, but merely a servant's entrance, the portal flush with the wood-paneled walls, simple and unadorned so as to draw no attention.

It certainly had not drawn hers.

Taking up the lamp, she opened the door. Her breath caught in her throat. *There* was the passage from her imagination, dark as a cave, the air stale and musty. She almost closed the door once more and left off her ideas of exploration, but right then came the sound of hurried steps from somewhere below her, deep in the pure darkness. There was a muffled curse and a heavy thud, and then a gravelly voice that she had no difficulty recognizing.

Aidan. His tone was brusque, though his words were muffled.

An hour past, he had pulled her hard against him and kissed her deep before he had ridden off. She *knew* he had gone. But it seemed he had returned.

She hesitated an instant, feeling a tingle of premonition, not exactly danger, but certainly a sense of wary reserve. Dark and light played across the walls and a draft caught the flame of her lamp, making it twist and bend despite the glass chimney.

Then Aidan's voice echoed from the darkness once more, and Jane pressed her lips together, certain that she was weaving her own unease. Lifting her lamp, she stepped through into the passage. But no amount of courage could make her pull the door closed behind her.

Each step took her in a gradual descent, lower and lower, and the murmur of conversation grew louder as she walked. She held the lamp before her, the paltry flame pulled by an unseen current. Flickering shadows touched the walls and floor, and cobwebs brushed her as she passed. The passageway was narrow, with an arched ceiling and stone on all sides.

Just as she wondered if it would take her all the way down to the ocean, the passage opened into a large, square room, with kegs stacked against the far wall. She stopped, feeling a cold draft on her skin. For an instant there was a peculiar stillness, an absence of sound that felt abnormal, even chilling, and then the wrath of the wind cut through the space, slicing the silence.

"Well look what the tide dragged in."

Jane whirled and almost lost both her balance and the lamp as cruel fingers curled into her upper arm in a bruising grip. She jerked away, her heart hammering a frantic pace.

"You've grown feisty." Digory Tubb sneered down at her, his eyes narrowed.

She stared at him in sick dismay. "What are you doing here?"

"Baiting the trap." Digory smiled in oily contempt, and Jane shook her head, beset by confusion. He leaned close and whispered in her ear, "But beware. The trap might bite."

With all her strength, she thrust her elbow against his belly, and as he grunted in surprise, she shifted to the side, beyond his reach. His head came up, his eyes narrowed in vicious intent, but he drew up short as Aidan stepped from the shadows. The glow of her candle touched his hair with gilt lights, and accented the hard, handsome planes of his face.

"Step away, Dig," he said, his expression giving nothing away. His gaze flicked to Jane, cold, aloof, and she felt a stark trepidation. Suddenly, he was a stranger to her, dark and lethal. A chill of premonition touched her, as it had when he had ridden away earlier in the night. Trusting in her instinct, she felt certain that she had stumbled upon a scene she had never been meant to see.

There was something heavy, something oppressive here, something strange and horrible that she sensed would end badly.

In that instant, she could not bear to look at him, and she could not bring herself to look away.

"Step away, Dig," Aidan said again, soft, so soft.

"Or what?" Digory patted the knife hilt that stuck from his belt, but the nervous catch in his voice gave him away. "You know what I can do with a knife."

"I do know," Aidan said, his tone like splintered glass. "And I know *now* that you prefer to ply your blade on those who cannot defend themselves. I had not thought it of you, Dig."

"Ah." Digory scraped out a laugh. "Figured that one out, did you? She saw more than she should have, my Gin, and didn't like what she saw. *She spurned me.* Tossed me aside like a withered apple. Threatened to tell the law. Can you imagine it?" He stroked the hilt of his knife. "I took my revenge and plugged a crack, both. 'Twas the easiest remedy." He sighed. "But I do miss her."

Jane swayed, a haze of red coming like a veil before her eyes. Digory's words, so carelessly tossed, horrified her. Off balance, she flung out one hand to press against the cold stone wall. *Ginny. Ginny. Ginny.* Digory Tubb had killed her. Because she had rejected him. Because she had seen more than she should, seen what he was. What he'd done.

And what exactly was that?

Her gaze slid to Aidan as her pulse slammed an erratic rhythm.

Digory's thumb flicked back and forth across the handle of his knife. His eyes darted about as though he searched for some escape as Aidan took a step closer, stalking him, prowling.

"Will you fight me with just your hands?" Digory asked, his voice edged in panic. "Against my knife?"

No. Jane took a half step forward.

"Yes." Aidan smiled. Gentle. Awful. "Shall I?"

A heartbeat. Two.

Before her eyes, Digory Tubb seemed to shrink into himself. His hand fell away from the hilt of his knife.

"My Ma would never forgive you. Never." He licked his lips, a nervous flick of his tongue.

"True. And because of my esteem for good Wenna, and for the fact that she once tended my wounds, you yet live." Aidan's gaze raked Digory, his expression one of disgust. "You'll leave here, Dig. Now. Sign on any vessel bound for distant climes, and do not return. If you do, I will know." His lips curved in a chilling expression of menace. Monstrous. Terrifying. "And then I *will* kill you."

Digory backed away, terror etched in his features.

"Oh, and Dig," Aidan said, his tone devoid of inflection. "Ginny Ward was guilty of nothing save having some fond emotion for you. Her murder will require retribution." He paused and then continued. "Were I you, I would never stop looking over my shoulder."

Jane looped her hands in the ends of her shawl, worrying the fabric as she stood watching Digory

Tubb backstep toward a shadowed nook in the far wall, his face a mask of hate. The wind came through, chill and bitter, as he was swallowed by the shadows, and two men appeared from that same recess.

She sensed Aidan come close beside her, though she did not look at him.

"Is there a door there?" she asked in hushed tones.

"Yes."

The silence was a heavy yoke. "There must be a price for what he did. He killed her. He tore her eyes—" She choked off, unable to continue.

"There are laws that deal with murderers."

She spun, startled by his reply. "And how will the law find him? How will they know what he has done?"

"I will tell them."

"But you said you would not. For the sake of his mother."

"No. I *said* that for Wenna's sake, I did not kill him." His tone was cold, hard. "I said nothing of guarding his secret."

"But you let him think—" She broke off, swallowed. Aidan looked a stranger to her, his eyes cold, his mouth hard. Here was the man of implacable resolve he had always described himself to be.

"It would have been better if you had not come here, Jane," he said, his tone perfectly conversational and for that, it was somehow frightening.

From the corner of her eye, she saw the two men she had noticed earlier. They carried barrels through the door, and then returned for a fresh load. Oddly, their actions struck her as sinister.

"Those barrels, they are from the New Inn, the

ones you stored at Wenna's cottage? The smuggled brandy?"

"They are. Brought here yesterday by Digory at my instruction."

Smuggled barrels, brought to Pentreath. For what purpose? A dark and gnawing unease took her, and she knew, *knew*, that those barrels had something to do with her father.

"I saw him," she blurted. "Digory Tubb. Yesterday. At my father's inn."

"Did you?" The glance Aidan slanted her made her wary.

"Are you surprised by that? Or did you send him to meet with my father?"

"No, I did not send him." He shrugged. "Perhaps he merely stopped there for a pint of ale."

But he did not believe that; she could sense it.

She stepped in front of him, demanding his full attention. "Tell me Aidan, what is your scheme, your plan?" Her voice rose, high and thin.

Did she know him? Did she know him at all?

She stared at him, seeing a stranger.

"It is tonight," she whispered, horrified by dawning understanding. "You do this thing tonight. Your grand scheme to destroy my father. Make him pay."

She had thought there was time, that with her steady love she would soften him, ease the torments that drove him. Oh, foolish girl. Foolish girl. There was such tragedy in this.

There was a small part of her that wished to protect her father, to save him from harm. The larger part understood that he had made his choices years ago, done things that he would need to atone for either in this world or the next. Gideon Heatherington had done tragedy to Aidan, and who knew

how many others. She knew that now. Her hand
convulsed in the fringe of her shawl. It was a terrible thing for a daughter to recognize, a thing that
could destroy her if she let it.

The larger part of her wanted to save Aidan from
himself, from his torments and shadows. Her own
demons had made her wise. She knew with certainty that whatever he did, he could never reclaim
his lost years, never clean the turbid river of his
sorrow, never strain his spilled blood from where
it stained the ground and mixed with the sea.

He thought his vengeance would heal him. She
was certain it would steal his humanity, leave him
an empty husk.

"How?" she demanded. "How will you do this?"

"The barrels will be left where they can be found
in the Crown Inn," he said. "The revenue men,
along with Squire Craddick, have been summoned.
Perhaps they are on their way there now."

"They will find the barrels. Use them as evidence
of his guilt." She shuddered. "You will see my father
convicted for a crime he did not commit?"

He studied her for a long moment. "Jane, he *did*
commit this crime, and worse. Perhaps not at this
time, with these barrels, but he is a wrecker, a killer."
He took a slow breath in, out. "He stole my life. The
life of my mother. The life of my father. He saw me
condemned to hell for no greater crime than surviv-
ing the wreck that killed my mother. I *will* see
Gideon Heatherington live the selfsame nightmare.
A fitting justice, is it not?"

Too fitting. Too perfect. She shook her head.

"This will bring you neither peace nor joy." When
it was done, her father made to pay, and Aidan
greeted a new day with his torment still biting at

him, she knew *that* would destroy him. She could not bear it.

He spread his hands before him, strong hands. Her lover's hands. "It *will* ease me, Jane."

"No," she said. "No."

"Do you think to convince me that he does not deserve retribution?" Words spoken in low, harsh tones.

"No. Not that." Her voice broke. "I had hoped that I could . . ."

"Could what, Jane?" His gaze burned into her, seeing her heart, baring her soul.

Her lips parted. The room darkened about her and she was lost in his eyes. Gray. Blue. Almost purple in the frugal light.

"Could what?" he asked again, softer, kinder.

There was a hard pressure in her chest. Tears clogged her throat, and her heart pounded so hard that it left her dizzy and choked. Feeling as though she was falling off a sharp cliff, she opened her mouth and let the words escape, praying, praying. If only she could sway him.

"I hoped I could make you love me," she said, defiant, desperate.

His eyes widened a fraction.

She tore her gaze away. From across the room, the scrape of the barrels on the stone floor as the men dragged and lifted them was loud in her ears, and the sound of her own pulse, so fast and wild.

Catching her chin between his thumb and first finger, Aidan tipped her face up, holding her only hard enough that she could not easily turn away. In his eyes she imagined a flicker of emotion, perhaps regret.

"I thought I could make you love me," she repeated, sad now.

The brush of his fingers on her cheek was gentle, and she realized she was crying. His chest expanded in a slow, deep breath.

"I do, Jane." Her breath stopped and her pulse stopped and the world fell away.

She wondered why his declaration brought only a sharp and terrible pain. And then, as he continued, she knew.

"I do love you, as much as I am able. But my vengeance I cannot renounce." His words shattered her. "I warned you, I am a man of dogged intent. I cannot betray the goals of more than a decade, forget the vows made in blood."

A tight and brutal fist closed around her heart. He *did* love her, and it was not enough to give him peace, not enough to free him from the shackles of hate.

"There is a difference between cannot and will not," she whispered.

"Aye. Will not, then." His thumb brushed her cheek. "Jane, love, I am sorry for your pain, but I have no regret for what I will do. You must know that."

She knew. She knew. Wordlessly, she stared at him.

He exhaled sharply. A hard press of his lips to hers, and then he was gone, leaving her standing with the clawed shreds of her emotions bleeding in her hands.

Light gone, air gone, only hopelessness and despair left behind. Jane felt frozen, as though she had fallen into the ocean and sunk into the darkest, coldest depths. Aidan loved her, a wonder, a gift, but one touched by darkness, shriveled and withered.

He loved her, he had said, as much as he was able. And it was not enough to save him.

She had not thought this. In all her imaginings, she had never considered that he *would* love her and still seek his vengeance. She recognized now her hubris, or perhaps it was only naivete. Still, the end was the same, and she was weary to the bone, heartsick. Her feet dragged as she trudged through the dark and damp corridor.

Stepping from the passageway into the library, she could summon no surprise at finding Hawker waiting for her. She hesitated, wary of him still. She had never ascertained exactly why he had been at her cousin Dolly's that day.

"Why are you not with him?" she asked dully.

Hawker took the lamp from her hand and pushed the door to the passage shut behind her. "He sent me to be with you."

"My gaoler?" she asked, and sighed at his obvious distress. "I am sorry. That was unkind of me."

"No, no. I understand."

"You know, then, what he has gone to do?"

"Yes."

"It will destroy him."

"Your father?"

She shook her head. "Aidan." Her voice caught. "He will find no peace in this, and what will be left to him then? What? He will have no one to hate. No one to blame. There will be only the poison in his heart with no release. It will turn in on itself, a rot that cannot be excised."

Hawker looked stricken, and she turned away, her composure near to shattering. After a long moment, she turned back to face him.

"So he set you to watch me, again."

"Yes." Hawker gave a lopsided smile. "To see you safe from harm, though I've been less than a fine hand at that job, haven't I?"

She thought of the time he had steered her from misstep as they walked on the moor, and the dangers they had faced together on the Bodmin Road.

"What harm did he think would befall me at my cousin's cottage?" she asked.

Hawker stared at her in obvious confusion, and she felt a stirring of suspicion, thinking of the flowered china on Dolly's table, and the feeling of being watched, and the odd coincidence of Hawker's arrival that day.

Nothing made sense. Nothing. She felt as though she was peering into a murky pond, desperately trying to see to the bottom. If she could only dip her hand and sweep aside the muck . . .

"You were to protect me at the New Inn, and again on the Bodmin Road, but what *were* you doing at my cousin Dolly's cottage?" she demanded. "No." She held up her hand, palm forward as she read his intent in his eyes. He meant to lie to her. "At least give me the courtesy of the truth."

His gaze slid away, then back. For an instant his lips tightened and she thought he would choose to prevaricate after all. He surprised her when he said, "Cap— I mean, Mr. Warrick has been working with Squire Craddick. There's wreckers about, and His Lordship has no tolerance for that. He wants them gone."

Jane nodded her encouragement, but said nothing.

"I was sent to your cousin's home looking for anything to tie to the wreck of the *Patience Grace*, near a month past, on a fine, clear night. The ship was there and then gone, and Squire Craddick knew she was carrying boxes of gold coins, blocks of tin, coffee, sugar. None of that washed ashore. Only a chest of books, and the captain's identification, and other small things. But *nothing*, not a *single* thing of great value. 'Twas as if someone had taken the finest pickings. The squire found it more than passing strange, and His Lordship agreed."

She remembered the man that Aidan had ridden off with on the Bodmin Road, the sensation that he had seemed familiar to her. Now she knew. Squire Craddick. Of course.

"And what has the *Patience Grace* to do with my cousin Dolly? Surely you do not imagine that she is a wrecker?"

"The *Patience Grace* had passengers, as well. Some brought goods with them. Clothes." He stared hard at her. "Fine china."

Jane swallowed a gasp, an image of Dolly's plate and cup shimmering through her thoughts.

"You see, nothing washed ashore. Nothing, save what I've told you, and then the body of that dead girl, Ginny Ward," he said.

So that is what Ginny had seen. She had watched Digory Tubb wreck a ship. She had died for what she had witnessed, and—based on what Digory had said earlier—her abhorrence of the deed. Wrapping her arms about herself, Jane felt her unease swell like a dark tide.

"Aidan was on the cliff that morning when Jem and Robert found her."

"I was with him. We came too late. It was a bitter thing. We had hoped to find her alive."

"Dolly Gwyn has no part in what you describe. Surely you know it was Digory Tubb. There is no connection there, none whatsoever. What could you imagine you would find in Dolly's cottage?" But she knew. She knew. Her fingertips went cold and numb.

Hawker's mouth tightened. "Not Dolly," he said. "But one who tosses her the occasional crumb."

Jane stared at him, appalled. She knew who helped support Dolly, who gave her the occasional extra coin, or little gift.

A gift like a plate and cup with flowers that were a perfect match to those on Wenna Tubb's table.

Gideon Heatherington.

"No," she breathed, and backed away. "No."

"His Lordship suspects your father leads the wreckers." Hawker ducked his head, looked away.

"Oh." An ugly coil of unease slithered to the pit of Jane's belly. Her father. A wrecker, still. 'Twas one thing to know her father had done terrible things in the past, another thing entirely to understand that he did them still. What had she imagined? That his deeds were buried in a time before he met her mother? That his crimes were limited to a dark and distant past?

She had deluded herself.

Suddenly, she thought of Aidan's story, the one that tarred her father with horrific deeds. She thought, too, of the night they had stood on the beach watching the dying ship. She recalled her father's dry clothes, and the light she had seen to the north, and the wagon.

Had her father been on that wagon? Had he set a light to lure the ship to its doom?

What was she to believe? What was the truth?

Dear heaven, she had spent weeks suspecting Aidan of every horror, and now she was forced to paint her own father with the colors of a villain.

Enough. Enough.

"I am going, right now," she said fiercely. "To Pentreath. To the Crown Inn."

Hawker stepped forward, and she glared him down.

"You may accompany me. Or you may remain here," she offered. "But you will *not* stop me."

"'Tis too late," he muttered. "The deed is surely done by now. The kegs in place for discovery. Perhaps your father has already been arrested."

"I will see it with my own eyes."

Jane limped to her chamber. Her hand hovered over the cloak Aidan had given her, soft, warm, beautiful. She narrowed her eyes in defiance and closed her fingers on her old scarlet mantle.

At the last moment, she took up Aidan's cloak instead.

Swinging it over her shoulders, she went in search of Hawker and found him waiting for her with a small, open trap that balanced on two wheels, harnessed to a pretty gray. For an instant, she wondered where the usual coach was, and then decided it did not matter.

She climbed into the trap and felt a moment's unease as Hawker took up the reins, wondering if perhaps she trusted too easily in his words and explanations. Then she looked to her own judgment, and decided that she spun needless complication here. The situation was dire enough without adding melodrama to the mix.

Heavy, low clouds blotted the moon. The night was damp and raw, the air bitter with a harsh wind. Drawing the hood of her cloak up, Jane was glad of her choice and the relative warmth. The crash of the waves came at her from what seemed like all sides as they crossed the causeway, and then faded to a dull and distant roar once they drew closer to Pentreath.

Hawker cleared his throat, and his hand strayed to the pistol at his belt. Her heart racing, Jane curled her fingers over the side of the trap. All she could hear was the *clop, clop, clop* of the horse's hooves on the road, too loud.

Finally, finally, the Crown Inn was there before her.

Oh, too late. Her heart near to stopped. There was Aidan's coach in the yard, and at least a dozen horses. Squire Craddick and his men. They milled in the yard, and strode into the bar. She wondered if they had found the barrels, if her father had been dragged away.

As the trap drew to a halt, she had to stop and force a breath before climbing down. She felt sick and dizzy, seized by a horrified desperation.

Watch out for your father. Do you understand, Jane? She had promised her mother. Promised her. And she had failed.

What had she imagined she could do here? Had she supposed she might turn back the hands of time and set all to rights? And even if she could, *what* was right? Everything Aidan had told her was true, but her father . . .

The quiet was cleaved apart as the sharp crack of

a pistol shot echoed, and then another, and then came a cruel and vicious silence that stopped dead the whispers of the night and stilled even the slightest current of air.

Chapter 16

Two shots. She had heard two shots.

Every dog in the village set to barking and baying. The noise slapped at Jane in waves from all around. She stumbled forward, away from Hawker and the two-wheeled cart, toward the open door of the bar and the crowd of men that blocked it.

Terror tore through her, hot as fire, a bright pain.

Aidan. Aidan.

Please, please, please—

Heart pounding, she skirted the edges of the group, but could get nowhere near the door. In desperation, she shoved her way forward into the thick of the throng. Above her head the familiar sign of the Crown Inn creaked back and forth, and the buzz of agitated conversation rushed around her, over her.

She smelled a faint tinge of gunpowder, the acrid scent out of place in the mingled miscellany of ale and smoke and sweat that wafted from the pub. A ghastly apprehension sucked at her. Raising her elbows, she tried to push through, but there were too many people blocking her way, too many bodies wrapped in heavy, padded coats for her to see anything save their backs.

Her skin felt clammy, her palms damp. She turned to her right, her left, rising up on her toes, her gaze raking the yard in frantic glimpses caught through the milling crowd. Her weak limb screamed in protest, but she held her vantage, desperate for some sign of Aidan.

He was not there. Oh, God. He was not there.

From the jumble of men's voices, she caught snippets of information that twisted a cruel knot of fear deep in her belly, tighter and tighter.

". . . shot him dead, cold as you please . . ."

"Clean through the heart."

". . . will be the better for his loss."

"Who?" Jane caught the arm of the man closest to her. Aidan? Her father? "Who is dead?"

The man she clutched glanced at her.

"*Who is dead?*" she asked again, her voice high and thin and desperate, her heart battering against her ribs.

"Go on with you, missy. There's no ale for you to serve tonight," he said, mistaking her for the barmaid. "But there'll be gossip aplenty to hear soon enough."

Dismissing her, he turned and pushed his way through the men. Wrapped in misery, Jane shifted and pressed, but she could not budge the crowd as he had with his broad bulk. She scanned the area, searching for Hawker. He was not by the trap, and she saw no sign of him.

"Out! Out!" boomed the voice of command from somewhere deep in the building. *Squire Craddick,* she thought. "You'll all wait in the yard now while I see the way of things."

Feet moved and shuffled, and those crammed in the entry to the pub spilled out the doorway and into the yard, taking Jane with them, farther and farther from the open door. She tried to enter then, ducking forward, but someone caught her arm.

"No, miss," said a man she did not know, likely one of the squire's. "Best you be spared what's within."

She tried to tear away, but he held her fast. The sucking undertow of her panic nearly overwhelmed her.

"What has happened?" she demanded.

"Murder," he said.

Murder. Death. An icy fist closed about her heart.

Jane gritted her teeth, holding back the wail that threatened to tear free. *Aidan.* Her legs wobbled, and she thought she would have fallen had the throng not been so close, with the press of someone's back against hers holding her up.

Trapping her.

Others began to speak, asking questions, offering conjectures.

"What did you find? Smuggled goods?" a man asked.

Jane swallowed the thick knot that clogged her throat. What had the squire and his men found? Smuggled kegs. False evidence to damn her father.

Oh, dear God.

Another man urged, "Tell us what you found."

Hearing the voice, Jane realized that the question came from Robert Dawe. She looked about, hoping to find him, hoping he might help her enter the inn. She saw only the unfamiliar faces of the squire's men crowded close around her.

"You ask what we found?" The squire's man

made a rude sound. "We found *nothing*. Nothing at all."

Jane's head jerked up. She could not fathom it. Aidan had had ample time to bait his terrible snare, to hide the kegs that would damn her father.

"Nothing?" she demanded, her fingers clutching at his sleeve. "Are you certain?"

"We found *nothing*, not a sign of the promised swag. We searched. Every room. Even the attic. Two good men climbed down the cliff face to the caves. There was nothing here, and nothing there." He shrugged. "Either there never was anything to find, or the landlord of the Crown is a wily fox."

She could not breathe, so thick and heavy was her terror. Was he dead? Was Aidan dead, shot before he had the chance to unload the barrels?

"And then?" another voice prodded.

Jane jerked her head toward the speaker, and for an instant, at the fringe of the crowd, she thought she caught a glimpse of Joss Gossin, the landlord of the New Inn. She rose on her toes, but after mere seconds was forced to fall back, her weak leg failing now to hold her weight. Disappointment scraped through her. She would have welcomed a familiar face and whatever assistance he might offer. Now, she regretted that she had not held close to Hawker. He would have stood a better chance than she to break through the throng.

With a desperate surge, she pushed against the crush of bodies once more. She made no headway, and changed her tactic, trying to move backward instead, and perhaps circle around. This approach met with greater success. She inched toward freedom with a sick urgency gnawing at her.

All around her was a slurry of words and voices.

". . . heard an argument . . ."

". . . a scuffle to the back, in the kitchen . . ."

". . . the sound of pistol shot . . ."

A scuffle to the back, in the kitchen.

Jane trembled as she let those behind her press forward, around her. She took a step back, then another, faster and faster, until finally she stumbled free of the crush.

She lurched away, hugging the shadows of the wall, dread surging in her throat. No one paid her any mind, and she was grateful for that. Hurrying now with her loping, uneven gait, she rounded the corner of the building, and skirted the patch of the garden she had tended for years.

In an instant, she stood before the familiar kitchen door, her entire body tense and trembling.

Walk away. Turn and walk away and wait for Squire Craddick to bring the tidings. She froze, taken by a slashing need to run, run, run. Away from here. Away from the tragedy that awaited her. There was no possible good end to this.

A deep, slow breath reined in her panic. No, she would not play the coward.

She set her fingers to the doorknob. The chill of the metal bit her skin. Slowly, slowly, she turned the knob, pushing the door open a little, and a little more.

There was only a weak peat fire in the hearth, and a single candle flickering gamely against the darkness. First, she saw the table, and the chairs beside it, one of them overturned on its side. Her gaze followed the broken crockery strewn across the floor, and the congealing trail of mutton stew that had spewed in a wide pattern.

For an instant, she felt cold, distanced, as though

she was not inside herself but somewhere else entirely. As though she stood far, far away and peered
at the scene through a smudged glass. And then
horror crashed in on her as she realized she stared
at a hand . . . an arm . . . a big body, face up on the
cold floor, eyes staring sightless to the ceiling.
There was a dark stain across his chest and blood
on the stone floor beneath him.

She sucked in a sharp breath. Catching hold of
the closest chair, she steadied herself, her gaze riveted on the bloody wound.

Shot through the heart, one of the men out front
had said.

She stared down at the body.

Digory Tubb was dead.

A shudder took her. What was he doing here, in
her father's kitchen?

The murmur of conversation made her aware
that she was not alone. Raising her head, she saw
two men at the opening of the hallway that led
from the kitchen to the bar. They were deep in discussion, both their faces turned away from the
kitchen door.

Jane swallowed and inched forward.

They paid her no notice as she rounded the
table, taking pains to walk as far from Digory Tubb
as she could.

Other voices, gruff and male, carried from the
front of the inn and the common room, the sound
nearly drowned out by the buzzing in her ears. Her
feet moved forward, though she did not will it, and
in a moment she stood looking down at a second
man, angled across the floor, close to the hearth.

For an infinity, she did not understand what she
saw, and then she understood too well.

"No," she whispered, and sank down in a grace-less slump, horror and grief tearing at her. With a shake of her head, she realized that someone knelt beside her in the shadows, hands pressed to a thick cloth, wet and stained a deep, deep red.

Raising her eyes, she saw it was Mary.

"Is he dead?" Jane asked, struggling for calm, her voice low and husky.

"Yes."

Her breath was torn from her in a brutal rush.

"Oh, God," she gasped.

Dead. Her father was dead. Shot.

She could barely understand the truth of it.

"I could not stop the blood," the barmaid said.

Jane closed her eyes. Opened them again. Her father was still there, sprawled across the cold, stone floor. She stared at him, her thoughts in turmoil, and through it came a prayer that he had not suf-fered, that he had died quickly, that he would be forgiven for his sins. Perhaps he was at peace now. She hoped for that. And she hoped that her mother was there to greet him, to find the goodness in him . . . surely there had been some goodness. . . .

Her mother *had* loved him. Hadn't she?

A sob choked her.

One of the men turned at the sound, and glanced in their direction. His eyes were a deep turquoise blue, set in a lined, weathered face, his brows thick and silvered. No recognition dawned on his face as he studied her, for he did not know her.

But she knew him. Squire Craddick. She had stepped to the side of the road many a time over the years so he could ride past.

"I'd thought there was only one of you." He frowned, and shook his head, bemused. "Well, I'll

ask that you both wait here. You were the last to see
these men alive, to hear what conversation took
place between them, and I'll have questions for you
in a moment or two."

He turned away once more.

The way he moved made her certain: it *was* Squire
Craddick that Aidan had met on the Bodmin Road
the night he had ridden off and left her alone. The
night Gaby was shot. They were together in this,
then, Aidan and the squire, together in this plan of
vengeance.

Or were they? Even in her distraught state, Jane
saw the fallacy of her logic, and a new terror jabbed
at her.

Was it Aidan the squire was after?

She inhaled on a ragged breath.

Clasping her hands in her lap, Jane rocked slowly
forward and back. She could not tear her gaze from
her father's face. His eyes were shut, his complexion
gray and waxy.

She reached out with a trembling hand, thinking
to smooth his hair, but stilled before she touched
him. A sharp, wrenching pain twisted through her.

With all she knew of her father now, of the things
he had done and the marks on his soul, what was
she to feel? What was she to think? There was only
a vast and barren wretchedness in her heart.

No, that was not true, for smoldering in a secret
corner was the clean, cold relief that neither of the
dead men was Aidan Warrick.

"'Twas a terrible thing," Mary said.

Jane jerked her gaze to the other woman. Mary
stared down at her hands where they yet pressed on
Gideon's chest, and as though she finally understood the futility of her efforts, she drew them away

at last. Her words were barely above a whisper, but they flowed quickly, in testament to her pressing need to set them free.

"That one"—Mary jerked her chin toward Digory's still form—"came looking for money. He was wild-eyed, and kept glancing about as though he expected someone to be behind him. They argued, him and Gideon, and he threatened your father. Said he'd tell everyone the truth, but he never said the truth of what."

A foul dread reared in Jane's heart. The truth of the company of wreckers and smugglers, the identity of the leader of the vile band.

Had the monster been Digory Tubb, or her own father?

Jagged slashes of hysteria threatened to shatter her control as all that had come to pass and the things she had come to know buffeted her. All this time, Aidan had planned to place false evidence to see her father convicted of a crime . . . what tragic and ghastly irony that in all likelihood, her father would ultimately have condemned himself by his own actions.

She drew a shuddering breath. "They shot each other?"

"No, no." Mary shook her head, her eyes dull. "That is the strangeness. That one there—Digory, your father called him—put a pistol ball in your father, and then your father's friend put a ball in him."

Jane stared at her for a long moment, unable to string her thoughts together to form a coherent chain.

She felt numb and heavy, as though she swam through mud, and a terrible lethargy tugged at her.

Her father was dead. Shot by Digory Tubb, who was himself then shot by . . .

"My father's friend?"

"You know him. He's been here before," Mary said.

Jane blinked, and her thoughts collided, clicking in place like a key in its lock.

Her father's friend. Joss Gossin.

Joss Gossin led the wreckers. The realization was so simple, so sensible, she could summon neither shock nor surprise. Perhaps her heart was frozen.

She had seen him outside only moments past.

"An odd one, he is. And cruel," Mary continued. "He said something about two perfect scapegoats, and then he laughed and shot Digory dead."

Joss Gossin had shot Digory Tubb.

"Did you tell the squire?" Jane asked.

"Not yet." Mary gave a strange little laugh. "He seems disinclined to listen until he is good and ready. He has spent the last minutes discussing the pistols that fired the shots, while your father lies cold on the floor."

Jane glanced at Squire Craddick. She opened her mouth, made to rise, to tell him that Joss Gossin had escaped, that he had tricked them all by blending with the crowd. In that instant there came a loud commotion from the common room, and the squire strode toward it.

"Wait," Jane called, but he paid her no mind, and her afforts to rise were hindered by her lame leg.

"They're mad, aren't they?" Mary said. "Leaving us here with two dead men." She gave a dark and ugly laugh. "Waiting for their pleasure in finding the time to ask us what we saw."

Mary heaved a sigh and set the bloodied cloth on

the floor. Her hands shook, and she clasped them tight, then jerked to her feet. She ladled water from the bucket and began to scrub her hands.

"Don't bother to try and tell him a thing," she said, glaring in the direction the squire had taken. "I tried. Twice. He'll listen only when he's ready."

Pressing her hand to the wall, Jane rose with measured care, and made her way to the barmaid's side.

"How is it that you are safe, Mary? I am glad and grateful that you witnessed this and live to tell the tale, but how?"

"There's my good luck." Mary gave a hollow laugh. "My husband was in a mood, and so I was late. Came rushing up the road just in time to see your Mr. Warrick leave. A frightening one, he is. Handsome as the devil, and twice as heartless, I'd wager."

"Leave?" Jane echoed. "Mr. Warrick left?" Her first instinct was relief. It surged past her fresh grief and horror. Here was her proof that Aidan had left the Crown Inn alive.

Then she thought on the oddity of it. He had left the inn without bearing witness to his vengeance.

Had he arrived too late to hide the barrels? That made little sense, for he had departed Trevisham more than two hours past. Yet, the squire's men had found no hidden bounty. She shook her head, confounded.

Mary shrugged. "I came to the kitchen door, with a thought to slip in and spare myself your father's temper. But they were already arguing, Gideon and the one what shot him, and I waited beside the open door. Heard the whole of it. Saw it, too. Saw your father shot, and then his killer killed . . ."

"Where did Joss Gossin go?" Jane asked.

"Out the front. Just before your Mr. Warrick came in the back."

Jane frowned at that. "I thought you said Mr. Warrick left."

"He did. And then he came back. He knelt by your father as he breathed his last, heard his dying words, same as me."

"Oh-h-h-h." Jane trembled. Tears stung her eyes, and it suddenly crashed in on her, all that had happened and come to pass. The weight of it was terrible, choking the breath from her and clutching a tight fist about her heart.

Her father's last words.

He truly was dead.

Mary sighed. "Your father looked straight at Mr. Warrick and he said the strangest thing. He said that they were paid up right and even, an eye for an eye. That 'twas a man from Mr. Warrick's crew that had brewed Jane's demons." Cocking her head to one side, Mary frowned. "What did he mean—Jane? What demons?"

A man from Mr. Warrick's crew.

The words droned around her thoughts, louder, louder. No, this could not be.

What bitter and cruel fate would do this? She could not breathe, her throat closed against the air, and her chest was bound in iron. She lurched away, feeling sick, a new grief assaulting her.

A man from Mr. Warrick's crew.

Bitter bile clawed up from her gut.

The smuggler on the beach who had stolen her youth, left her with a ruined leg . . . whose actions had led to her mother's death. The smuggler on the beach whose actions had brewed her demons.

He was a man from Mr. Warrick's crew, and she

was battered by the possibility that 'twas all part of Aidan's vengeance. Her ruined limb. Her mother's death.

No. No.

Squire Craddick's footsteps sounded in the passageway. Wildly, Jane glanced about.

Her father lay dead on the kitchen floor, and his dying breath condemned the man she loved as the architect of all the tragedies that had dogged her life.

Watch out for your father. Do you understand, Jane?

Her mother's voice was there, clear in her mind. How many times had she told Jane that? *Yes, Mama, I understand.*

Jane stared down at her father's lifeless face and felt her heart crumble to dust.

She had understood nothing.

She had not watched out for him.

Without a word, she turned and walked quietly out the kitchen door and into the night.

Jane traced the words engraved on her mother's headstone, silently mouthing them from memory.

Sacred to the memory of Margaret Alice Heatherington the wife of Gideon Heatherington of this Parish who departed this life 18th day of July in the year of our Lord 1802 aged 29 years. In this life a loving wife, a tender mother dear.

"Did you love him?" she whispered, her words sharp with pain. So many memories crashed over her. Arguments overheard. Words never understood as a child, taking on new and dark meanings now. Yet, she remembered too her father's inconsolable grief at her mother's death.

Her only answer was the mournful howl of the wind.

She stilled, her hand frozen in place against the stone, sensing him. *Aidan.*

Turning, she let her hands fall to her sides. She saw him at the far edge of the churchyard, beneath the dead and blackened elm, separated from her by the low stone wall. The wind caught the tiers of his long black greatcoat, making it billow about him.

Once, she had thought him a man of mist and dreams. Now, she knew he was a creature of fog and grim shadows.

Aidan opened the gate and stepped inside, the sound of his booted feet as they crunched the dead leaves was loud in the stillness. He stopped some three feet from her.

The sight of his handsome face, etched with lines of tension and worry, made her want to weep. Beautiful, golden Aidan Warrick. What had he once told her? That his heart was shriveled and black as coal.

She reached back, behind her, and rested her hand on the cold stone of her mother's grave.

"Joss Gossin—" Jane began, stiff and wary.

"—has been taken into custody by Squire Craddick and his men," Aidan finished, remote.

Jane sucked in a breath, finding a tiny comfort in his reply. The moonlight caught his brow, the curve of his cheek, the angle of his jaw. He looked carved of stone.

"What did my father say to you?" she asked, her voice shaking. "His dying words. Tell me."

So long was his reply in coming, she had ample time to wonder if he would speak at all. If he would speak the truth or a lie. Each second was an agony.

"He said that he had paid in full. An eye for an eye. That it was a man from my crew that had attacked you and, in effect, killed your mother." His tone was cold, removed, offering her no hint of his thoughts.

Her heart stuttered, but she forged on. There must be an end to this, and it would only come if she was brave enough to seek it. "And is that true, Aidan?"

Again there was a dreadful and lengthy silence.

"I don't know, Jane." The harsh, clipped words seemed to bear out his honesty. "Maybe." He raked one hand through his hair. "I do not recall the exact date that I first came to Pentreath looking for Gideon Heatherington, the first day that I began to set in motion my plan of revenge. And I cannot swear to the whereabouts of my crew for every moment."

She nodded. Ever honorable, he would not lie, even if it suited his purpose.

"Jane, if I could kill the man again for you, I would," he said, grim.

Yes, she knew that. It was of no comfort.

Swallowing, she met his gaze. "Did my father . . . did he say anything else?"

Now he did not pause or hesitate. "That he loved you with all his heart." The words were a whisper, smoke and gravel.

No, her father had not said that, however much she might wish he had.

She wanted to weep. To howl and scream and beat her fists against the ground and vent her grief and her agony. But she did none of those things. Instead, she asked, "How could such a poor liar be a pirate and thief?"

"Jane, I—"

"No, don't." She waited a heartbeat, gathering

her thoughts, *needing* to make him understand. "My father was an *excellent* liar. So very good. I heard him lie to merchants and customers and even his brother's wife." She gave a huff of uneasy laughter. "Silly that I never realized he lied to *me*. But, of course, he did. And likely to my mother for many years." She well remembered her mother's tears.

Aidan's gaze was no longer cold, but laced with pain. For her. He suffered for her.

"Tell me when your father died, Aidan. Tell me the date of his death."

"Jane, what has that to do with this? " He stood before her, so stiff, so unhappy. She could *feel* the harsh wave of his torment.

"Tell me."

"The twenty-fifth of July, 1802."

"Are you very certain? There can be no mistake?" she asked, solemn.

"The date is branded in my mind."

"You said that your father died one day before your feet touched English soil, one day before you made your way to his door. Was that true? Your ship did not land until July twenty-sixth?"

"Yes."

Just that one word, and she felt as though a barbed chain about her heart slipped free, a tiny petal of hope unfurling deep within.

"Then I will tell you the truth, as well." She reached out and laid her palm over his heart. He stiffened but made no other move. The muscles of his chest were smooth and hard.

"I know you lied just now when you said my father claimed he loved me," she said softly, and beneath her hand, she felt his sigh. "You made that up to ease me. The truth is, he never loved me. Strange how different things look when viewed in hindsight."

Finally, finally she understood her mother's admonitions to watch out for her father. She had never meant for Jane to watch out in the sense of *taking care* of him, but rather, in the sense of being *wary* of him. Jane wondered at her own naivete, that she had been so blind.

Letting her head fall back she stepped closer and held Aidan's gaze. Her hand slid up his chest to his shoulder, and her fingertips skimmed the silky strands of his hair.

"His dying words were pure venom, Aidan. An accusation against you, meant to reach my ears and meant to cause me pain. And they do. They do."

"Jane, sweet—"

She shook her head and slid her fingers along the angle of his jaw to his lips.

"They hurt because I know he said them with malice in his heart, his every intent to destroy any happiness we found together." Tears threatened and she looked away, then back, mastering her emotion by sheer strength of will. "You lied just now to ease my heart, telling me that my father said he loved me. But in truth, *you* ease my heart. What you sacrificed—"

Hope flared in his eyes.

The tears came now and she could not hold them back.

He caught her wrist and turned her hand to press a kiss to her palm.

"Squire Craddick and his men found no smuggled brandy," she said, her voice trembling and thin. "Where were the kegs?"

"In the carriage." He gestured to the dark shape

beyond the church. "I piled them in, knowing no one would look there. Closed the shades. Hid them in plain sight. None of the squire's men thought to check *my* coach." His gaze was steady, so focused, so intent.

"You gave up your *vengeance* for *me*." It took her breath.

He gave a small smile, sad and beautiful at once. "Jane, love, when it came to it, when it came to choosing between my vengeance and you, I did not hesitate. I chose you."

Emotion trembled in her heart, so great and limitless that she shook with it.

"I would die for you, Jane." A dark laugh escaped him. "When success was in my grasp, I could think of nothing but you. Your face. Your smile. Your brave heart. And even my hatred, steeped for so many years in blood and pain, could not compete with the strength of my love for you."

"Oh." The word was no more than a gasp. She trembled so she could barely stand.

He stepped closer until their thighs brushed, and she could smell the scent of him and feel his warmth. His gaze never left hers and his voice was a low rasp, painted with the colors of his emotion. "What I said at Trevisham was a half-truth. I do *not* love you only as much as I am able. I love you more than my life. I steer my path by your light."

Oh, God. She loved him. With her heart and her mind and her body and her soul. She loved him with all she was and all she could ever be.

His voice roughened and shook. "I never meant to see you harmed. Not you. Not your mother. Though I know it for a poor excuse, if it was my man who did the deed, it was without my instruction or knowledge. I swear it, Jane. I swear it."

"And I know it. I have grieving to do, Aidan, for lies and heartbreak aplenty. But I lay none of it at your feet. You see, your ship arrived on July twenty-sixth and my mother died on July eighteenth. A week's difference, Aidan. So you see, it was not your man. *It could never have been your man.*"

He froze, and then laughed, incredulous. Relieved.

"My brave and brilliant Jane." He caught her to him, lifting her feet clear off the ground, and spun her about. Then he shifted her in his arms and carried her from the graveyard to the waiting carriage.

She could only hold fast to him and try to catch her breath, so chaotic were her thoughts.

"Do you love me?" he demanded, setting her before him and holding her arms with his hands. His expression was fierce, intent. "My God, Jane, do you love me?"

Without waiting for her answer, he pressed his mouth to hers, reckless and fierce and wild, dragging her hard against him. His kiss sang through her blood and settled in her heart.

"Yes. Yes, I love you," she breathed against his lips, her hand resting on his chest. "Don't you know that?"

He stared down at her for a long moment, serious, focused. "I know it," he said at last, and she felt the steady beat of his heart. It beat for her.

"My heart. My love," he murmured, and kissed her again, deep and lush, sending emotion spilling through her.

"Marry me," he said. "At dawn. We'll wake the vicar. I'll wait no longer than that."

"At dawn?" She laughed.

"Or dusk." Aidan kissed her again, and then bent his head to press his lips to her neck. "Or noon. Midnight. Name the hour that pleases you."

She almost chose midnight, for she had learned to love the darkest of shadows.

And then she drew back and looked into his eyes, pale in the moonlight. In sunlight they would glow the gray-blue of the ocean, the color of hope and healing and dreams. The color of a winter dawn.

"Dawn, then," she said. The beginning of a new day.

Jane curved her body into his, and smiled, slow and sensual. Rising up on her toes, she nipped his neck with her teeth, the underside of his jaw, his lower lip.

"And I have such lovely ideas of how we might fill the hours until then," she whispered, as his arms closed tight about her.

Turn the page for an exciting sneak peek of
Eve Silver's (writing as Eve Kenin)
Driven

Coming to bookstores everywhere
September 2007

The air was stale, rank with the stink of smoke, sweat and old beer. Bob's Truck Stop. Nice place for a meal.

Raina Bowen sat at a small table, back to the wall, posture deceptively relaxed. Inside, she was coiled tighter than the Merckle shocks that were installed in her rig, but it was better to appear unruffled. Never let 'em see you sweat. That had been one of Sam's many mottoes.

She glanced around the crowded room, mentally cataloguing the Siberian gun truckers at the counter, the cadaverous pimp in the corner and his ferret-faced companion, the harried waitress who deftly dodged the questing hand that reached out to snag her as she passed. In the center of the room was a small raised platform with a metal pole extending to the grime-darkened ceiling. A scantily clad girl, barely out of puberty, wiggled and twirled around the pole. Raina looked away. But for a single desperate act, one that had earned her freedom, she might have been that girl.

Idly spinning the same half-empty glass of warm

beer that she'd been nursing for the past hour, she looked through the grimy windows at the front of the truck stop. Frozen, colorless, the bleak expanse stretched with endless monotony until the high-powered floodlights tapered off and the landscape was swallowed by the black night sky.

A balmy minus thirty outside. And it would only get colder the farther north they went. Raina had a keen dislike of the cold, but if she were the first to reach Gladow Station with her load of genetically engineered grain, there'd be a fat bonus of 50,000,000 interdollars. That'd be more than enough to warm her to the cockles of her frozen heart.

More than enough to buy Beth's safety.

Keeping her gaze on the door, Raina willed it to open. She couldn't wait much longer. Where the hell was Wizard? Sitting here—a woman alone in a place like this—drew too much attention. She wanted no one to remember her face. Anonymity was a precious commodity, one she realized had slipped through her fingers as from the corner of her eye she watched one of the Siberians begin to weave drunkenly across the room.

"Well, hello, sweet thing." He stopped directly in front of her, kicked the extra chair out from the table and shifted it closer before dropping his bulk onto the torn Naugahyde. He was shrouded in layers of tattered cloth, stained and frayed, the stink of him hitting her nostrils before he finished his greeting.

"Leave. Now." Keeping her voice low and even, Raina snaked one hand along her waist toward the small of her back, resting her fingers on the smooth handle of her knife.

The Siberian smiled at her, revealing the brown stubs of three rotting teeth. "You can't chase me off

so easy. I've been watching you." He gestured at the
front of his pants. "You need a man, sweet thing."

Uh, huh. "And you think you're a man?"

The trucker frowned at her question, then his
thick brows shot up as he realized he'd been insulted. Undeterred, he leaned forward, catching her
ponytail with one scarred and dirty hand. "I'll show
you how much man I am. Give us a kiss, sweet thing."

His tongue was already out and reaching as he
pulled her face closer to his.

"Last warning," Raina said softly, wishing he
would listen.

He gave a hard tug on her ponytail. Raina slid her
knife from its sheath, bringing it up with a sharp
twist, neatly slicing through the tip of the trucker's
tongue. Blood splattered in all directions, thick and
hot. With an enraged howl he jerked back, letting
loose his hold on her as he clapped both hands over
his mouth. Dark blood dripped down his unshaven
chin to pool on the tabletop.

Raina sent a quick look at the rest of the Siberians. Their attention was firmly fixed on the girl
who was shimmying up and down the pole. Returning her gaze to the moaning trucker, she picked up
the stained scrap of cloth that passed for a serviette
and slowly wiped her blade clean. She knew that
once serviettes had been made of paper, but that
was a long time ago when there had still been
enough trees to provide pulp.

"Name's Raina Bowen. Not sweet thing." She
sighed. So much for anonymity. "And the last thing
I need is a man."

Well, that wasn't exactly true. She needed one
man in particular, Wizard and his precious trucking
license, but he was nowhere to be seen.

The trucker's eyes widened as he registered her name, and a flicker of recognition flared in their dull depths. Nice to have a reputation, even if she didn't quite deserve it. This lovely little encounter would just add to the mystique. Unfortunately, it would also add to the risk of being found. Damn.

He reached for her again, his hands rough, his expression stormy. He was mad, challenged, belittled, and he wanted revenge. What was it with Siberian gun truckers?

Twirling her hair around one finger, Raina shifted her expression, lowering her lashes over her blue eyes in a "come-hither" invitation, curving her lips in a winsome smile. The trucker blinked, clearly confused by her abrupt change in manner. He leaned in—Lord, some people never learned—and Raina deftly clipped him hard under the chin with the hilt of her knife.

He slumped across the Formica table, unconscious, mouth hanging open, leaving her with a blood-splattered tabletop, a ruined beer and an end to her patience.

His companions were looking this way now. Raina lowered her head as though enthralled by her table-mate, using her body to shield his inert form from view. Her ruse worked and the men nudged each other and laughed before turning back to the stripper.

Well, that had bought her about three minutes.

A sudden blast of light sliced through the frost-dusted window, spreading a glowing circle across the floor. Hope flared as Raina wondered if Wizard had finally arrived, but no, there was too much light for just one vehicle.

Trucks. Lots of 'em. They parked in a circle, the

beams of their headlights illuminating a circum-
scribed area.

Like an arena.

She'd seen this set-up before. The new arrivals
were expecting entertainment, the kind that in-
volved fists, and they were using their rigs to create
the venue. She stared through the glass, the muscles
of her shoulders and neck knotting with tension.
Illegal gladiator games. There was going to be
a bloodbath.

Hell. Wizard or not, she'd outstayed her time
here. Tossing a handful of interdollars on the table,
Raina shrugged into her parka and headed outside,
sticking well back in the shadows as she watched
the scene unfold. The trucks were huge, as tall as
two-storied houses, painted slate gray, and on the
front in bold silver letters, the name JANSON.

Men were emerging from the cabs. Big, burly guys,
dressed in hides and skins, bristling with weapons.
Janson company men. How nice. The Janson owned
the ICW—Intercontinental Worldwide—the longest
highway ever built. Or at least, they acted like they did.

She could feel the tension in the air. Taste it.
Someone had pissed these guys off, big time.

At the far end of the lot was a lone truck. Black.
Clean. Nameless. Nice transport, she noticed. A
non-company driver, just like her. Poor bastard. He
was obviously tonight's planned entertainment.

"Hey, Big Luc," one of the Jansons yelled, moving
into place in the circle that had formed. "That's the
worthless parasite who jumped line. We gotta teach
him some manners."

Jumped line? What moron would jump line on
Janson trucks? They went first. It was an unwritten law.
Anyone who flouted it was either insane or bent on a

quick death. Raina watched as money exchanged hands. Odds were obviously in favor of Big Luc.

"His pressure looks low, don't it? Can't have an unsafe rig on the highway," a second man called, then laughed at his own lame joke. "Wizard's got some balls coming here tonight. He shoulda kept driving. Maybe we'd have let him live another day."

Wizard. Oh, no. Of all the morons in the frozen north, she had to hook up with the one who had picked a fight with a good portion of the Janson army. She narrowed her eyes at the huge black rig, the one at the far end of the lot. Wizard's rig. Damn, damn, damn.

He was of no use to her now. Still, she couldn't help but try to figure a way that she could salvage the trucking pass he was supposed to give her.

"Luc. Luc. Luc." The crowd was calling their champion.

In response to the cry, a huge man swaggered into the circle of light, raising his arms as he slowly spun around and around, egging his admirers on. Beneath the flat wool cap that clung to his skull, bushy brows drew down over a nose flattened and skewed to one side, and just below it bristled a thick thatch of mud-colored whiskers. An animal pelt hung over his massive shoulders. The head was still intact, the jagged teeth catching the light.

Raina glanced back at the black rig at the far end of the lot. She'd never met Wizard, had contacted him on Sam's instructions—which in and of itself was a questionable recommendation—but she couldn't imagine he'd be any match for Luc. She had a hard time imagining *anyone* as a match for Luc.

The door of the cab opened, and a man swung down. He was tall, dressed in a black parka, the

hood pulled up, obscuring his features. She felt a
moment's pity, and then squelched the unwelcome
emotion. Not her fight. Not her business. Sam's
words of loving fatherly advice rang in her head as
clear as if he was standing beside her. *If there's no
profit in it for you, stupid girl, then walk away. Just walk
away. What do you care for some sucker's lousy luck?*

Not only was there no profit in it for her, but the
jackass had cost her. Wizard was supposed to show
up an hour past with a temporary Janson trucking
license that would allow her to jump the queue all
nice and legal, behind the Jansons but ahead of the
other indies. Instead, he was an hour late, and he'd
dragged a frigging army with him. Too bad the
army wasn't on his side.

Wizard strode forward. He made it halfway
across the parking lot, halfway to the door of the
truck stop before Luc's fist connected with his face.
Raina winced. She had a brief impression of long
dark hair as the hood fell back and Wizard's head
snapped sideways. He went down, rolling head over
heels across the inflexible sheet of solid ice.

In three strides Luc was on him, the steel reinforced toe of his company issue boot finding a nice
home right between Wizard's ribs. Wizard didn't
move, didn't moan, and for a second Raina wondered if that first punch had knocked him out cold.
With a laugh, Luc kicked him again, and then
nudged him with his boot, once, twice. He backed
off, waving at the group that surrounded him, shaking hands as he slowly made his way toward the
door of the diner, acting as though he'd just rid the
world of public enemy number one.

The remaining Jansons closed in, a pack of avid
rats, eyes glittering with malevolent intent. There

was no doubt in Raina's mind that they were going to beat Wizard within an inch of his life, a warning to anyone who tried to cross them.

Raina glanced at her snowscooter. She'd been smart enough to park her rig in a safe place and use the scooter to get her to the truck stop. No sense inviting trouble. Now she wondered if she could maneuver into the circle of men surrounding Wizard's prone form, nab him, and get them both out of here before someone got killed. She hesitated, the thought going against her every instinct of self-preservation. Why she was even considering this she couldn't say. Hadn't Sam Bowen beaten all compassion out of her? *Stupid girl. Empathy will only get you killed.*

Squelching the voice in her head, she focused on the guy sprawled across the frozen ground. He had the damned trucking license, and she needed it. All she needed to do was figure a way to get it.

She cringed as Wizard pushed himself to his feet. Shaking his head as if to clear it, he wiped the back of his hand across his mouth. God, he didn't even have the sense to stay down.

"Hey, Luc," he called softly, the sound of his voice drawing Raina up short. Low, rich, a sensual baritone that sent a shiver up her spine. "While you're in there, you want to fetch me a beer?"

Raina closed her eyes and sighed. Dim. Thick. Brainless. He was a dead man. And all for the sake of what? His machismo? She shifted, trying to get a look at his face, but he'd pulled his hood up again.

Big Luc turned slowly to face him. "You got a death wish, boy?"

"Name's Wizard, and the only thing I'm wishing for is a long cold beer." Oh, that slow, lazy drawl. It should be illegal for a guy that dumb to have a voice that smooth.

"Well, Wiiiiz-aaard . . ." Luc guffawed, slapping one fleshy palm on his thigh. "You ready to die?"

Run. Run. Run. You might have a chance. Raina willed him to move, because she knew Big Luc would kill him and leave his frozen carcass in the snow. The wild dogs would pick him clean, and no one would care. She'd make herself not care.

Luc lunged at him. Raina expected Wizard to step back, to dodge, to move. Instead, he shot out one fist with lightning speed, dropping Luc in his tracks.

She blinked, certain her brain was processing something other than what her eyes had seen.

For a moment, she waited, convinced that Luc would get up, would charge like an enraged bull and cut Wizard down. Without a backward look, Wizard turned and strode in the direction of the diner, as if he hadn't just accomplished the impossible. As if he hadn't just invited his own assassination.

And, oh, the *way* he moved . . . confident, fluid, a man comfortable in his own skin. Raina watched him for a long minute, and then looked away, wondering what the hell was wrong with her. Why should she care about the easy way some useless gun trucker moved his hips?

Whoooo. Get it together, Bowen.

No one spoke. No one moved. It felt like no one dared breathe, and then two guys stepped forward, hauled Big Luc up by his armpits and dragged him away.

Stupid man. Stupid, stupid man. Wizard had just made a mighty powerful enemy in the Janson Trucking Company. Actually, they'd been his enemy from the second he'd jumped line, but they might have let him live . . . suffer, but live. Maybe. Now, she didn't think so. They were likely to gut him and feed his intestines down his own throat.

Her breath hissed from between her teeth. She needed the Gladow winnings. For herself. For Beth.

Frig. She *needed* that temporary license, which meant she was just as stupid as Wizard was because she was about to step into his fight.

Hugging the shadows, she sprinted to the edge of the wall, climbed onto her snowscooter and gunned the engine. She spun the scooter in an arc. Heart racing, she stopped sharply near the door of the truck stop, just behind the dumb jackass who had so thoroughly messed up her plans.

"Get on," Raina shouted. Several of the Janson men were closing in, and she was glad that the hood of her anorak hid her features from view. She could only pray that they wouldn't recognize her. Yeah, right. "If you have one iota of sense, *get on.*"

Wizard whipped around to face her. For a frozen moment he stood silhouetted against the light streaming from the window behind him. She thought he would prove that he lacked even that one iota of sense she'd mentioned, for he just stood there, his head tilted as he watched the line of Janson truckers who were slowly stalking him, closing in behind her. She could sense them, see the hazy reflection of their faces in the windows of the truck stop at Wizard's back.

Then with a shrug, he swung one long leg over the seat of the snowscooter, his arms coming around her waist as he climbed on.

Dragging in a deep breath, Raina gunned the engine and took off into the star-tossed night. Heart racing, she set the speed as fast as she dared, knowing the dangers of hitting a deep rut at high speed. Knowing, too, that there was a strong likelihood they'd be followed. Even over the noise of the engine she could hear the roar of a mob denied.

Heat exploded in a shimmering wave, and for an instant, night turned to day as someone fired a round of plas-shot.

Wizard's reaction had to be instinctive. He pushed up tight against her back, protecting her with his body. With a hiss, she jerked her elbow sharply into his gut, sending the message that she didn't need him to act like human armor. *Moron.*

She could feel him behind her, pressed up against her back, his muscled thighs melded to hers, his arms forming a solid vice around her waist. He was bigger than she had expected. When he'd stepped down from his truck, all she'd registered was the size of Big Luc, the danger posed by the Janson drivers.

She'd thought Wizard some harmless prey. Now, with the feel of his long, hard body pushed up against her, she wondered how she could have been so wrong.